I AM THUNDER

I AM THUNDER

MUHAMMAD KHAN

MACMILLAN

First published 2018 by Macmillan Children's Books
an imprint of Pan Macmillan
The Smithson, 6 Briset Street, London EC1M 5NR
Associated companies throughout the world
www.panmacmillan.com

ISBN 978-1-5098-7405-7

9 8

A CIP catalogue record for this book is available from
the British Library.

Printed and bound by CPI Group (UK) Ltd, Croydon CR0 4YY

*For Suraiya, who told me to write this,
and for Mama, who made sure I did*

A NOTE FROM THE AUTHOR

In February 2015 news broke of three British schoolgirls who flew out to Syria to join the self-proclaimed 'Islamic State'. As a Muslim and a high-school teacher, I found this shocking on many levels. The girls, by all accounts, were academically gifted with caring families and friends. So what prompted their disastrous decision – one that would cost them their lives?

For someone who has lost a relative to religious extremism, the incident reopened old wounds. So in April 2015, over the two-week Easter break from teaching, I sat down and wrote the first draft of the book you now hold in your hands. Writing it was painful, but I needed to understand what might lead someone to make those choices.

Once I began writing, I realized it was going to be harder than I thought. Why? Because being a Muslim – even a British one – means different things to different people. Muzna's daily life is the very real experience of some, but not all of my Muslim students. But her teenage experience is something each and every one of us can relate to, whatever our background.

I wrote Muzna's story for you. Muslim or non-Muslim? It doesn't matter to me. It shouldn't matter to you.

You are thunder. Don't keep quiet.

Muhammad Khan

'The most common way people give up their power is by thinking they don't have any.'

Alice Walker, Pulitzer Prize-winning author

'I tell my story not because it is unique, but because it is not. It is the story of many girls.'

Malala Yousafzai, winner of the Nobel Peace Prize

PART 1

YEAR 8: END OF SUMMER HOLIDAYS

CHAPTER 1

'Oh-em-gee! Are you playing with your Barbie?!'

My doll face-planted on to her dining-room table. Plates and cutlery went flying as the plastic roast dinner catapulted into the miniature sink. Salma had a knack for turning up at the worst possible moment. I still hadn't recovered from the time she'd caught me 'perving on the naked guy' in my science book. For the record: I was doing *homework*.

'As if!' I scoffed, scrambling to my feet. 'Just tidying up a few old things.'

Salma wasn't buying it. Of course she wasn't – you can't pull the wool over a bestie's eyes.

'Shame, Muzna!' she mocked. 'We start Year Nine in, like, *three weeks*. Think they'll have playtime on the curriculum?'

My cheeks prickled. Playing with dolls kept the peace at home; let my parents go on thinking I was 'innocent'. Plus I still thought it was actually kind of fun. But admitting this would be asking for a lifetime of teasing.

'Laugh all you want,' I said. 'This stuff will shift on eBay, *easy*.'

'Dream on. No one wants your curry-stinking dollies . . .' Salma trailed off, spotting my laptop lying open. I saw her lips curve into a mischievous grin.

'Salma, no! Don't!' I cried, trying not to step on Barbie's best china.

'Hmm, looks like somebody's been staring at naked people again!' Easily beating me to it, she sat down in front of my laptop. Puzzlement replaced glee. 'What the hell is *Dono Aanke Khuli*?'

'An info site,' I said, hobbling over. '*Both Eyes Open*. Like WikiLeaks, only . . . leakier.'

'Boring,' Salma said absently.

'I'm working on an edgy new story,' I explained.

'And what's "bride burning"?' she asked, reading the words off the screen.

'Not too sure, actually. Hence the research – but it's bound to be super-edgy!'

Salma didn't look impressed. 'Where'd you hear about it?' she asked.

I picked at a bobble on my sleeve. 'I kind of . . .' I licked my lips. 'I was just . . .'

'Spit it out, bruv!'

'So, I overheard Ami chatting to her friends about it last night. They were whispering so loudly, you couldn't *not* hear.'

'Listening in on your mum's private conversations?' Salma said, clucking her tongue. 'You're *so* Asian!'

In spite of her trademark put-downs, Salma Chaudhry was my sister-from-another-mister, born on the same day, in the exact same hospital. It wasn't until nursery that we bonded over a Beanie Boo with eyes like bin lids. Can't remember now who the rainbow-coloured unicorn belonged to, but that toy became our mascot. And by the time it got left behind on a bus somewhere, our friendship was solid as.

'That's it!' I slid into the chair vacated by Salma, excitedly slapping my cheeks. 'You fixed a major plot hole. *Eavesdropping.* Better add it in before I forget.'

'Do it later,' Salma said, shutting the laptop on my stumpy fingers. 'I made plans. We are going shopping, girlfriend!'

'It won't take long,' I promised, reopening the laptop.

'You and your stories!' Salma snarked. 'Ever heard of *Hare Krishna and the Prisoner of Afghanistan*?'

I blinked. 'No . . .'

'Exactly!' she said snapping her fingers. 'Who wants to read Asian fairy tales? Nobody, that's who.'

I shook my head. 'I don't write fairy tales, I write—'

'And that's your problem, right there. Think Beyoncé got rich off of writing stuff?'

'Well actually . . .'

'Bey stuck out her hand, and Jay-Z put a ring on it. That's how you make money!'

I narrowed my eyes. 'So you're basically telling me to marry a guy for his money?'

'Hell no!' she said, giving me stink eye. Four fingers hovered inches from my face, then dropped one by one, like dominoes. 'Looks. Bod. More looks. *Then* money.'

We both burst out laughing. Salma was a crazy genius; she knew exactly how to wind me up. And me being dumb, I fell for it. Every. Single. Time.

'Grab your purse and prepare to splash the cash!' she announced.

'Five minutes and we'll shop-till-you-drop,' I promised, turning back to my laptop.

I heard the sharp intake of breath, could sense the protest building up in her, but then something totally unexpected happened.

'Oh-em-gee!' she shrieked. 'You got messaged by a hunk.'

A chat box had popped open in the middle of the screen.

Salams, how are you today?

I closed it. Automated customer service pop-ups were *so* annoying. But within seconds it had sprung open again.

Are you Muslim?

Salma giggled. 'Don't leave a brother hanging, Muzi.' The user ID showed us that someone called Kasim Iqbal was chatting.

Why? What's it to you, nosy? I typed. Sass came easy from behind a laptop screen.

I'm Muslim too, and looking for buddies. How old are you?

Taking this as an opportunity to show Salma exactly how unboring I could be, I replied. *Thirteen. How old are you, mate?*

Seventeen. Wanna see a pic? he typed.

My laptop pinged as a file was received. I glanced over at Salma – Excited Puppy Face. Without another thought, I clicked it open: a selfie taken in a slightly smudgy locker-room mirror. The boy was shirtless, squinting at his phone from under a carefully sculpted quiff. A gemstone in his left ear had caught the flash, sending light rays scattering across smooth pecs and ridged abs.

'Sexy boi!' Salma squealed, pretending to lick the screen.

I gave her a severe poke. But honestly, it *was* kind of impressive how much Kasim looked just like one of Barbie's boyfriends. An Asian one.

You go school? he asked.

Obvs. Why – don't you?

Don't need to. Got my own house, swimming pool, and car to boot. No more money worries for Kasim.

I bit my lip. Poverty was like the fourth member of my family. It chose where we shopped, made us buy in bulk, and stopped us from ever going on holiday. Whenever Ami and Dad argued, you could be sure money was at the bottom of it.

What do you do? I asked.

This and that. Mostly I pray. Allah hooks me up with everything I need.

That was his secret formula for getting rich quick?

Praying doesn't work like that! I replied.

Or maybe it does, and you just been doing it wrong? he typed.

Salma pretended to gag. 'Tell him to shut up and send another shirtless pic.'

I ignored her.

Know those little flash games you can download on phones? Kasim wrote. **That's me.**

Seriously?

Yeah, make a lot of money from ad revenue and add-ons. You into games?

Kind of. Writing stories is my thing, I admitted, feeling kind of shy as I typed.

'Oh-em-gee! Is there no one you won't tell?' Salma said. 'Look, there's a dustman on the street. Go tell him before he gets away.'

No way! Kasim typed. **I'm working on a detective game at the minute, but I can't come up with a decent plot.**

I could totally help!!! I'd never met anyone who needed my input on a story before. I was practically slavering.

I knew you were special! Wallahi you give off good vibes.

Thanks! I wrote, getting the warm and fuzzies. *So who are your main characters? What's the setting?*

Here's all I've got so far—

Suddenly the screen went blank. I gasped, wondering what cruel twist of fate had made my ancient laptop die at such a crucial moment.

Salma held the answer – literally. The plug dangled limply at the end of the cord, ripped from the socket that was the only thing keeping it running. 'You'll thank me later.'

'How could you?' I asked, welling up.

'Oh puh-leeze! You really think hot guys hang out on random websites that aren't even chat sites wanting story advice from thirteen-year-olds? Two words: stranger danger.'

Put like that, it sounded textbook dumb.

'As I was saying, before you so rudely started drooling over six-packs – *I've made plans*. Your dad's picking us up from the shopping centre at three. Time's a wastin', girlfriend . . .'

She swept out of the room, dangling my purse behind her like bait. I sprang up, ready to chase her down for it, but something made me stop.

Salma said 'Jump!' and I said 'How high?' It had always been like that. Glancing over my shoulder at the disconnected laptop, a lump formed in my throat. For about thirty seconds, Kasim Iqbal had made me feel special.

CHAPTER 2

I examined a Hello Kitty pencil case with cute little charms. Little out of my price range, but I did need one for the new term . . .

'Step away from the tat!' Salma said, coming over all *fashion police*. 'Pencil cases are *so* primary school. Get a make-up bag instead.'

A boy, who seemed around our age, backed into me and started to apologize. The apology died on his lips, replaced by fits of laughter. 'Look, Dan!' he called to his mate, pointing at me like I was an animal at the zoo. 'Zayn Malik!'

A beard joke. I was dizzy with humiliation.

'Yeah!' His friend laughed, as two more gathered round to stare. 'She's got more tache than you have, mate!'

'You got a half-inch willy and zero pubes, bruh!' Salma shot back, slipping into Ghetto Gal mode. 'You get me?'

The first boy turned beetroot red as his friends howled with laughter. They reminded me of a pack of hyenas. 'Oooh, you got owned!' they mocked.

'*Shut up, you dirty Paki!*' the boy roared, spritzing us with spit.

An old man's hand shot out, catching the boy's arm in a death-grip. 'Apologize to these young ladies, right now!' he demanded. His eyes were chips of ice.

'What's it to you, gramps?' The boy was clearly fronting. He looked like he was going to wet himself.

'Don't they teach you nothing in school?' asked the old man. 'Look where racism got Hitler. Be a man and say you're sorry!'

Deciding not to chance it, the boy threw an apology Salma's

way. A second glare from the old man won me a mumbled one too. The hyenas clutched their bellies and laughed.

I stormed out of the shop and beelined for the toilets, too upset to think straight. Hot tears spilt over my cheeks as I flopped on to a toilet seat, slamming the cubicle door shut. Why did boys always have to pick on me?

Kasim liked you, drawled the voice that lived in my head.

Minutes later, I got a text from Salma.

whr r u???

toilets by mcdonalds

wait 4 me k?

It seemed like an hour before a rap on the cubicle signalled my mate's arrival. By now the humiliation had had a chance to work its way out of my system. All that remained was a soggy nose and hurt pride.

'*Happy birthday to you!*' Salma sang tunelessly, dropping a small green box on to my lap.

She knew it wasn't my birthday – what with us sharing the date. But a present was a present. Turning the box over in my hands, I looked at the label.

'*Lightens excess dark hair?*' I read aloud. 'I can't use this! Ami'll kill me. This stuff gives you cancer, you know!'

'And breathe!' Salma commanded, snapping her fingers inches from my face. 'First off, Mum's been using this stuff for years, and she ain't got no cancer. Secondly, it's the summer. If your eagle-eyed Ami notices, we can pretend it got sun-bleached.'

Salma's mum was cool – my mate's beautiful highlights being a case in point. I wished my own parents would let me add threads of pure gold to my boring black hair. But it was never going to happen. Imagine what they'd say about moustache cream!

'So . . .' Salma prompted, popping open the lid and taking a whiff. 'Oh shit!' The ammonia made her eyes water. We giggled, and the dead feeling in my soul began to lift. 'Wanna give this stuff a try?'

I took a steeling breath. 'Girl, let's blitz this beard!' I said, giving her the z-snap.

Salma high-fived me twice. She liked me fierce, and it *was* kind of exhilarating to imagine I was Li'l Miss Sass from some American TV show, instead of boring Muzna Saleem from Haringey.

Two measly minutes was all it took for Salma to whip up the dream potion. The shadow of facial hair, which had been mildly embarrassing way back in Year 7, had gone on to become fluffy enough to notice. But now it lay trapped under a layer of crème bleach, and I was about to get even.

'What now?' I asked, feeling the bleach tingle against my skin.

She consulted the instruction leaflet. 'We wait. Budge up.'

'Loo for two!' I joked, shifting across the toilet seat.

'Oh grow up,' she said, then farted.

We both cracked up.

Fifteen minutes later, it was time for the big reveal, and I prayed I wasn't about to be disappointed. Salma returned to the cubicle with a wodge of wet tissues. I lifted my chin into the air, feeling self-conscious as she wiped away the crème.

'What?' I cried, watching her eyebrows slither up her forehead. Had I broken out in blisters?

But Salma wasn't saying. Instead she snapped a pic, then held her phone out for me to view. I prepared myself for the worst . . .

My first thought was the picture was of somebody else. My second, that she must've applied a filter. It was too good to be true – how could all my ugly facial fuzz just vanish?

Zooming in revealed it was still there, but *camouflaged*. My eyes filled with tears.

'I love you forever!' I squealed, hugging the life out of her. The warm mango scent of my friend's perfume filled my heart with joy. She was like a real-life fairy godmother.

I glanced back at the phone, and my smile was gone.

''Sup?' Salma asked.

'It's 3.45 p.m.!' I choked. 'Dad's gonna kill us!'

Before I knew it, I had broken into a frantic sprint, blasting out of the toilets like a cannonball, praying to God that Dad had been delayed in traffic. I didn't want to make him mad. He'd ground me and take my phone away.

Gripping on to the edge of the balcony, I scanned the car park below, mentally willing Dad's Vectra to be at least five miles away.

But there it stood, as stark as an exclamation mark.

CHAPTER 3

My heart dropped like a stone.

A relic from the nineties, Dad liked to boast that our car was the same shade of green as the Pakistani flag. Under the dim car-park lighting, it looked like toxic waste to me. How long had Dad been waiting for us? Was he going to shout at me in front of Salma?

Not trusting the lift to be quick enough, I hurtled down the stairs. Salma stayed hot on my heels. She knew the deal; she'd had a strict Pakistani father of her own, before a heart attack stole him away.

I yanked open the back door of our car. 'Assalaamu alaykum, Dad!' I called cheerfully. Or at least I tried to. All I heard was the bleat of a slaughtered lamb.

'What time is it?' Dad asked, his expression unreadable.

'Sorry I'm late. I lost track of—'

'Salams, uncle-ji!' Salma interrupted, all sugary sweet. 'It was totally *my* fault. I was trying to buy—'

'I am speaking to my daughter, Salma. Kindly keep quiet,' Dad said.

Cut by his abruptness, Salma dropped her eyes.

'Again I ask,' he said in that same dangerously calm tone. 'What time is it?'

I glanced at my phone. 'It's 3.50, but—'

'Your father must be getting stupid,' he said slowly. 'He was certain your friend requested a 3 p.m. pick-up. You know, it's a *very* hot day. This car park is like a—'

'Sorry . . .' I mumbled, growing more miserable by the second.

'Stop interrupting!' His words echoed round the car park, announcing my rudeness to the world. Shame filled my heart. 'This car park is hot and stuffy, like a bloody oven, and your father can't afford air conditioning because the racist people he works for won't give him a promotion. As if my life wasn't hard enough, now you also want to punish me, Muzna?'

I shook my head, a tear rolling down my cheek. Time stood still as I stewed in humiliation. Finally he relented and told us to get in.

To say the ride back to Salma's was awkward would be an understatement. Good old Salma kept squeezing my hand, but I was drowning in guilt. I couldn't help thinking that none of this would've happened if I hadn't tried to get rid of my facial hair. Perhaps Allah was punishing me for defying my mum?

'Khuda hafiz, uncle-ji!' Salma said cheerily, slamming the car door shut and waving at Dad as we pulled up outside her house.

Silence foamed around us. I wished he'd just yell at me and be done with it.

When he finally did speak, it was to say something completely unexpected.

'Muchi, I think I'm going to lose my job.'

'What? Why?' I asked in horror.

Whenever Dad had a tough day at work, he called his colleagues 'racists'. Other times, he'd sing their praises, buying them boxes of mangoes we couldn't afford, or luxury Christmas cards and presents. Totally confusing. But losing his job? That sounded pretty final.

Dad sighed and shook his head. 'This is why it is so important for you to become a doctor, beyta. Nobody can touch doctors. Insh'Allah, you'll make a lot of money and live a comfortable life. Maybe you'll also think of your poor Ami and Daddy when we become old and useless . . .'

A career in medicine had been chosen for me on the day I'd been born. I wouldn't have minded if I'd been any good at science, but I was *crap*. Writing was my talent. My *only* talent. Dad'd read my school reports, heard English teachers rave about me at parents' evenings. He'd even smiled at my 'Crazy Wall' of one hundred and one story ideas. But the truth was, he couldn't care less.

Salma had these crazy ideas about becoming Hollywood royalty. Maybe she'd even pull it off. But I was different, and scared. Like I was so often reminded: Allah punished kids who disobeyed their parents.

'I'll try to make you and Ami proud of me,' I promised, my voice cracking.

And I *would* try. If I kept at it, maybe at some point science would start making sense in the effortless way that English did?

'You're a good girl, Muchi,' Dad said. 'Your Ami and I love you very much.'

I glanced at his face in the rear-view mirror. It was beaten down and fragile, yet hope shone through the network of worry lines. Me becoming a doctor meant the world to him. How could I break his heart after all the sacrifices he'd made?

He broke into a smile, seeming instantly years younger. 'Look, Muchi,' he whispered. 'Kites!'

I glanced out of the window. The common had been freshly mown, and the meadow scent of it filled my nose. A man ran parallel to us, flying an enormous kite shaped like a Chinese dragon. In his shadow scampered a kid, trying to get his own Pokémon kite airborne, but without much luck.

From the way Dad's face lit up, you'd think he'd seen the most beautiful thing in all Creation.

When I'd been younger, Dad had told me stories about his

adventures as a champion kite flier. *Basant* – the spring festival of kites and yellow clothes – was big business in Pakistan. Paper kites took to the sky, fluttering like butterflies, enticing people out of their houses with every colour of the rainbow. But it wasn't just about beauty. Fighter kites battled it out in the heavens like angry gods. A yank here, a tear there, and before you knew it, a kite's line had been cut. '*Bo Kata!*' the victor would taunt. '*Bo Kata!*'

Resting my cheek on a palm, I stared up at the sky. Two imaginary kites floated into existence: Dr Muzna vs Writer Muzna. They bobbed and danced in circles, sizing each other up like boxers in a ring. Then, without warning, they lunged.

Bo Kata!

In the end, it was over before it had even begun. Doctor trumped Writer.

It was time for me to stop living up in the clouds.

CHAPTER 4

At 9 p.m. my mother brought up a plate of Oreos and a glass of warm milk. Another thing Salma would take the mickey out of, if she knew. Ami stroked my hair, telling me in Punjabi not to stay up too late. Unlike Dad, my mum didn't speak a word of English.

'I wish I had gone to school,' she said, squinting at the words on my laptop screen as if they were mysterious hieroglyphs.

'You could take adult classes?' I suggested, dunking a cookie in my milk. 'Loads of people do.'

She laughed. 'But Allah did not give your mother brains! Still, I am not complaining. He gave me you, Muchi. And you are cleverer than most sons.'

With a rattle of her gold bangles, and a swish of her apple-green *dupatta*, she was gone, leaving me to think on her words. I realized Ami didn't want me ending up like *her*. That made me sad because to me, she was the most special woman in the whole world.

I turned my attention back to my story about bride burning. Even if I had to be a doctor, there wasn't any reason I couldn't be a writer too. Like, in my spare time. Turned out bride burning *was* a thing. The internet had the gory photos to prove it. It was a way for in-laws to get rid of a bride they didn't like. If you weren't immediately killed in the blast of an exploding oven, you were stuck with looking like an alien from *Doctor Who* for the rest of your life. What was my stupid facial-hair problem compared to fourth-degree burns?

In that moment, I resolved to become the kind of doctor who

specialized in treating burns victims. But in the meantime, I'd write my story. A tribute to my wronged sisters.

My laptop pinged, startling me. A chat box had opened in the centre of the screen.

Salams. Can't stop thinking about you.

Kasim Iqbal had found me again.

Unable to move a muscle, I stared at the message. My blood pumped like thunder in my ears. How was this even possible? I'd gone nowhere near the *Dono Aanke Khuli* website again . . .

Don't be scared. I'm Muslim. You got nothing to fear.

Life returned to my fingers and I typed out a reply.

How did you find me???

Allah guided me. Even better – we don't have your dirty friend getting in the way.

I felt myself blush remembering how Salma had behaved when she'd seen his photo. But how could Kasim know that? Come to think of it, how did he know Salma wasn't with me *now*?

I stared at my webcam lens, and it stared right back. OMG, I'd been *hacked*. I was about to slam the laptop shut, when another message sprang up.

Please don't shut me out! I feel like we have a connection. At least help me with my detective game. What harm can it do? Please!

WHY ARE YOU WATCHING ME?????? I stuck my thumb over the lens, seriously creeped out.

Sorry. Just you seem like a really nice person. And you're really pretty.

My hand flew to my mouth. I was the type of girl who regularly got bullied for being butters. Could the bleaching crème have made all the difference?

Look, I've shut down the webcam link. It was stupid and haram. Forgive me?

Sure enough the pinprick of light beside the lens – the thing I'd so stupidly missed earlier – had gone out.

I glowered, hammering out my reply. *That was creepy af!!!*

He inserted the blushing emoji. **I know. I was curious. I mean, I showed you a picture of me so. . .**

You could've asked for one back.

You're right. So right. But now that we've seen each other, can we call it even and move on? I really want to get to know you.

Me?

Absolutely. Not everyday you meet a future Booker Prize winner on the interwebs.

I smiled in spite of myself. Kasim didn't seem like a perv. No creepy requests and he seemed ashamed of the webcam snooping.

Come on, sis. Use your skills to help a brother. Whaddya say? Folded hand emojis stretched the width of the chat box, pleading for my help.

I stared at the blinking vertical line in the message space, still undecided. My eyes drifted to the webcam lens. It had stayed off. If things got creepy, I could always pull the plug.

My mate thinks I'm nuts, I finally replied. *She's, like: no one's gonna want to read your stories, so stop wasting your life.*

Sounds like jealousy to me.

She's the pretty one. What does she have to be jealous of?

Pretty fades – smart is forever.

A smile crept across my face. *Writing stories isn't smart . . .*

I can't do it. Doubt your mate can, either. That makes YOU the smart one. Amirite or amirite?

I hugged myself. I wasn't used to getting compliments.

You gonna tell me your name?

I hesitated. *Smarty Pants.*

Hahaha! You're witty.

Really?

100%. I think you're amazing.

I took a moment to let that sink in. A seventeen-year-old thought I was *amazing*. Being worth the time of day to anyone other than my parents or Salma was a revelation for someone as lonely as me.

You still up for helping me with my detective story? Kasim typed.

Can I see a pic of you first?

Sent you a selfie before. Remember?

You were posing. I want to see you, like right now. Sometimes Salma talked crap, but the stranger-danger stuff she mentioned earlier was eating me.

One sec . . .

It seemed to take forever. Enough time for me to wonder whether I'd put him off being mates. Then I got a message notification and relaxed.

In the fresh selfie, Kasim was waving at me, the glow of his computer screen illuminating a cheesy grin on his face. He looked younger. But maybe that was just because he'd put a top on. I was glad. I'd been brought up to think boys and sex went hand in hand, all aboard a one-way train to Hell. But maybe the world wasn't quite as evil as my parents made out? Salma wasn't scared of boys, so why should I be?

I'll put the basics of the game in a doc and send it to you tomorrow. Then you can work your writer magic over it and come up with a plot. You should go bed now, little sis.

OK Bossy Boots.

Night-night, Smarty Pants. Insh'Allah we'll be making so much money with our game, you won't even know what to do with it. xo

*

Bossy Boots and Smarty Pants. Smarty Pants and Bossy Boots.

I found I couldn't concentrate on my story. Or anything really. I paced around my bedroom, smiling like a crazy person. Had I really been chatting to Kasim Iqbal – an actual, real live person, and not just a character from one of my stories? Had he really called me '*AMAZING*'? I'd heard of kids getting rich by inventing apps. If we made megabucks from his game, maybe my parents would never have to argue again. And maybe becoming a doctor would no longer be that important.

It was like the 5th of November in my head. Any reservations I might have had were lost in colourful explosions.

'Muzna, have you done something to your moustache?' Ami asked at breakfast.

She could have said 'upper-lip fuzz' or 'shadow'. Or even the slightly less offensive 'facial hair'. But no. Ami always went in for the kill.

'No,' I said. 'It's just a side effect of my acne gel. I think it bleaches hair . . .' Not the excuse Salma had dreamed up, but it actually sounded way more believable.

Ami coiled a finger round my chin and examined my face. I pulled my best innocent expression.

'Use less medicine,' she instructed.

'But don't you think it's sort of *good*?' I said, gripping the sides of my stool. 'I get called Movember Gal and Ned Flanders at school. It hurts, Ami! And my legs look like loo brushes.'

'Allah! Did you shave your legs too?' Ami demanded, yanking up my shalwar. Met by the cringe-worthy sight of a hairy leg, she breathed a sigh of relief. 'Thank God for that.'

'But *you* shave your legs!' I protested. 'Why can't I?'

'I am a married woman,' she explained. 'It is my duty to make myself attractive for your father. But you are my baby, Muchi. Only bad girls try to grow up too fast.'

'So?' Salma prompted.

My cheeks burned as I held the phone to my ear.

'I'm not sure . . . what was option number one again?' I'd zoned out and was totally fishing for clues.

'Rude!' she trilled. 'I just asked if you wanted to see that new movie with the hottie off Disney Channel. Guess you've got better plans!'

'Sorry, Salma,' I said, twisting my fingers, 'but I *really* want to finish my story.'

'Fine!' came the unforgiving reply. 'Two weeks before Year Nine, and my BFF turns into an old lady. You're gonna end up alone, girl, talking to yourself and writing books about your ten stray cats.'

'Don't be like that, Salma—' I began.

But she'd already hung up.

I'd always been so careful not to upset her. Pretty much a given when you had just the one mate. But now Kasim Iqbal was in the picture. Was I being a cow? Possibly . . . But maybe letting Salma know I wouldn't always be at her beck and call was healthy for our friendship?

Do you ever miss your parents? I asked Kasim.

He'd told me he lived abroad with a bunch of friends in a big mansion. Just like a second family, they had each other's backs and shared everything. It sounded great.

Sometimes, Kasim replied. **My parents weren't proper Muslims. Like all the stuff you learn in RS about Islam was the stuff we never did. Pakistani Culture was their god.**

His description was savage, yet familiar. According to the

Gospel of Dad, being a 'good Pakistani' was everything and being a 'good Muslim' came second. I could belt out Noor Jehan's top five hits in Punjabi, but don't ask me to recite five surahs from the Qur'an.

Every time I miss my parents, all I got to do is remember what they tried to do to me, he wrote.

What did they do?

No answer. I started to type an apology when his reply came through.

My parents were forcing me to marry a girl from back home.

But you're only 17!!!

When I get married, it'll be to a British Muslim girl. And I'll spend my whole life looking after her and making her laugh.

That was too cute. Kasim was a solid guy.

Thank you.

I wrinkled my brow. *For what?*

Just. I don't usually tell people personal stuff. But with you, the words come easy.

My lips stretched into the widest smile.

Any time, I typed.

'Ami, would you like some help?' I asked.

Ami peered over a mountain of carrots – peeler in hand, and sweat on her brow.

'Then I would ask Allah to grant all your wishes,' she said gratefully.

The spare peeler was right at the back of the drawer. Had it been *that* long since I'd helped out in the kitchen? Determined to make up for lost time, I raked the peeler across the knobbly carrots as fast as I could. Soon my fingertips were stained orange, and a sweet tartness hung in the air.

'This lot's going to last us till next year!' I said, wondering how much curried carrot we could take.

Ami furrowed her brow, 'Then maybe I'll also make *gajar murabba*.'

I licked my lips, imagining the heavenly taste of candied carrots. Glancing down at my belly filled me with shame. Then I remembered Kasim's words:

All those stick-thin women you see on TV is just the West stuffing their demented ideals down our throats. TV has become one big advert for plastic surgery.

I'm not perfect, I thought, *but I am one hundred per cent plastic-free*.

'When I was a girl,' Ami began, with a shake of her head, '*gajar murabba* was like my drug. In our village, I came to be known as *Murabbi Chor*.'

'You were a candied-carrot thief?!' I gasped, wondering if she was pulling my leg.

'Are *you* telling the story, or me?' she asked with annoyance.

Was she kidding? I hadn't heard Ami tell a story in forever. I mimed zipping my lips.

Satisfied, she continued. 'The village elders all loved me because I offered to do little jobs for them. "Parveen is such a hard worker!" they'd say. It was true, but I worked with one eye on the *gajar murabba* jar. By the time I finished their chores, everyone's jars would be empty, and my belly would be full. Not wanting to be beaten, I hid the empty jars in Grandpa's bed. He was half senile anyway, so no one believed him when he protested his innocence.'

'Ami!' I gasped as we both laughed. 'That's horrible.'

'Yes, *beyta*,' she said, tears streaming down her cheeks. 'Your Ami was a little devil. And like all devils, one day I got my comeuppance. Grandpa set a trap, lacing a jar of *murabba* with chilli flakes. What a time to discover the old duffer wasn't senile! Overcome by my burning tongue, I leaped straight into the well. As if that wasn't humiliating enough, my mother forced me to cook Grandpa meals for a whole month as an apology!'

I laughed even harder. God, I loved my Ami. She might not have been born in this country, or even gone to school, but she could make you laugh till your sides split. Pakistani village life seemed so fun. Some day, I decided, I'd write a book about her. Who knew, maybe the BBC might want to turn it into a biopic? Imagine: my humble Ami's life on British TV!

I wanna meet you.

Four words that transformed my belly into a nest of snakes. I stared at the laptop screen.

Can't we stay virtual BFFs? I typed hopefully.

Kasim and I had been chatting like this for days. He was kind and smart and *never* PMSing. Best of all, he was convinced the story I'd written for his game was a real money-spinner.

So why were those four words splashed across my screen freaking me out?

Don't be scared, he typed. **I told you, I'm a good Muslim boy. Besides we're business partners now. Smarty Pants & Bossy Boots, Inc. You can totally trust me.**

It's not that . . . My skin grew clammy.

Then what?

I hung my head. The thing was: I did want to meet him, but I was worried what my parents would think. He was an awesome friend but that didn't change the fact that he was a boy.

Only reason I came back to London was to meet the girl behind the brains of our soon-to-be award-winning game. Also to personally deliver your story fee. He'd been suggesting visiting for days now, but I figured it was one of those things you said without really meaning it. Had I led him on? **I feel like you're my actual sister, Muzna. Don't you?**

Totally. Or maybe a hot boy-next-door would be better? Was it fair my parents wouldn't let me hang with him just because he'd been born a boy? Surely they'd understand once I explained it to them that we were working together.

I want you to be the writer for all my games. You'll make easy cash. Then you got options. Buy your own house, share it with your parents, or give it to charity. Please don't say I wasted money flying over!

My stomach flip-flopped. Airline tickets weren't cheap – it was just about the only thing keeping my parents from taking me to Pakistan every summer.

OK . . .

OMG! Had I really just gone and typed that?

But I'm REALLY shy . . . I added, as a disclaimer.

Me too. But if I'm right about us, we'll be chatting and laughing in no time. See you soon, sis. xo

'Best Day Ever!' Salma chirped happily, as we rode the escalators up to Debenhams. 'Seriously, Muzi, you had me worried there for a minute. Thought you'd gone all boring and I'd have to find myself a new BFF.'

'You ever do,' I said, 'you know I'll murder them.'

We looked into each other's eyes and burst out laughing.

Salma stopped and squinted. 'That eyeliner?'

'A little,' I said, shrugging it off as no big deal.

Salma cackled. 'Check you out, you li'l slut!'

She wouldn't get it if I told her. I just wanted to look nice for Kasim. Romance had nothing to do with it.

I glanced at my watch. Eleven minutes to go before me and

Kasim found out whether we clicked in the real world. I was nervous as hell, but he'd become like family. This *had* to happen.

Salma was all over the perfume testers. Barely batted an eyelid when I told her I was going to the toilet. My conscience tugged at me. Should I fill her in? No – this was *my* secret. Salma had put Kasim right off when she'd pretended to lick his abs on screen. She wasn't like us.

The coffee shop on the upper floor was where we'd arranged to meet. Kasim told me he'd be wearing a blue shirt and black trousers. But when I got there, there wasn't a teenager in sight. I checked my watch again, compared it to the clock on the wall. Exactly on time. So where the heck was he?

Just then, I caught a blue blur at the corner of my vision. Slowly I craned my head round for a better view: blue shirt, black trousers – *check*. Sipping from a cup of coffee at a table for two, he swiped away on a tablet.

That's not him!

Apart from the fact he looked nothing like his pictures, this guy hadn't been seventeen for at least *ten years*. The dress code had to be a nasty coincidence.

Or was it?

I stole behind a column just as the man glanced up. Closing my eyes, I counted away the seconds, praying I hadn't been seen. Biting my lip, I tried to figure out my next move, struggling to hold back the tidal wave of emotions that threatened to overwhelm me. In a flash of inspiration, I speed-dialled the number Kasim had given me.

My world came crashing down to the theme of *Game of Thrones*. The man's phone skittered across the surface of the table blaring its ringtone.

There had to be some mistake. Kasim was seventeen. *Seventeen*.

'Hello?' said the man at the table, though I heard his voice clearer through my phone. It was as if he'd pressed his lips to my ear. I ended the call – heart pounding, tears pricking.

I'd been catfished by a paedophile. How could something like this happen to someone like me? I was too smart, too wise, too careful. I hadn't even been looking for a boyfriend . . .

News stories about missing teenagers rampaged through my head. Girls found dead, mutilated, or not at all. I felt physically sick.

Run! my mind screamed at me. *Run, because in a moment he's going to ring you back, and your phone will give you away.*

A sob escaped my throat as I broke into a sprint. I threw myself down the escalators. Had to get out of there. Had to put as much distance between myself and HIM as possible.

Scalding tears and rib-racking sobs. That's what Kasim had done to me. Good thing the Debenhams toilets were completely deserted. I punched the walls and screamed and cried. Then my stomach groaned and, before I knew it, I was throwing up. Last night's spaghetti sprayed on to the wall like silly string. I gasped for breath, stumbling over to a stall, before a second wave hit. I just wanted to curl up and die.

By the time I'd got myself cleaned up and gone to find Salma, it was ages later. But she was still enjoying herself up on the third floor. Only she'd moved on to cosmetics. I touched her hand, letting her know I was back.

'Oh-em-gee!' she said, smelling of a thousand different testers. 'You just *have* to try this colour.'

I filed the whole Kasim Iqbal thing under 'Never-to-be-Spoken-of-Again'. Thinking about it made me feel dirty and used. Salma would laugh at me. My parents would confiscate my laptop. The only reason I had a laptop in the first place was because Uncle

Tanveer had given me his old one. No – sharing was definitely out.

I still couldn't understand it. Kasim had almost seemed like a twin. Of course he had. The paedo had lured me in by pretending to be on the same wavelength and bigging up my stories. Man, was I lucky to be *alive*.

Back at home, I managed to locate the spyware on my laptop and deleted it. I followed that up with two full-system scans. No such thing as overkill where paedos were concerned. Only after I'd stuck a square of masking tape over my webcam lens did I start feeling like myself again. Less dirty.

Still – couldn't hurt to take one more shower . . .

PART 2

YEAR 11: AUTUMN TERM

CHAPTER 5

By Year 11, crème bleach had lost its edge. My facial hair had turned into bramble, and a minefield of acne littered my T-zone. As if this wasn't soul-destroying enough, the hairiness had spread to the rest of my body too. Neither knuckles nor toes were spared. *Oh well*, I thought. *Dad always wanted a son* . . .

Joking aside, I was not in a good place emotionally. Rigsby Academy boasted more bullies per square centimetre than the comments sections on social media. I felt like I'd landed on Planet of the Super Models or something. Seventy per cent of the time, I got through by keeping my head down. Salma was there for the rest, zapping bullies with disses that could make a gangsta weep.

I was grateful for Salma's support. Really, I was. I just wished I could stand up for myself. I was 'articulate and able to make keen logical arguments' – at least that's what my last English report said. But at fifteen, I'd arrived at a discouraging conclusion. Life favoured the white and the pretty. Salma got by on the latter. Me? I was neither of those things.

'We could try wax strips?' Salma suggested at break-time, epilating the leaves off a hedge. 'I mean, if you want?'

Though it was mid-October, the sun had missed the memo. Global Warming, probably. Sun-worshippers were scattered across the school field, working on their tans. In my world, good weather equalled bad news. The sun made my beard glow like a fricking fibre-optic bush. No wonder Salma was banging on about wax strips.

'I'm not allowed to, OK?' I said, scowling. Why did she have to keep bringing up my embarrassing problem?

'God! I was only trying to help!' she snapped.

'Well you're not. Just because you lucked out, doesn't mean we all did.'

'Everybody's got problems,' she said quietly.

'Really? Let's compare. You're pretty; I'm butters. Your mum was born here, so she gets you; mine can't even read. And I'm sorry your dad's gone, but at least he wasn't a control freak like—'

'My dad was a violent bastard!' she bellowed.

The air seemed to ripple, and a couple of sparrows flew out of the hedge in alarm. I stared.

'My dad was ten times worse than yours,' Salma added quietly.

I shook my head, struggling. He'd passed away during our first term at primary school.

'I remember uncle-ji,' I said. 'He was always smiling.'

'That was his Outside Face,' she said. 'We got the other one. He bare beat on Mum for acting like a white-girl *gori*.'

I gawped. 'I can't . . . How come I never knew this?'

'Cos Dad wanted it that way,' she said darkly. 'Said that if we ever told anyone, he'd kill Mum and me first, then drown himself in the Thames.'

My breath came out in a dull whistle. No wonder she'd always been so loud and practically lived over at our place. Probably trying to drown out her home life. I felt ashamed for never having noticed.

'There are worse things than not being allowed to wax,' Salma said.

'I'm sorry,' I whispered, hating that I'd shouted at her.

She shrugged. 'Ten years ago, mate. Me and Mum survived.'

'Sometimes I wonder why our parents came over here,' I

grumbled. 'I mean, all this "don't forget your roots" stuff is so extra.'

'Dumb and dumber,' Salma agreed, chucking leaves into the air like confetti. 'Learned one thing, though. I ain't letting nobody push me around ever again.'

That afternoon, in the spooky way you sometimes know it's going to rain before it actually happens, I sensed trouble brewing. Ami and I stood side by side at the sink, washing the dishes. Steam rose off the wet plates, making my acne itch, and a rotten smell seeped out of the drain. *Mental note to self: chuck half a bottle of bleach in later.*

'*Beyta*,' Ami said, popping the awkward silence like a soap bubble. 'I don't want you becoming like Salma, OK?'

Never minced her words, my Ami. So she'd finally picked up on all the subtle changes in Salma's style and attitude.

'Ami!' I said, nearly dropping a dish. 'She's my twin. You said so yourself, remember?'

'Once upon a time, yes. But her mother didn't take our advice.' She twisted the sponge sharply, draining it of filth. 'She gives Salma too much freedom-sheedom.'

'Freedom? Are you serious? Her father was stricter than Dad!' I said, barely holding back on telling Ami what he'd really been like.

'Yes, but that good man died,' she said with a sigh. 'Salma's mummy is so busy trying to fit in with her white friends at work that she has little time to see what her daughter is getting up to.'

'You mean like you and Dad?' I said with bitterness.

Ami gave me a slighted look. 'You act like we do you a great disservice. When we came to this country, we came for a better life. But not everything here is better. Kissing in the streets, nakedness on TV, girls lying drunk in the gutter!'

'Yeah, but Salma's not like that!' I said, nearly scrubbing the pattern off a dinner plate. 'She's a good Pakistani, just like us.'

Ami studied me coolly for a moment. 'Let us hope,' she replied.

Though she kissed my forehead, there was a stiffness to her lips.

The weirdness continued into the rest of the evening, with Ami keeping to herself, muttering under her breath as she counted onyx prayer beads. Even Dad raised an eyebrow though he knew better than to question her unless he wanted to spend the night on the couch.

I was furious at Ami. If it wasn't for Salma, I'd *still* be playing with my Barbie. Sure, Salma had a naughty sense of humour, but that's all it was: jokes. I was lucky to have her as a friend.

'I want you to meet someone,' Salma announced, her lips shimmering with coral lip gloss.

Someone? My heart sank. The thing I'd long been dreading had finally happened.

Until now, I'd always wondered why Salma stuck by me when she could have her pick of any of the pretty, popular girls. Last week she'd confided in me that her dad was violent behind closed doors. That would give anyone trust issues, for sure. But hanging out with Gorilla Gal had to be a strain too.

'You've made a new friend?' I said, trying to keep the accusation out of my voice.

'Yes!' she said, bouncing on the balls of her feet. 'Just promise me you'll be nice, OK?'

Ouch. Was that how little she thought of me?

As if reading my mind, she threw her arms round me. 'Oh God, Muzi! You're my bestie, right? Of course I can count on you.' She flashed me a smile then skipped towards the drinks machine.

'Come on, you!' she said, grabbing her friend's hand and tugging playfully.

Why on earth was my replacement acting so shy? Could she be even uglier than *me*?

A skinny boy with a nose like a shark's fin stumbled out. 'Hey,' he said, tipping his shaggy head. Then he snorted, eyes blinking slightly out of sync.

A boyfriend?

No wonder Ami had been warning me off. Mum Radar had been activated. Make-up, sexy clothes, secret desires. If you were hiding something, Ami'd know about it – sometimes even before *you* did.

'Um, hi,' I said, shooting quizzical looks Salma's way. 'Is this your cousin?'

The boy laughed. 'Just cos we're both Asian, don't mean we're related!'

Definitely a boyfriend, then. Though not like any I would've imagined. Salma loved flicking through magazines, gloating over every hooked nose, blemish, or Photoshop Fail she could find. Something that always made me way uncomfortable, though I never let on. But out of all the boys she could have had – and trust me, there were tons who wanted my beautiful mate – she'd picked *him*. Really? Maybe love was blind . . .

'Tariq, Muzna's like my evil twin,' Salma explained by way of introduction.

Why was she putting on that fake voice and making all those girly gestures? It ticked me off. She was brilliant just the way she was.

'So . . .' I began, racking my brains for something to say. 'Do you go here?'

He exchanged a look with Salma and burst out laughing. 'Nah, just climbed over the gate when I saw the titties on this one!'

I gasped.

'What Muzna's trying to say,' Salma cut in, 'is she'll mess you up if you ever cheat on me. Don't let the *good girl* look fool you. She's like Jackie Chan and Malala Yousafzai rolled into one.'

Tariq laughed so hard, he showered us with spittle. The best I could manage was a lukewarm smile.

'Oh man, that is classic!' Tariq said, wiping away imaginary tears. He glanced at his watch, pinching the dial to stop it from hula-hooping round his skinny wrist. 'Shit! Gotta go detention.'

'Rude *boi*! What you getting detention for?' Salma asked, batting her eyelids.

Her fake lashes were *cringe*.

'Nothing,' he said, throwing a couple of punches at an imaginary person. 'Stupid teacher! Gives detentions for *no reason*.'

He pressed his open mouth to Salma's as if sucking out her soul. I stifled a gasp, cutting my eyes away.

'He's gooooooone!' Salma shouted in my ear, half scaring me to death. 'So, what'd ya think?'

'Amazeballs!' I gave her a thumbs-up. What else could I do? Tell her I was afraid of ending up a third wheel? Salma was my first and only mate. The thought of losing her to a boyfriend was more than I could bear.

'Ew, no one says that any more!' she said, wrinkling her nose. 'But yeah, got myself a man. With actual man parts.'

I covered my mouth and giggled. 'Does your mum know?'

She scowled, raking her hair back. 'Mum's too fussed trying to hold down a job to keep tabs on my *private* life!'

I winced. I hadn't meant to sound judgemental. 'I'm sorry.'

'Don't be,' she said. 'Glad my mum can't poke her nose in. Think it's natural the way your mum and dad control every inch of your life?'

'They care about me,' I replied automatically.

'Care?! That's a good one!' Her sarcasm sliced and diced. 'Your dad decides you have to be a doctor, and you're too scared to tell him what you'd really like to do. How is that caring? Your mum won't let you wax, so you go round looking like a friggin' yeti! How the hell is that caring?'

'My parents *do* care!' I said, glowering. 'They just don't want me ending up pregnant at fifteen and ranting about my "baby daddy" on *Jeremy Kyle*!'

'Actually,' she said, 'all they care about is you not embarrassing them in front of the bitchy-arse Pakistani community. Meanwhile you're so damaged, you think dating is *perverted*.'

'I never said—'

'Oh shut up! I saw it on your face.' She snapped her fingers inches from my nose, making me flinch. 'Bitch, you're gonna need years of therapy!'

My lips trembled. 'Well . . . you're going to catch an STI off Tariq!' I turned and fled, wishing I could hit DELETE on the last five minutes of my life.

Where had it all gone wrong? I should be *happy* for Salma – she was living large. True, I thought Tariq was low-key pervy, but maybe he'd just been acting out.

So why had I opened my big, fat trap and brought her mum into it? My traditional upbringing? Ami's spooky warning? Or maybe none of that mattered and I was just being overprotective.

I sighed heavily, confused and guilty and ashamed of how quickly the whole thing had escalated. Though my parents were dead against it, I didn't think having a boyfriend had to get all X-rated and haram. Salma and I were both fifteen now. OK, so try-before-you-buy was out, obvs. But if you dated a Muslim guy, he'd respect that, right? And maybe down the road, you'd end up getting married anyway. So what was the big deal?

CHAPTER 6

When I got home, I knew something major was going down. The depressing soundtrack of old Indian songs drifting out of Dad's bedroom made that clear.

'Ami, is Dad sick?' I asked, immediately forgetting my troubles with Salma.

'His heart is broken,' Ami said in a reverent whisper.

'You guys didn't have another argument, did you?' I asked, casting my school bag aside.

'*Bevakoof!* Go and ask your daddy to explain it to you.'

I went upstairs, a fist already forming round my heart. I knocked quietly on Dad's door, before going in. I crossed the room and perched on the side of his bed.

'Dad, are you OK?'

He was so deep in the doldrums, I had to ask twice before he even acknowledged me.

'No, Muchi – it is as I foretold.' He stared ominously at the ceiling. 'I worked for racists, I was attacked by a racist, and now I am deemed worthless by racists. This is what stupid ISIS and al-Qaeda have done!'

Dad was on a rant. Mixing up racism with terrorism was a bit like switching chilli powder for gunpowder. He was smarter than that. But when Dad got depressed, logic left the building. He channelled Dilip Kumar – Bollywood's 'Tragedy King' – and every bad thing that had ever happened to him, real or imagined, just added to the drama.

'Come on, Dad,' I said, gently. 'It can't be *that* bad.'

He looked at me as if he'd just spotted Judas. 'I've been *fired*.'

The bomb dropped. Without Dad's small-but-steady income, how would we survive?

A few questions later, I had pieced the story together. A woman got reported to social services for keeping her son off school to look after his younger brothers and sisters. Dad went round to investigate, and once the woman cottoned on to why Dad was there, it was like a switch had been flipped. Coming over all Psycho, she chased him round the house with a butcher knife. Dad tried to fend her off with a chair and accidently knocked her over. He was immediately suspended pending investigation.

Trouble was, Dad was convinced he already knew what the outcome would be.

'Maybe we should go back to Pakistan . . .' he said, stroking my head.

My heart stopped. Had he forgotten I was born here, and England was the only home I'd ever known?

The doorbell rang, making us both jump.

'It's the police!' Ami cried.

'They've come to take me away,' Dad said, stepping into his slippers, and shuffling off to answer the door.

It wasn't another Dilip Kumar Moment. The police really had rocked up, and they wanted Dad to accompany them down to the station. He wasn't being arrested, but they needed a statement. As the stone-faced officers spoke to my father, Ami wept like a child.

I might've been embarrassed, had I not been paralysed by fear. I had never seen Dad looking more devastated. I wanted to scream at the police, to ask them why they weren't out catching real criminals instead of terrorizing a respectable family man who had never so much as got a parking ticket. But I was a coward. I had no voice.

Dad wouldn't hear of me going with them. Ami and I watched

helplessly from the front door as the officers escorted Dad to their car. He was still in his slippers.

Glancing over his shoulder with mournful eyes, he said, 'Look after your Ami, *beyta*.'

It broke my heart.

At least they didn't cuff him, I thought. The neighbours were out in force, watching the spectacle unfold as if it was an episode of *EastEnders* being filmed right here on our street. *Pakistani man being taken away by the police?* They were bound to think terrorism was involved.

'Salma!' I called, spotting her by the lockers. *Time to end this stupid feud.*

'*What?* I'm busy.' She spun the discs on her combination lock.

'Look, I was totally out of order,' I admitted, rushing over before she bounced. 'I'm sorry, OK? Bringing your mum into it was stupid.' I swallowed, trying to stop my throat from sealing up. 'And I was *jealous*.' Now my cheeks were on fire. 'I was afraid that . . . It's always been: Salma and Muzna Against the World, starring you and me and nobody else. I thought I was losing you.'

Salma glared, not impressed by my lame apology.

At least I'd tried. My feet were blocks of cement as I tried to walk away from the only friend I'd ever had. A playful shove startled me.

'Sisters before misters, girlfriend. 'Member dat!' Salma said, grinning.

I tried to match her smile.

'What's up?' she asked, BFF-sense kicking in.

'Sharing is scaring.'

She raised a well-defined eyebrow. 'Mhm? Situation like that calls for a skinny latte. My treat.'

*

Five minutes later, I was stirring my latte, watching the caramel-brown swirls melt into each other.

'You sure he can't get another social work job elsewhere?' Salma asked.

I shook my head. 'Nobody's interested in employing someone with a criminal record.'

'That's crap! Your dad gave them the best years of his life. Then they go fire *him* cos some crazy woman tried to cut him?' She shook her head ominously. 'What goes around comes around.'

'Shh!' I glanced around nervously.

Salma was talking karma, but you couldn't say stuff like that any more. People got triggered. Society was waiting for the next brown person to snap and run around screaming 'Death to infidels!'

'Don't worry, Muzi,' Salma continued. 'Your dad's smart, yeah? He'll get a better job lickety-split. Have a little faith in the Big Guy. That's Allah, by the way, not your dad . . . Now, excuse me, but if you're not going to drink that, I know someone who could do with a double.'

I relaxed, sliding my cup over. 'Not worried you'll end up a fatty, like me?'

'First of all, hon, you're thicc not fat. Second of all, they call it *skinny* for a reason. It melts the blubber, and shoots it all out the other end.' She blew a wet raspberry at me, then downed the latte.

'So, how're things with you and Tariq?' I asked. I wanted to know what having a boyfriend was like for someone who shared all the baggage of being a Pakistani girl.

'OK-ish . . . Truth be told, he's going through a rough patch at the minute. You know? Parents rowing twenty-four seven.'

'Marriage: that sacred union of bliss and bust-ups.'

'I know, right?' she agreed, but the smile never touched her eyes. 'He's scared they'll end up getting divorced. Then him and his brother will get separated.'

'Oh,' I said. 'That sucks.'

Poor Tariq. As if being split up wasn't bad enough, news of it would go viral. The gossip queens in our community would see to it. And then people would start looking down on their whole family.

'Muzna, get down here right now!' roared my father, the next day.

My heart was in my mouth. *He's finally found out about Kasim!*

After all this time, he was still the first thing I thought of whenever my dad was angry.

I rushed downstairs, to see what was up. My parents wore identical scowls. Ami was cradling the phone to her chest.

'It's Salma's mummy!' she hissed. 'She was under the impression Salma had been here since five o'clock yesterday! I bet a boy's involved.'

The phone was thrust into my trembling hand. 'H-h-hello?'

'Muzna, *beyti*? This is Salma's mum. I'm going out of my mind here a bit. Salma's switched her phone off, and Parveen tells me she didn't come over for a sleepover yesterday. Is that right?'

'No, auntie-ji,' I confirmed in a small voice. 'She's not here.'

'Oh God! She's been gone nearly twenty-four hours. Where could she be?' she asked, her voice shrill with worry.

'I'm sure she's fine,' I said, with fake confidence. 'Salma's super-sensible.'

'If you know something, you tell her right now!' Ami snapped unhelpfully.

'Do you have any idea where she might be?' her mum said, almost as if she was embarrassed to ask.

'I don't know,' I said, wishing I did. 'She, um . . . She didn't come here though. Maybe she went round another friend's house?'

'You're the only person she's ever trusted.' She gave a long, suffering sigh. 'OK, I'll call round her cousin's . . . If you hear anything, let me know. Please.'

She hung up.

My heart thudded. Where could Salma have vanished off to for a whole day? And why had she dropped me in it? I didn't want to jump to conclusions, but Tariq's name kept blinking in my head like a red alert. Had he abducted my mate and left her lifeless body in a ditch somewhere? No. That was the sort of nonsense my parents had programmed me into believing to scare me off boys – which after Kasim-gate, had worked like a charm.

'Where are you going?' Ami asked Dad as he grabbed his car keys.

'Twenty-four hours!' He shook his head in disbelief. 'I'm going to round up a few friends to help her look.' He rubbed the back of his head. 'These are not good times, Parveen, and poor Salma no longer has a daddy.'

'I'm coming too,' I said, snagging my jacket off the coat tree.

'No!'

I saw the look in his eyes, and I backed off. I realized my parents actually believed I was in on her disappearance.

Salma's phone kept going straight to voicemail. I'd left tons of messages, each more hysterical than the last. I told her to call me back immediately, letting her know there was a search party headed her way.

With nothing more I could do, I turned to prayer. I don't mean the full-body movements, facing-Mecca type of prayer. We just weren't that sort of family.

I raised cupped hands, and whispered hopefully to God.

'Allah, please don't let my friend be in trouble.'

As an afterthought, I added, 'Don't let Tariq have murdered her either!'

I awoke to the sound of an argument downstairs. Groggily I detached myself from the bean bag I'd fallen asleep in. My face felt like it was made of putty, and my brain throbbed. I crept towards the banisters to eavesdrop. My parents spoke in harsh, garbled whispers. As I crept closer, a squeaky floorboard betrayed me.

'Muzna!' Dad cried.

Spooked out of my skin, I stumbled down the stairs.

'Sit,' he instructed, pointing to an armchair in the sitting room.

I glanced at Ami, but she wouldn't meet my eyes. I began to wonder if Salma was dead.

'I have been a liberal father,' Dad began, placing his hands on his hips. 'But I am having to draw the line somewhere. From this point on, I am forbidding you from ever speaking to Salma again. No speaking, texting, emailing or anything else. OK? Not even in school. Understand?'

I blinked, unable to believe what he was saying.

'If you defy me, Muzna, I will know,' Dad warned. '*Everyone* in the community will come to know, and they will call your father *shameless*! I have lost my job, yes. I have unjustly been given a criminal record, yes. But at least I am still respected in my own community. Do you understand me, *beyta*?'

Tears fell freely from my eyes. When had they started? 'W-what did she do?'

'I am too ashamed to say,' Dad said, looking very uncomfortable.

'I will tell you this much,' my father continued, launching into it like I knew he would. 'One of my friends had his flight to Islamabad cancelled. Returning home, he found his house had been broken into and called us. A few of us left the search to assist the poor man. Imagine our shock when we discovered that girl upstairs in bed with his nephew – *naked*!'

I dropped my eyes, as if I'd been the one caught instead of Salma. Shame boiled in my chest.

'Her poor mother,' he lamented. 'Tomorrow, everyone from London to Lahore will know about it. They will say, "Saleem's daughter was her best friend, so she must be like that too." You cut all ties with that wicked child right now, Muzna! Do I make myself clear?'

I stared at him, gaping in horror. Salma was my sister. He had no right to—

'DO I MAKE MYSELF CLEAR?!' he bellowed, a vein throbbing dangerously on his forehead.

'Yes!' I squealed in terror. I had never seen my father so angry.

'You listen to your father!' Ami ranted. 'No daughter of mine will bring shame on this family as long as I live!'

It was over. The friendship that meant everything to me would cease with immediate effect. Yet again, my parents were calling the shots. And yet again, I was too much of a coward to challenge them.

Dear Salma,

My parents have forbidden me from ever speaking to you again. They've taken my phone and made me delete you from WhatsApp, Snapchat, Insta - everything. Dad even cut you out of the school photo on the mantel! Now there's a hole where your face used to be, like the gaping hole in my heart.

   I see the rest of my life as one big, shapeless lump of grey - an ugly thing I will never have any control over. Your friendship gave me life; you gave me hope.

Why did you have to do that stuff with Tariq in somebody else's house, anyway? You've got the community calling you and your mum filthy names! They're boycotting your family and attacking anyone who won't follow their rules.

If I speak to you, some snitch is going to snap a pic and show it to my parents. Then I'll get shipped off to Pakistan and probably have to marry one of my cousins! Please try to understand there's nothing I can do. I know I'll never make another friend again. But you, Salma, are beautiful and cool and funny - you'll land on your feet. You always have, always will. You just need to learn to trust people.

Maybe some day, when the crazy has blown over, we can be friends again. I really hope so.

I love you, Salma. Don't you ever forget that! You are my life and soul. But it turns out I'm not allowed to have those things.

Goodbye.

CHAPTER 7

'Muzna!'

It was the moment I'd been dreading.

I glanced up at Salma. Oh God, she did not look good. Frazzled hair and hollowed eyes. I scanned the canteen. Suddenly it seemed like every Asian kid had their phone out. *Bada Bhai* was watching.

'Muzi, for God's sake, speak to me!' Salma said, giving a strained chuckle. 'Please?'

Would it really cost me so much to defy my parents?

My eyes filled with tears as I pressed my lips shut. Shakily I got up, barely aware of the plastic tray I was gripping so tightly it might have fractured. I was too afraid to hand Salma the envelope I'd been carrying around for days. *Too many eyes. Too many eyes.* So I left it on the table instead, praying it wouldn't end up in the bin.

'Muzna!' she shouted after me as I hurried towards the exit. 'I'll never forgive you for this!'

I legged it out of there, sobbing, wishing with all my heart I was a better friend.

I'll never know whether it was because someone reported the incident in the canteen or just an unhappy coincidence. Either way, my fate was sealed.

Ami broke the news while applying Amla oil to my hair. Working the fragrant liquid into my scalp, she grumbled over how much her own hair had thinned with age.

'Your uncle Tanveer is offering your father a job at his

restaurant in Ether Downs,' she said, her voice strangely flat.

'South London?' I said in surprise. 'How's Dad supposed to manage that commute?'

Ami took a quivering breath. Had she been crying? 'We are moving, Muchi. This costly place will be sold off to pay our debts. We will live like refugees in a small flat above the restaurant.'

'Ami!' I said, whipping round to face her. 'Are you . . . Is this because of Salma?'

A shadow fell over her face. 'Have you not listened to a word I've said? Nobody wants to employ your father. His brother is offering a lifeline. We must take it.'

'But what about me?' I said, devastated.

Ami shut me down with a look that had fangs.

'What's this *Me*?' she asked. 'Growing up in this country has made you selfish. We are Pakistani, Muzna! Never forget that. Family comes first.'

'You know, without my job, we cannot afford to live here any more,' Dad announced at the dinner table, eyes protruding like boiled gooseberries.

I glanced over at Ami, who immediately shook her head.

'Really?' I replied, acting like this was the first I'd heard.

His moustache twitched with indignation. 'We are moving to Ether Downs. Uncle Tanveer has offered me a job at his restaurant, and I have accepted. He's a three-star Michelin chef, you know!' He beamed with pride.

First they'd taken my friend; now they were taking my home. Did he expect me to jump for joy?

'It's not intellectual work, like social work,' he admitted. 'But Allah works in mysterious ways . . .'

'I'm in my final year, Dad,' I pleaded, seconds from blubbing, the calm protest I'd so carefully worked out forgotten.

'Don't worry, Muchi,' he said, patting my shoulder. 'I would never sacrifice your future because of my own misfortune. Tanveer has recommended a top school, a thousand times better than Rigsby. Ofsted rated them "outstanding"!'

Between Three Stars and Outstanding, my last hope faded.

CHAPTER 8

'Hurry up, *beyta*!' Ami called for the third time.

I peered out of my narrow bedroom window at the green Vectra parked by the kerb. Dad was clutching the steering wheel so tightly, his knuckles stood out like pickled onions. Ami stood on the pavement in her thin *shalwar kameez*, fighting off a breeze that wanted her *dupatta*.

I stared at my small, gutted bedroom, trying to commit every last bit of it to memory. It was dank and – like the rest of the house – smelt faintly of curry. But once upon a time, it had held my hopes and dreams. And memories of Salma . . .

I'm so sorry.

The horn blared like a bull elephant.

'Coming!' I yelled, skittering down the stairs.

A week had passed since I was informed we had to move, and my sadness was mostly internalized. I'd even begun to think a second chance in Ether Downs might be good for me. 'Life is what you make it' – someone wise once said that. 'YOLO' – someone less wise said *that*. It all means the same thing. But what I had was not a *life* – it was a fake life that my parents controlled.

Somewhere along the line, I'd become a Loser. I needed to stop feeling sorry for myself and put myself out there. Freedom and opportunity waited behind every door.

'Goodbye, house,' I whispered, pausing in the hallway to run my fingers over the dark patches where two paintings and a mirror had once hung. 'You broke my heart. I don't even like you very much, but I'm still going to miss you.'

*

So there we were: the Brit-Pak family Saleem, pretending to be super-excited about our new life above a curry house, and temporarily stuck in traffic on the A5203.

Dad waited at the zebra crossing for a girl in a hijab to cross. She raised a hand in thanks. 'Don't thank me!' Dad seethed. 'Rubbish people with your hideous hijabs and your bastard beards and your hate preaching!'

Sometimes I thought Dad should join Britain First. He had major beef with religious types. I'd asked him about it before. Dad insisted it was only the 'ignorant' who clung to Islamic teachings. 'We live in modern times, so religion must evolve,' he'd said. Still couldn't see what that had to do with dissing someone's beard or hijab.

When Dad yanked the Vectra's handbrake with the sound of a breaking bone, I knew we'd arrived. I sat up, eyes darting from window to window, checking out our new neighbourhood.

For once, Dad hadn't been exaggerating. Zindabad was classy as hell. Through the smoked-glass windows, I could make out an illuminated certificate on the wall. Michelin had rated Zindabad with two of the three stars Dad had bragged about.

'Come, come!' Dad said, wrapping an arm around my shoulders, guiding me through the entrance.

'Saleem *bhai*!' cried a man in an elegant black suit, drawing curious stares from the customers.

I recognized my uncle Tanveer at once, though I hadn't seen him in years. He'd resorted to a dodgy comb-over, which I did my best not to stare at. My uncle hugged the life out of Dad, beating his back like a drum, and nodded politely to Ami.

'But who is this charming young lady?' he asked, his amber eyes settling on me. 'And where is little Muzna-*beyti*?'

'*Assalaamu alaykum*, uncle-ji,' I said, shyly.

'Shouldn't you be wearing a chef's outfit?' Dad asked, confused.

Uncle Tanveer chuckled and told us God had blessed him. He now employed a full-time chef *and* sous-chef to take over cooking duties. He only dabbled at Christmas or Eid.

'You know what the English say –' he waggled his unibrow for effect – 'too many chefs spoil the soup.'

Uncle took us round the back, to a concealed flight of stairs. Every now and then he patted the comb-over, as if making sure it hadn't flipped open like a bin lid.

'These humble steps will lead you to a most spacious and highly modern apartment,' he said, winking at me.

I grinned guiltily, hoping he hadn't caught me goggling at his hair.

Dad began grovelling in the traditional way, saying that Tanveer was one of God's Own to be helping us out in our moment of need. Ami weighed in, showering him with blessings. Uncle beamed with pride.

Turning the key in the lock, he threw open the door, and gestured like a ringmaster. 'Ladies and gentlemen, welcome to your new home!'

Dad ushered me through the door first. I don't know what I'd been expecting. Not much, given Ami's 'living like refugees' comment. But the place was *dope*. Open-plan kitchen, front room, and dining area, ringed in by huge picture windows. Further along lay two spacious bedrooms with en-suite bathrooms. *Me with my own private bathroom!* But the crowning glory had to be the mini chandelier. Hanging above the horseshoe-shaped sofa, its pendants glistened like gigantic dewdrops. Staring up at it transported me to a golden ballroom, where a prince twirled me round and round until I felt like I was floating.

Uncle Tanveer had splashed the cash, and no mistake.

'*Vah, vah!*' Dad said, taking it all in. 'First class!'

'Look at her face!' Uncle said, nearly poking my eye out. 'She's like a kid in a sweet shop.'

Hands down, this was the kindest thing anyone had ever done for our family.

'Uncle, this place is amazing!' I said, folding my hands over my heart. 'Thank you so much. How can we ever repay you?'

Too late, I caught Ami's chastising glare. *Oops.* If Uncle Tanveer asked for rent, it would be entirely my fault. God, I was such a liability . . .

'Muzna, *beyti*,' he began, patting my head like I was five instead of fifteen. 'Your good father took care of me when I first came to England. I am only returning the favour. Besides, I know some day you will be becoming a big doctor and cure cancer. On that day I will come to live with you at Buckingham Palace!'

My parents burst into obligatory laughter. Another voice pressuring me into becoming a doctor – #BrownGirlProblems.

I left them to it, eager to explore every inch of the amazing flat. It was fully furnished. Just as well, since our jumble-sale crap would've looked so wrong here. A switch above the sink caught my attention. I flicked it on and heard a ferocious growl.

'Waste disposal unit,' Uncle Tanveer called, making an *OK* hand signal. 'From *Amreeka*!'

'Why do Americans put a chopper in the sink?' Ami asked, horrified by the idea.

Uncle laughed, clapping his hands. Then he explained it to her.

I gazed out of the massive window on the east side. Traffic whizzed by on the main road, controlled by a red-amber-and-green god. I wondered if it would be just as busy at night. Sleeping through that much noise didn't seem possible. But I supposed I'd just have to adapt.

I tried to spot my new school. Dad had claimed it was one of the best.

An outstanding school, I thought. *With outstanding bullies?*

That's when it hit home that for the first time in my life, Salma wouldn't have my back.

That evening, my family sat at an exclusive table down in the restaurant, with a prime view of the water feature. Uncle boasted it had cost two thousand pounds. Looked a lot like rain hammering against a window to me. Maybe I was just too ghetto to appreciate it?

'So when do you start here?' I asked Dad, picking up my knife and fork.

My father sucked the marrow from a chop bone with relish. 'Day after tomorrow.'

'Are you going to be a –' I stopped. If I said 'waiter', Dad would probably be offended. 'Manager?' I finished weakly.

'I will be the maître d'hôtel!' he said, lifting his head high.

'Better not speak French, or they'll think you're serving frog's legs and snails!' Ami quipped.

My parents laughed loudly.

'Don't look so glum, princess,' Dad said, noticing my discomfort. 'Save that for tomorrow.'

I stopped eating. 'Why? What happens tomorrow?'

'I'll be dropping you off at your new school – Falstrum Academy!' The way he said it, you'd think he was on about Eton.

My face dropped.

'*Leh!*' Ami chided, jerking her hand at me like a spade. 'You thought you could have a holiday just because your dad got fired?'

Dad hushed Ami, throwing furtive glances over the privacy panels. My parents believed the Asian community was an information highway of gossip, and misfortune was the news that fuelled it.

'I can't go tomorrow!' I said, really panicking. 'I mean, what about stuff like uniform and . . . and equipment?'

'All settled,' Dad said, smiling smugly.

'The nice principal told us you won't have to wear uniform until next Monday,' Ami said.

Fantastic. I'd stick out like a dork on my very first day.

I was silent for the rest of dinner, idly picking at my food, lost in gloomy thought. Ami and Dad managed to polish off seconds. I wished I could be as optimistic as they were about our new life in Ether Downs. But honestly, I was bricking it. Now that I had this perfect opportunity to redefine myself, I was afraid I was going to mess up.

That night, I lay awake in a bed that was far too big and way too comfortable, listening to cars rushing by in the night. I turned over, hugging Laddu: my teddy bear. Once upon a time, he'd been as bright yellow as the Asian sweet I'd named him after. Now my cheap teddy's fur was a miserable shade of ochre and rougher than a doormat.

You can take the girl out of the ghetto . . .

I hoped to God Falstrum Academy wasn't a school for rich kids. Being a brown kid was tough. Being a poor brown kid was way harder. But no matter how things swung, I promised myself this time would be different. I would stand up for myself.

PART 3

YEAR 11: SPRING TERM
FALSTRUM ACADEMY

CHAPTER 9

'Wake up, Muzna!' Ami cried brightly, fluttering round the room like an insanely cheerful canary. 'Wake, oh wake, oh wake!'

She tickled my palm like sweet torture. I hid it under the covers. So she tickled my ribs instead. I groaned, desperate for more sleep. But one glimpse at the clothes Ami had laid out for me was enough to wake the dead.

No way was I going to school in a hot-pink shalwar kameez.

Once I'd finished in the bathroom, I fished out a pair of jeans that didn't make my bum look big (not easy), and paired them up with a slouchy red hoody. The only make-up I ever wore was spot-control related. That, and a sneaky bit of eyeliner.

'I want you in the car in fifteen minutes,' Dad said, pointing at his watch.

'Mmmf!' I agreed, guzzling down my Coco Pops at the kitchen table.

Ami made a face. 'Oh-ho! I ironed your pretty pink suit, and you wear this English rubbish?!'

For once Dad came to my rescue. 'Parveen, she's going to school not a *mela*. I don't want her catching young boys' eyes with that alluring suit.'

Blinding them, more like, I thought. I wished my parents would just trust me to uphold the morals I'd been brought up with. But since Salma-gate, trust was in short supply.

Oh Ami and Dad, I thought ruefully, *don't you realize my face is all the contraception I'm ever gonna need?*

*

Falstrum was shiny and new. Four years ago the academy had been funded by the National Lottery to be renovated and updated. I was going to a school that gambling had paid for. Maybe they'd have extra classes to teach me how to be a croupier.

The school complex was made up of five gigantic tomb-like buildings. They were called things like 'Building A' and 'Building B'. If I'd been in charge, I would've given them dope names and added a splash of colour. After all, wasn't learning supposed to be fun?

Me and Dad followed the bold signs round to reception, and after an extended goodbye that was straight out of a Bollywood weepy, I waited nervously in reception for a student to take me up to my new form room.

Be cool, I told myself, like some bargain-basement life coach. *Things sucked at Rigsby because you let them. This is your last chance to shine. Use everything Salma taught you. Use the friggin' Force, if you have to. But BE COOL.*

'Hi! My name's Amie,' announced a girl, making me jump. She wore her rust-coloured hair in a tight bun. Beneath her maroon blazer was a slate-grey uniform. The school crest was a stag leaping in front of a flaming torch. 'What's yours?'

'Muzna,' I said, trying to smile, only my lips kept twitching. God I hoped I wasn't having a stroke.

Be cool! Be cool! Be cool!

'That's a nice name,' she said, checking out the timetable I'd been given by the receptionist. 'Used to go out with a bloke called Mustafa.'

A Muslim boy? 'What happened?' I asked, biting my lip.

Her forehead creased. 'Huh? Oh, you mean with Mustafa! Er, nothing really. We just sorta drifted apart.' She gave me a naughty wink. 'He had a really big one, though!'

I covered my mouth and giggled.

'Is that why you dumped him?' I ventured.

'No, you dirty cow!' she shrieked, cackling with laughter. 'Some of his habits were bare nasty. I'm not even lying! Listen to this, yeah! He used to pick his nose, then try touching me with the *same finger*.'

'Who does that?' I asked with gleeful disgust.

'I know, right?' she said, swatting my arm gratefully. 'I weren't having none of it, so I dumped him!'

I nodded, imagining what it might be like to have a boyfriend – even a gross one. Then I remembered Salma's boyfriend and how that had worked out for her. Fantasy over.

'There you go.' Amie pointed to a classroom. 'You've got Dunthorpe as your tutor. He's, like, so friggin' amazin'! Come on, I'll introduce you and stuff.'

I needed to take a moment to figure out how New Muzna was going to act, but Amie had already thrown open the door. Conversations evaporated, and everyone turned to stare at me. I sank deeper inside my hoody.

'Why's everyone gone quiet?' some wise guy asked, getting a round of laughs.

'Hello, you must be Muzna Saleem!' said my new tutor, a guy in his thirties. Argyle tank, nerd glasses and wavy, sandy-blond hair – he was working the geek-chic look like nobody's business. 'My name's Mr Dunthorpe. Nice to meet you.'

'Hey,' I said, with the charisma of a wet sponge. I cursed Amie for not giving me time to get into character.

'Oh Lord, it's a terrorist!' bellowed a large mixed-race girl in the front row.

BE COOL switched to *DON'T CRY*.

'Sade!' Mr Dunthorpe snapped.

'Well make it take its hood off, then!' Sade said, flapping a hand at me. 'How'm I supposed to know it ain't Anjem Choudary under there?'

'You need to shut your face!' growled a boy by the window. Kicking back in a black hoody, manspreading with the latest Nikes, you could just smell the 'Rude *Boi*' vibes coming off him. I glanced up at his face.

OH. MY. GAWD.

He looked like a marble statue from the V&A. You know the type: angular brow, dominant nose, noble cheekbones. His hair was so intensely black, and his complexion seemed to glow. The goatee hugging his square chin killed it. One hundred and ten per cent Guy Candy.

Sade glowered, but the look in her eyes told a story of fear. 'Wish you'd never come to this school,' she grumbled.

'Aw, but Arif's so *beautiful*!' squealed a girl in the back row.

'Beautiful terrorist, more like . . .' muttered Sade, though I don't think anyone else heard.

'I'd do him,' volunteered another girl, setting off a wave of sniggering.

Arif stayed focused on Sade, turning his death-glare up to a solid ten.

'Sade and Arif, you both have ten-minute detentions with me at break-time,' Mr Dunthorpe announced, his green eyes suddenly piercing. 'Everyone else, be quiet.'

'Sorry, sir,' the hot boy said, looking like a naughty puppy. 'My third day at Falstrum, right?' (Which explained the lack of uniform.) 'Definitely not looking for trouble, me. But Sade's got no right to bully the new girl, innit?'

'We'll discuss it at break,' Mr Dunthorpe said firmly. 'Now Sade, apologize to Muzna so we can get on with the day.'

'For what?' she boomed.

He ignored her question. 'Quickly, please.'

'Sor-ree!' she said, glaring at me. 'Not sorry.' she muttered under her breath.

My tutor turned to me with a smile. 'Muzna, I'm afraid I *am* going to have to ask you to remove the hood, please. It's school rules here at Falstrum.'

Oh God, how I wished I'd entered the room with my hood down in the first place. I felt like a bride at a wedding – one with a Halloween surprise lurking beneath her veil. And for some mad reason, the fear of disappointing Arif made me feel like I was going to puke.

I ripped the hood off like a plaster. Twenty-two pairs of judgemental eyes gave me epic vertigo. 'Hey, guys!' I said, giving a cheerful little wave.

'Hey, guys!' mimicked a boy with Justin Bieber's old hairstyle.

'Afraid you'll be seeing an awful lot of me, since I'm also going to be your English teacher,' my new tutor said. 'Congratulations! You'll be in Set One.'

As the teacher of the subject I cared about most, I was going to make it my mission to impress him. Download one of those word-of-the-day apps, devour past papers, read an intimidating classic like *War and Peace* or *Anna Karenina*. Whatever it took, I was on it.

The pips sounded, signalling the end of registration.

'Sarabi, could you join us here for a minute, please,' Mr Dunthorpe said.

A petite Asian girl with a mile-long plait walked over, ignoring the taunts from Sade telling her to run for her life.

'Could I get you to look after Muzna for a week? Do a good job, and I'll stick a whole load of achievement points on SIMs for you.'

'It's fine, sir,' Sarabi said, giving Mr Dunthorpe a really pretty smile. 'I'll show her the ropes.'

'OK, Muzna? And I want to apologize again for Sade's poor behaviour. If anybody upsets you, please inform me right away. We operate a zero-tolerance bullying policy at Falstrum.'

I nodded, though honestly I wanted to forget the whole thing. It wasn't the first time I'd had the T-word flung at me. But what it had done was make me drop my New Muzna persona. If I didn't want to end up as Doormat Muzna, I couldn't afford for it to happen again.

'Have a great day, girls!' Mr Dunthorpe said, waving like an overenthusiastic kid.

'He seems friendly,' I said, as Sarabi walked me to my first class.

The corridors were wider than they'd been at Rigsby. Less pushing and shoving had to be part of the reason the kids were behaving better. Then there were the uniforms. Nobody seemed to be pushing it – no mini ties, no rolled-up skirts. And when I spotted a boy holding a door open for a teacher, I felt like I'd died and gone to grammar school.

'Trust me: the word you're looking for is "awesome",' Sarabi said – the second person to describe Mr Dunthorpe that way.

'Actually it's "porn star",' interrupted a boy, casually slipping arms around us. The stench of BO and Lynx were toxic.

Sarabi brushed him off with a glare.

'What?' he asked, all innocence. 'Don't pretend like you ain't seen Dunthorpe doin' his ting on the internet!' He thrust his pelvis a few times, sniggered, then spotted someone else to torment, and was off like a bullet. I imagined cartoon clouds of dust trailing him.

'Are all the boys here like that?' I asked, trying to pick Arif out of the steady stream of students.

'Aren't they everywhere?' Sarabi retorted.

'High-five!' I said laughing.

But even as we clapped hands, something told me *Arif* was different. Aside from the fact he looked more sixth form than Year 11 (and let's not forget *drop-dead gorgeous*), he had stuck up for a complete nobody and ended up in detention for his troubles. That was the mark of a true hero.

CHAPTER 10

Dad had the news on in the background as we gathered round the dining table. I was starved, and the tempting flavours Ami was wafting around the flat made me drool. She'd pulled out all the stops to cook us an amazing dinner. It felt like Eid. Maybe living above a two-star restaurant had brought out her competitive side?

As we tucked in, the newsreader on TV grimly announced that another Western journalist had been beheaded in Syria. Abu Bakr al-Baghdadi was calling it 'a victory for Islam'. My blood ran cold.

'Saleem, turn this rubbish off!' Ami said.

'Parveen, we need to know what they're saying about us,' Dad replied.

'But they're *not* us,' I said, eyes watering from the zing of black cardamom.

'I know that!' he said, batting away my protest. 'But do the public know?'

'Truth shines through in the end,' I said, but I was having my own doubts. The scary girl in my tutor group, Sade, was a prime example of what Dad meant. It hurt because she didn't even know me, but judged me all the same. Sometimes you figured people of colour would be more sensitive about stuff like that. Then you got proven wrong.

'Off – at least while we eat,' Ami said authoritatively, killing the power. 'I'm not having ISIS-shysis spoiling my meal!'

'We are not going to bury our heads in the sand like ostriches!' Dad protested. 'Islam was once a well-respected religion. Now these bloody Taliban and ISIS bastards come along and make it a thing to be reviled!'

'How was your first day at school?' Ami asked, pointedly changing the subject.

I took a sip of water. 'Yeah. So my tutor, Mr Dunthorpe, is really nice . . .'

'Young man, is he?' Ami asked.

'Ancient. All his kids are at uni.'

Cheered by this news, Ami piled more food on her plate. Sometimes it seemed the only way to keep your parents happy was to feed them lies.

'What about maths and science?' Dad asked, eyes bulging. 'You know you need both of these to become a doctor.'

Picturing a Well of Calm, I imagined sticking my head in it.

'Everything was fine, Dad.'

It was the best I could do. Being forced to do well in subjects you were crap at was really not helping my self-esteem issues.

As my parents chatted away in Punjabi, I silently reviewed my first day. Unfortunately, Muzna 2.0 had turned out to be pretty much like the beta version. Bummer. Perhaps going from '0 to 100 (Real Quick)' was the stuff of hip-hop dreams? People called it the 'social ladder', but it was more like a mountain.

Sarabi had seemed nice. But did she want to be mates, or was she just being polite? Guess the jury was still out. My mind turned back to Sade. With one insult, she'd reduced me to a victim. But Arif's takedown had been *epic*. His dark eyes had smouldered, just like Heathcliff's from *Wuthering Heights*. Even *I* wasn't dumb enough to think it was because he fancied me. Buff boys like Arif didn't notice bottom feeders. Just looking out for a 'sister', I guessed . . .

I jerked my head, dissolving Arif in a puff of mental smoke. Thinking about boys was asking for trouble. High GCSE grades: *that* was goals.

CHAPTER 11

The next day, I found out I'd got nicknames: 'Red Riding Hoody' and 'Sarabi's Friend'. Not that I minded. I was just grateful no one had been mean about my facial-hair problem. Yet . . .

By lunchtime, any delusions of being mates with Sarabi were laid to rest. I'd been ditched – well and truly. I got it, having the new kid tag along wasn't exactly the must-have fashion accessory of the season. Plans of becoming Ms Congeniality were indefinitely put on hold.

I smelt him before I saw him. Musk and cedar, and something I couldn't quite put my finger on. Whatever it was, it got my heart thumping.

'A'ight?' Arif said, sounding like he'd been running a marathon.

I turned round and stuttered a 'hey'. He might have sounded like he'd been running a marathon, but he looked like he'd been pumping iron. A grey ribbed vest cupped unbelievable pecs, hugging every bend and curve of his corrugated abs. Tubular veins ran the lengths of his arms, and his smooth vanilla skin glistened with sweat.

'Sorry,' he said, misunderstanding my goggling. 'Me and the lads been playing a bit o' footie.' Tall white teeth gleamed between kissable lips.

'Are you Pakistani?' he asked abruptly.

For the first time I picked up on his Mancunian accent. It was *cute*. I nodded, still unable to find my voice. He must have liked my answer, though, because his wonderful smile reappeared.

'Me too, fam. Pakistan *zindabad*!' He punched the air and chuckled. His friends yelled at him to get his head back in the game. He looked at me and rolled his eyes. 'Where's your mate, then?' he asked, glancing over my shoulder as if Sarabi might be hiding there.

'Sick,' I lied, instantly regretting it. But admitting I'd been dumped was so embarrassing. Arif had only been at Falstrum three days longer than I had, yet he'd already made friends. A whole mandem of footballers.

'Need anything, you come to us, yeah? Even if it's just to sort out that miserable cow Sade.'

'Thanks,' I said, feeling sweat trickle down my back. I racked my brains for something cool to say. A joke. A one-liner. Anything.

I had nothing.

He nodded as if sensing this, then headed back to his game of football.

Suddenly a dam burst in my head, and my mind overflowed with all the cool things I could've said. I sighed watching Arif head the ball. *Please don't injure that beautiful face!* None of the other boys came close to his level of hotness.

'Hi, Muzna,' Sarabi called, bringing me down to earth with a bump.

'Oh, hey!' I cried, a little too hyper. Had she caught me gawking at Arif?

'Sorry, had an orthodontist appointment,' she explained.

I realized how silly I'd been imagining the 'abandonment' was some kind of karmic payback for the way I'd treated Salma. *The way my parents* made me *treat Salma.*

'So, what do you think?' she asked, checking her watch. 'About Falstrum, I mean.'

'It's . . . overwhelming,' I confessed, bumping my fists together nervously. 'Waaaay bigger than my last school.'

'Why'd you switch anyway?' she said, offering me a sweet.

I gladly accepted a couple of Skittles. Sugar was energy, and seeing Arif in that vest had worn me out. 'My dad got a job down here. Do you know Zindabad's on the Broadway?'

'What, the big, flashy restaurant?'

I nodded. 'Uncle-ji owns it. He invited my dad to come and work for him.'

'Cool. Does that mean you guys get free curries and kebabs?'

I chuckled. 'Sometimes. Mostly we let Mum handle the cooking. Otherwise she sulks. And when Asian women sulk, plates start breaking—'

'Get to your lessons, please, ladies!' barked a PE teacher.

I looked round and instantly regretted it. Those bicycle shorts were so NSFW. Or Planet Earth, for that matter.

'Aw man, that's nasty!' commented a boy, snapping a pic on his phone. The poor woman's crotch was guaranteed ten seconds of Snapchat fame.

As if on cue, raucous laughter erupted all around us as camel toes and moose knuckles were discussed.

'Too much *freedom-sheedom*,' I muttered, with a shiver.

Friday rolled around, and I was glad to find I shared my textiles class with Sarabi. This was my last chance to earn the mate tag. Next week I'd be expected to find my own way round Falstrum. I definitely liked her – everyone did. But as far as I could tell, she didn't have a specific friendship group. So, unless I'd read the signs wrong, there was an opening.

Unfortunately, friend-making was my Kryptonite. Salma and me only happened because our mums were friends. All my other mates lived between pages on shelves. Joining the human race was a move that was long overdue.

Cautiously I pulled up a stool next to Sarabi. She flashed me a smile. Good sign. Meant I hadn't entered stalker territory yet.

Ms Greenberg, our textiles teacher, was a curly-haired woman with large watery eyes and a permanently confused expression. She spoke in whispers, like she was at a séance or something. 'Embroidering wallets,' she murmured, was today's task. This got a massive groan, which I thought was a bit of an overreaction.

'Did it last year,' Sarabi explained.

'Oh,' I said.

Four baskets of coloured thread were spread across the classroom. I headed for the least popular one. A lanky boy stood in front of me, carelessly tossing the skeins about. I recognized him from my tutor group. Couldn't remember his name for the life of me, but his blond topknot was unforgettable. Suddenly he turned around and thrust his hands at me.

'Which one do you reckon's best?' he asked.

I blinked in surprise, not used to being asked for my opinion.

'Um, that one sort of matches your hair,' I said shyly, pointing at the golden skein in his left hand.

'Yeah, man. Big up my weave,' he said, connecting it to his topknot and whirling it round like a propeller. 'I'm Beyoncé!' He gave a tone-deaf burst of 'Formation' while krumping.

I laughed out loud.

Ms Greenberg snatched the skein from his hand, glaring like a resentful owl. 'If you can't be trusted to behave sensibly, Malachy, I will have you copying out of a book!'

Malachy – that was it.

Nabbing a baby-pink skein, I booked it back to my stool.

'Sarabi,' I began conversationally, trying to thread my needle. 'Remember how you asked me earlier in the week if I liked it here?'

'Made up your mind?'

I nodded. 'Falstrum wins the "Muzna Saleem Seal of Approval".'

'Is it?' Malachy asked, en route to his seat. 'Even with Slim Sade mouthing off the day you come?'

'That part sucked,' I admitted.

'Some people,' he said, kissing his teeth, 'ain't got no manners!'

I shifted about uncomfortably. 'Guess stuff is going on in the world. Gotta roll with it.'

'No you don't,' he said, pointing a finger at me. 'Don't be taking shit from Sade or anyone. My G Dunthorpe'll sort it. Dude's mint.'

'Malachy!' hissed Ms Greenberg. 'Language.'

He swore under his breath, then ducked back over to his seat. I liked Malachy, he was funny.

I glanced over at Sarabi. The tip of her tongue was poking out of her mouth as she worked on her wallet. I tried to figure out what she was embroidering, but soon gave up.

'So is Sade the only one I have to watch out for then?' I asked.

'You mean bullies? Oh there's a few. But if you mean Islamophobia – I think Sade's Queen.'

'I feel sorry for the girls wearing hijabs, then,' I said.

'Guess they must be dedicated to their faith,' Sarabi said simply.

I didn't want to argue the point. Dad told me wearing a headscarf was never part of Islam, just an extremist add-on that came later. But then Dad said a lot of things – not all of them were true.

My eyes roamed the classroom, taking in an emo's electric-blue hair, a black girl's corn rows, finally settling on Sarabi's long plait. Whether wearing a headscarf was part of Islam or not, I couldn't see why it got singled out for hate at school.

Fifteen minutes later, I'd pricked myself for the twentieth time. Knots like tumours hung off drunken stitching. My wallet basically belonged in the bin. I stole a glance at Sarabi's work.

'Oh that's so cool!' I cried, smiling. Sarabi had embroidered henna patterns all over her wallet. They swooped and swirled like dancing wisps of smoke. 'I'd totally buy one.'

'Thanks!' she said. Then her eyes fell on my wallet and her smile faltered. 'I, er, could help you with that, if you want?'

'Yes please!' I said, shamelessly thrusting my work at her. 'Let me guess: you were a sewing machine in a previous life?'

Sarabi snorted. 'I'm surprised you can't embroider. Or maybe my parents are just traditional-traditional? Mum insisted we learn all those embroidery, crochet and knitting skills while we were practically still in nappies.'

'Aw, ickle babies embroidering their nappies!' I said, clasping my hands together.

Sarabi laughed at the mental image.

'How many sisters do you have?' I asked.

'Just one. Older than me, and soon to be married.' A sigh escaped her lips. 'I'll miss Taran, but inheriting her massive bedroom is going to be sweet! I've also got an older brother, Sukhdev, who works in IT.'

'Man, you are so lucky. I'm an only child.'

Her look said it all. Asians had to have large families.

'I know, right? This is brown paint,' I said, patting my cheek and making her laugh. 'Mum had an emergency hysterectomy a few months after I was born,' I explained.

'Oh,' Sarabi said, touching my shoulder. 'That's so sad.'

'Yep, you're looking at the Saleem family's sole "pride and joy".'

Sarabi grinned. 'Bet they spoil you rotten.'

I stared at her like she was from a different planet. 'I wish! Mostly I get mile-high expectations dumped on me.'

'I hear you,' she said. 'Let me guess. Could they, by any

chance, want you to become a doctor?'

I placed my forehead on the table and groaned.

'And medicine doesn't float your boat?' Even without looking, her needle continued to move back and forth through the cloth like it was enchanted.

I sat up. 'Try *sinks* my boat! I *love* English, Sarabi. Writing – painting pictures with words – it's *everything*. I know it sounds dumb—'

'It doesn't,' she said quickly. 'So what would you do with an English degree, then?'

'Novelist!' I said, making jazz hands. I hadn't told anyone about my dreams for the longest time. Little bubbles of excitement fluttered in my belly.

'What do you want to be a *novelist* for?' The way Sarabi looked at me, you'd think I'd said 'killer clown'.

I shrugged. 'Hard to explain. I just have these stories inside me. Clawing away, trying to get out.'

'Sounds painful.'

'I guess it kind of is,' I said, smiling. 'But man, *nothing* beats the buzz you get when you type those magical words "The End".'

Sarabi raised her eyebrows.

'Don't look at me like that!' I said, flushing with embarrassment.

'Not judging,' Sarabi promised, raising a slim hand. 'It's just . . . well, you don't hear about many Muslim authors, do you?'

I remembered Salma saying the same thing once.

'You don't hear about Muslims *period*. Unless it's to do with something bad. The media's got the world believing we're a bloodthirsty cult or something.'

'Groups like ISIS don't help either,' she replied.

'Truth,' I agreed. 'We definitely need to fire whoever's in charge of our PR. I want people to read my books and go, "You know what? Muslims are all right."'

Sarabi's face darkened. 'My dad got beaten up one time because a group of thugs thought he was a Muslim.'

'That's terrible!' I said, covering my mouth.

She nodded. 'Hope your books get turned into movies. Something tells me thugs aren't massive readers.'

We sat in comfortable silence: Sarabi nimbly unpicking my crappy stitching; me watching in awe.

'So your parents know nothing about your plans?' she asked, sewing claret circles.

I propped my chin up on an elbow. 'Nope. No matter how many times I try breaking it to them, it's like they're fixated on this stupid idea of me becoming a doctor. When I was younger, Ami was my number one fan. Now it's almost like she and Dad have become the same boring person.'

'That sucks,' Sarabi said.

'Focus on your projects, please, girls!' Ms Greenberg warbled. 'And why is Sarabjit decorating your wallet for you, Muzna?'

I tried to dream up an excuse. Sarabi beat me to it.

'I'm not, miss. Just helping out, cos that's what friends are for.'

I met her eyes and received the warmest smile. I hadn't even *remembered* to be the new version of myself, and she still wanted to be my friend. I could have cried.

'Why don't we sit here, in the shade?' I asked Sarabi.

It was Monday of the following week, and a beautiful leafy oak had caught my attention. Prime real estate.

'Are you mad?' Sarabi asked, eyes like a spooked mare. 'That's where Tallulah and her gang hang out!'

'What kind of a name is *Tallulah*?' I said, chuckling.

'Hush!' she pleaded. 'Trust me; you really don't wanna have her on your back. She has spies everywhere.'

Sarabi guided me over to a patch of grass beside an aluminium fence. The mottled shade of an elm offered some protection from the sun. Being Asian girls, we'd been brought up to think tanning was all kinds of evil.

'What do you wanna do after school – career-wise, I mean?' I asked, unpeeling one of my small oranges – the ones Ami bought in bulk at Lidl.

'Honestly, I don't have a clue!' she said, blushing. 'I like so many different things. I like the idea of being a lawyer. And dance rocks. But overall, I think Spanish is my favourite.'

'So combine them.' I shrugged.

'How?'

'Defend a client in Spain,' I said, thinking off the cuff. 'After making your opening statement in Spanish, obviously, you could challenge the prosecution to a dance-off. You know? Best *paso doble* wins the case!'

'That's some imagination you have there!' Sarabi said, giggling.

I glanced up as a group of kids walked towards the coveted oak. Only, 'walking' was the wrong word for it. 'Strutting' came a little closer. From the way people scooted out of their way, you'd think they were actual celebs. In the middle strode a tall brunette, every bit as stunning as a Victoria's Secret Angel. In a single fluid motion, she'd propped Chanel sunglasses on top of her head and settled into the nook of the tree. This was her throne. No wonder Sarabi had warned me off. A broad-shouldered meathead crashed down beside her, staking his claim. They shared a lingering kiss and about a gallon of saliva.

Say hola to Falstrum's first couple, I thought.

'Shameless,' Sarabi muttered, scowling. 'That's Team Tallulah, in case you were wondering.'

But instead of feeling disgusted, something new happened. I found myself imagining snogging Arif. I coughed. 'Do you ever wonder what kissing's like?'

Sarabi's head snapped up in shock. 'Muzna! You mustn't think like that.'

'Why not?' I knew the answer, but in that moment, I guess I was Sasha Fierce.

She ballooned her cheeks in frustration. 'Because you'll end up pregnant and break your parents' hearts!'

'What?' I said, trying not to laugh. 'You do realize it doesn't quite work like that?'

Shutters came down over Sarabi's eyes, and her expression hardened. 'Your funeral,' she muttered, packing away her things with prim little movements.

'Oh don't be like that,' I said, reaching out for her arm. 'I was having a laugh. You know? Imagining what it would be like to be the bad girl I'm never allowed to be.'

She thawed a little. 'I guess it must be the writer in you again. Just make sure you don't get carried away and end up writing some god-awful romance book.'

'Don't you worry about that,' I said. 'My first novel's going to be called . . . *Filthy Sheets Gone Grey*.'

Sarabi jabbed me, and we both cracked up.

CHAPTER 12

It was time for my first English lesson with Mr Dunthorpe. I tried not to get my hopes up too much, but everyone I'd spoken to seemed to think Mr Dunthorpe was like the Jay-Z of the teaching world. A quick search on RateMyTeacher.com backed this up.

However, things got off to a bad start when I was instructed to sit next to the Queen Bee herself. Tallulah gave me a quick once-over, then resumed sexting beneath the table. I felt like I'd been scanned for communicable diseases.

'Today we're going to practise writing discursive essays,' Mr Dunthorpe announced to a chorus of groans.

'You,' he said, pointing at Gary – the kid from my tutor group with a greasier version of the Bieber mop.

'Me?' Gary said. 'Why me? I wasn't the only one complaining, but you always go and pick on me! Fancy me, do ya?'

Some people laughed nervously.

'Gary,' Mr Dunthorpe said, his face impassive. 'Sorry to disappoint, but teachers never look at students in that way. What I'd like you to tell me is what you think a discursive essay might be.'

Gary shrugged like he couldn't care less.

'Well, then your reaction was completely uncalled for.' He included us all in a sweeping gaze. 'Anyone else care to hazard a guess?'

I remembered my promise to myself about going all out. My hand shot into the air like a spear.

'Yes, Muzna?' Mr Dunthorpe said, giving me an encouraging smile.

Every pair of eyes turned to stare at me as if seeing me for the first time. Even Tallulah stopped taking pictures between her thighs. It was make-or-break time.

'I think it's the kind of essay that discusses something in detail. Like showing both sides of an argument?' I said. 'Oh, and you have to include a conclusion,' I added breathlessly.

'Well done!' he exclaimed. 'Ten achievement points on SIMs, I think.'

The deal with achievement points was that if you collected enough, they got converted into Amazon vouchers. With my pocket money situation best described as 'tragic', I needed all the achievement points I could get.

'That ain't fair!' Gary complained. 'She probably did them in her last school, while we've been stuck with *you* for a teacher.'

Wow. Gary was a complete douche. What on earth was someone like that doing in Set One?

Mr Dunthorpe didn't take the bait. Instead he drew a spider diagram on the board and fired up our imaginations with a couple of killer examples.

'This is the idea phase,' he told us, when the responses slowed down. 'If you can think it, you should write it. Separating the wheat from the chaff comes later.' His enthusiasm spread like a mental Mexican wave. Everybody wanted in, and the suggestions came thick and fast.

'OK, ladies and gentlemen,' Mr Dunthorpe whispered dramatically. 'Let's make discursive-essay magic!' He caught my eye and winked. I got the feels. He made me feel like I *mattered*.

'So,' Tallulah said, placing her iPhone face down on the desk between us. 'What's your little essay going to be about?'

That accent, though. It was like sitting next to Kate Middleton.

Turning to face her properly for the first time, my heart skipped a beat. How on earth could her boyfriend kiss that perfect face without being burned to a crisp? Why, oh why, could *I* not look that amazing?

Aware that I was staring, I shifted my focus to my blank sheet of A4. 'I'm . . . not really sure . . .'

'I'm Tallulah, by the way,' she said.

'I know. *Everyone* knows you!' Realizing I was sounding like a pathetic cheerleader, I popped on the brakes. 'I'm Muzna. I, uh, transferred here from Rigsby. It's this small academy in Haringey.'

'Cool. Want to know what my essay's going to be about?' she asked, arching her back like a cat. Perky breasts stuck out like ripe mangoes. I spotted at least two boys copping an eyeful. Couldn't blame them.

'Sure,' I said, flattered that the Queen was still speaking to me. *In a parallel universe, we could even be friends!*

'Cyber bullying.' She held her hands up, as if framing a headline. '*Should cyber bullies be sent to prison for murder if a victim commits suicide?*'

'That's actually really smart,' I said, without thinking.

'For a bimbo, you mean?'

'What? No. Totally not what I meant,' I blabbered. 'I mean compared to *me*. You know, No Ideas Gal.'

'You'll think of something,' she said with a wink. 'Unlike *him*.'

I followed her eyes to Gary.

'What is he even *doing* in this class?' I asked, instantly embarrassed by how bitchy it sounded. But Tallulah either didn't notice or didn't care.

'Gary has "special needs",' she explained, complete with air quotes. 'Dunthorpe's the only one that can handle that level of bad.'

'Like detention-bad?' I asked hopefully.

'*Exclusion*-bad. The revolving-door kind – otherwise Falstrum gets fined, and Principal Dillinger misses out on his trip to Monte Carlo.'

Then lightning struck. 'I *think* my essay's going to be on the hierarchy of high school!'

'Cool, but where's the "discursive" part?' Tallulah asked, raising her eyebrows like scythes.

'Well,' I said, slightly less confidently. 'I'm going to look at the pros and cons of joining cliques versus . . . finding yourself?' I twisted my hands.

'Impressive!' Mr Dunthorpe said, popping out of nowhere.

'Really?' Tallulah said. 'Sounds like the plot from *Mean Girls* to me.'

I sank in my seat, exposed as a fraud.

'*Mean Girls* was a satire, not a discursive essay,' Mr Dunthorpe pointed out with a smile. 'In the intervening fifteen-ish years, I'd say the world has become a very different place. If you get it right, Muzna, it's just the sort of thing examiners are looking for.'

'I'll probably make a complete mess of it . . .' I said, feeling my cheeks burn.

'Nonsense,' he said. 'What's the point of writing a run-of-the-mill piece, which we both know you could do in your sleep? Far more interesting to stretch yourself a bit.'

My mouth dropped open.

He nodded, confirming my suspicions. 'Yes, I read your last report. Your previous teacher and I both have high hopes for you.'

Boosted by his praise, I put pen to paper, ready to take on the world.

Nothing happened.

Crap!

It wasn't that I couldn't think of anything. I had way *too much*.

Each time I tried to focus on an idea, another would drop, distracting me with its major potential. My poor head was a hive on fire, idea-bees zigging and zagging just out of reach. I was about to give up, when one idea suddenly outshone the rest. The bees quickly settled, bowing before royalty. *Slay queen!* I thought, as I started my opening paragraph.

Twenty minutes later, I got that feeling. When you know you've got something special on your hands. It wasn't great – not yet – but it *could* be. Only when I slipped out of my crazy writer's haze did I register Tallulah. She was staring. I smiled uncertainly.

'Are you a lesbian?' she said, grey eyes flecked with steel.

'N-n-no,' I stammered, welling up with alarming speed.

'Not that it matters,' she blithely went on. 'I'm a regular fag hag, ask anyone. Just curious about your butch-dyke look, is all.' She pitched forward, dropping her voice to a theatrical whisper. 'Oh my God, you're a boy, aren't you?'

I shook my head, now struggling to breathe. What a fool I was to think someone as popular as Tallulah could resist crushing me beneath her fashionable Vans.

Waiting a full three minutes, so it didn't look like a reaction, I raised my hand and asked if I could go to the toilet. Mr Dunthorpe studied my expression, then signed my diary, giving me permission to leave.

I locked myself in a cubicle. The air came whooshing out of my lungs. I choked and coughed and cried. I looked down at my shapeless uniform. Was it my fault Ami wouldn't let me pick a more flattering size? With a sinking feeling, I realized Tallulah might have caught me staring at her massive boobs. Or was my beard to blame? Was that why she thought I was a legit boy? I buried my face in my hands and sobbed my heart out.

*

The pips went as I returned to my seat. I'd planned it that way. The sound of chairs scraping back and people making lunch plans rose like a storm.

'No one is going *anywhere* until I have silence!' Mr Dunthorpe warned, hands on hips.

Nobody wanted to be late for lunch, so he promptly got his wish.

'Thank you. The first draft of your essay is due next week Monday. Muzna, can I see you for a minute? The rest of you go and enjoy a *healthy* meal, please!'

I sighed, stashing my stuff in my bag, then dragged myself over to Mr Dunthorpe's desk. He was going to read me the riot act for my ridiculously long toilet break. Girls were always texting each other to meet up in the loos for a gossip, and he looked like the kind of teacher who called you out on it.

'Take a seat, please,' he said.

Uh-oh, this was going to be serious.

Mr Dunthorpe removed his glasses and massaged the bridge of his elegant nose. Weird – he was actually pretty good looking for an old guy. I hoped his partner appreciated him.

'Muzna, I'm not here to tell you off or judge you,' he finally said. 'As your tutor, it's part of my remit to ensure your well-being at Falstrum.'

Great. But I couldn't relax. I was picking up those lull-before-the-storm vibes.

'Tallulah was unkind to you.' He said it as gentle as a whisper.

'*That?*' Oh my God – he must have the classroom bugged. No way did Tallulah's voice carry that far. 'Psh, total non-issue!' I lied.

His eyes burned brightly. 'At Falstrum we celebrate diversity in all its forms. After lunch, I'm going to pull her out of class to remind her of this. Would you also like her to apologize to you?'

My eyes nearly popped out of my skull. 'No!' I shook my head firmly. 'I mean, I'm fine, sir. Really.'

He nodded. 'She's intimidated by you.'

What had the man been smoking? Tallulah was a goddess. Even Taylor Swift would feel a little insecure around her.

'Your ability to consider multiple viewpoints in your writing and the speed with which you do it is uncommon in most students,' he finished.

I blinked. *He's only trying to make you feel better*, said the voice in my head.

'Your discursive essay,' he continued. '"Hierarchy of High School" – you're on to a winner there.'

I smiled sheepishly. 'Thank you.'

'One more thing. In her report, your tutor described you as "extremely shy" and "unwilling to contribute to class discussions",' he said, eyes crinkling.

I cringed. Me and Mrs Gideon had never got on. She'd had her favourites, and I hadn't been one of them.

'But everything I've seen of you this week tells me she was mistaken,' he continued. 'When you feel passionately about something, you transform into a powerhouse. It's amazing to watch! Don't let *anybody* knock your confidence.'

I began to see that Mr Dunthorpe wasn't trying to cheer me up after all. Strange as it seemed, the dude was speaking from the heart.

'Can I go, please?' I said, fearing I was going to ugly-cry and embarrass us both.

'Of course. Thanks for the company!' And with that, he whipped out a Spider-Man lunch bag.

CHAPTER 13

'Muzna!' Sarabi called as I hurtled past her in the corridor. 'What's up?'

'I'll tell you, but not here,' I said, side-eyeing the randoms that were hanging around.

I followed Sarabi to our private place by the aluminium fence.

'So spill,' she said, leaning forward, as if she could inhale the story out of me.

'Sarabi, do you think I look like a butch dyke?'

'Huh?' Sarabi looked baffled.

'How about a boy, then?'

Sarabi laughed.

'It's what Tallulah said.' I sniffed, the pain made new.

'Oh don't listen to *her*. She's a bad person.'

'But she's so pretty . . .' I said.

'Not on the inside,' Sarabi said matter-of-factly. 'Sure: she sings in the chamber choir, goes on all the trips, and gets a free pass from most teachers. But Dunthorpe sees right through her.'

I tugged at a daisy, remembering what he'd said to me earlier: *She's intimidated by you.*

Could it be true? Because, honestly? Anyone would rather be *her* than me.

'What got her triggered?' Sarabi asked, tucking into a pie.

'I don't know. Mr Dunthorpe said he liked my work. Then she was staring at my . . .'

'Yes?'

'. . . beard,' I finished, in a small voice. 'And she went off on one. Like totally unprovoked.'

Sarabi looked at my chin with sympathy. 'I know exactly how you feel.'

'How could you?' I snapped. 'Your face is more hair-free than a shaved egg!'

'Not me,' she admitted. 'My aunt. Compared to her, you're lucky. Her beard was lo-o-ong. And she's religious-religious, so no plucking either. Her family thought they'd never get her married. But then her doctor prescribed some tablets.'

'Tablets?' I repeated. What was she on about? Having a beard wasn't the same as having a headache. 'Like antidepressants?'

Sarabi shook her head. 'Tablets that control hormones and facial hair, I think.'

'Did they work?' I asked, with naked desperation.

'I think so. She's married now, at any rate.'

Polishing off her pie, she changed the subject. Apparently some Bollywood star was going to be filming a scene for his new movie in Southall. Sarabi was on a mission to get a selfie with him for her Instagram. I squealed for her. But really I was obsessing over the wonder pills.

All my life I'd wanted to look pretty but I knew my parents would freak and think I was hooking up with a guy, but lately, every time Arif walked past, hashtags swam around in my head like little bubbles of inappropriateness: #DesiHunk, #MrSexyPex, #MuznasFutureHusband. I had no control over it.

If Salma was around, I knew she'd tell me to go for it. And if I never took risks, then complaining about the Tallulahs of the world was just plain bitching.

My gaze shifted to the spot beneath the great oak. The ice queen was in residence, getting handsy with a flock of male admirers. It still boggled my mind how someone *that* beautiful could be so evil. Disney lied. Tallulah was slutty and cruel, but she lived the way she wanted and made no apologies for it. In spite of everything, I could actually respect that.

I pictured Arif with a beard-free version of myself, lying together under the oak, holding hands.

Dream on, Muzna . . .

'Hullo, Muzna! Have a seat, my dear,' called Dr Agyemang enthusiastically.

Having made an appointment online, I'd sneaked over to the surgery after school. I was snap, crackle and popping with nervous excitement. Somewhere inside me lurked the same hopeful girl who'd fantasized about Hermione lending her a *hairus goneus* charm. But what with living in the muggle world, I'd just have to hope the NHS could get me sorted instead.

'So, what can I help you with?' my GP asked, interlacing her fingers. She was rocking banana cornrows, which spiralled round her scalp in burgundy and black ripples.

'Well, it's super-embarrassing.' I giggled. God knows why.

'You know I'm here for you,' she said, dimpling.

Cautiously, I began dropping hints and clues, like we were playing a game. *Guess my condition – win a prize!* But before long, the details came tumbling out. I even ended up telling her about Tallulah's bitchery (and that she sang soprano in chamber choir – though I'm not sure why). Dr Agyemang listened to all of it, nodding at all the right moments, nudging a tissue box closer the weepier I got.

'So I hear there's a pill, maybe, that I could take?' I ventured, sniffing into a tissue.

'Indeed there is. Good ol' internet, I suppose?' she queried.

Actually it was my bestie's bearded aunt, I thought. But a simple nod made up for wasting her time earlier with Twenty Questions: The Medical Edition.

'We'll have to run some blood tests first. Make sure the problem *is* hormonal in nature. Probably need to check for polycystic ovary syndrome too . . .'

'What's that?' I asked, going rigid.

'Nothing to get het up about,' she promised. 'PCOS is a treatable condition many women suffer from. There may be fertility issues, of course. Are your periods regular?'

'Yes,' I said quickly. 'I mean, mostly. It varies . . .'

'Hmm. Let me run off a blood test request. You can get it done here today. Results should be back with me by early next week, and I'll give you a bell. Sound good?' She smiled reassuringly.

'As for the anti-androgens,' she continued, 'think of them as little sponges that soak up excess male hormones. Don't look so worried! Every human being has a balance of both male and female hormones. Sometimes these can go off-kilter. It usually sorts itself out as you get older. But I think you'd like better skin sooner rather than later?'

I nodded, desperate to be like every other girl, but worried about what Ami would say.

Dr Agyemang was as good as her word. The following week, her news gave me life. I didn't have PCOS, but I did have excess testosterone. The simple fix was Diane-35. Pills that would make my periods regular and take care of my 'hirsutism' and acne.

A life without spots or hairiness? *Bring it on!*

CHAPTER 14

Three weeks later, Dr Agyemang's pills had become my new best friends. The war on spots and bearded-lady syndrome had finally been won. I was as feminine on the outside as I was on the inside. I binned the crème bleach product I'd used faithfully since I was thirteen. This was the beginning of my totally awesome new life.

The changes didn't go unnoticed at home. Ami's hyperactive imagination went into overdrive. She demanded to be told what I'd done to my facial hair, and more importantly, whose benefit it was for.

'Relax, Ami,' I said. 'Dr Agyemang gave me some medicine for it. I'm better now. See? No more pimples.'

'*Bevakoof!*' she cried. 'Don't you know this sort of medicine can damage a girl's womb? Who's going to marry you if you can't have children?'

'What's that supposed to mean?'

'Look, Muzna – you are my only daughter, and I love you very much. But this world is cruel and you are not beautiful.' Her eyes filled with tears. 'Your only chance for a husband, *beyta*, is if you become a doctor.'

Every instinct told me to storm off. My cheeks burned with shame, and a powerful sob ballooned in my throat, but I forced myself to stay put. Ami's eyes widened as if she too had been expecting this lame reaction. Enough was enough.

'I know I'm not as pretty as you were,' I began, struggling to find the right words in Punjabi to make her understand. 'But you should be encouraging me to get educated for *myself*. Not for some imaginary husband. With one breath you tell me boys are evil, and with the other you try to sell me off to one. Who tells their own daughter she's ugly? You're a rubbish mum and I hate you!'

One hundred years of matchmaking tradition bitch-slapped by a repressed fifteen-year-old. My big speech might even have meant something had I not immediately burst into tears and fled to my bedroom. The clichéd door-slam sealed the deal. Bog-standard teen tantrum: move along, folks – nothing to see here.

Even as I lay on my bed crying my guts out, I knew Ami hadn't meant to be cruel. She was stating facts in her own *desi* way because she knew how hard things would be for girls like me. Money might not be able to buy you happiness, but apparently it could buy you a husband, especially if you didn't look like a supermodel.

Frustrated, I glanced into the mirror. No acne, no beard. No beauty either. Ami was right. Beneath the superficial changes, I was still the same, slightly dumpy, two-shades-too-dark girl, with nothing going for her. And worst of all, I knew I was turning out to be just as boy-mad as Ami feared.

I begged Allah to help me. I was crushing on Arif big time, but I didn't want to go to Hell. Neither did I want to end up in a loveless marriage with a man who saw me as a cash cow instead of the person I was.

CHAPTER 15

I drifted down the corridor, humming to myself. It was a rainy Wednesday lunchtime, and Sarabi was at Manga Club. She'd invited me along, but I'd said no. All those huge eyes and spiky hairstyles gave me nightmares.

At the end of the corridor, I doubled back. Glancing through the glass panel in the middle of a door, I spotted someone standing in the otherwise deserted classroom hugging himself. His height made me think he was a teacher, but then I spotted the Falstrum uniform. As I watched, his shoulders began to tremble. Was he crying?

When he dropped to the floor — legs tucked under, hands on thighs — I twigged that he was praying. His head swept first one way, *salaam*ing the angel on the right, then to the left. Now I could see the guy was Arif, but why were there tears on his cheeks?

'Are you OK?' I asked, popping my head round the door.

'Shit! Don't do that to me, man!' he said, scrambling like a spooked cat. 'Thought it were a teacher.'

'Sorry . . .' I said, cheeks burning. 'I thought you were . . . upset.'

'What, this?' he asked, wiping his wet eyes. 'Praying from the heart does it.'

'Oh,' I said slightly confused, but also impressed. Boys pretended that they didn't cry, but Arif was owning it. 'Sorry.'

'Me too, fam. Way I spoke to you just now? Out of order.' He pulled a sock on. 'Stupid *kuffar* got me on high alert, innit?'

Kuffar. Disbelievers.

'I feel like that sometimes,' I admitted, lingering in the doorway. 'But honestly, I doubt anyone would have a problem with you praying. It's your right, isn't it? And it's super-noble and all.'

He chuckled and patted the floor. 'Have a seat, fam, and let Uncle Arif tell you summat about the world.'

My body tingled. There was something seriously *wrong* about getting on the floor with a sexy boy in a darkened room. I knelt on the carpet tiles, my heart pounding so loud I was afraid he could hear it. His feet were *massive* . . .

Know what that means, don't you! leered a dirty voice in my head.

I was definitely changing. When I used to hear girls lusting over the latest hottie, I found it a little pathetic. I had eyes, sure, and I knew what a 'pretty boy' was, but for the first time in my life Arif was awakening something. It was scary and thrilling at the same time.

'They hate us, Muzna,' Arif said, his eyes wide and intense. 'Islam proper scares 'em. Teachers here, yeah, all nice to your face and that, but behind closed doors it's a different story. Don't believe me? Google "Prevent Duty".'

'Is that the anti-radicalization thing?' I asked.

'Anti-Islamic, more like!' He rubbed his lips, furrowing his brow. 'The government wants teachers to report students with "extreme views". Like if some kid in Year Six says, "The West is always starting wars in Muslim countries," teachers are supposed to snake 'em out to the feds. This half-pint, who's pissing himself, gets dragged down to the police station for speaking truth!'

My mouth fell open. *Was that true?*

'Double standards,' he said, shaking his head.

'How do you mean?'

'Insult the Prophet or burn a Qur'an, and it gets defended as "freedom of speech",' he said, pounding the floor with a fist. 'But Prevent is all about gagging Muslims. Funny how they get to pick and choose what you can and can't say.'

'You've thought about this a lot.'

He nodded. 'Pretty hard not to when it's shoved in your face twenty-four seven. Jameel – my big brother, yeah – proper smart, he is. Knows bags more stuff than I do about the hypocrisy of the West. You should come over and meet him. Have you woke in no time—'

The pips sounded.

'Better get to class now, eh?' he said, stepping into his trainers. 'Later.'

I watched him leave. A teacher snapped the light on, but the gloom stayed in my heart.

'The way she keeps you guessing till the very end is pure genius!' I babbled. 'And she leaves this –' I tried to recall what my word-of-the-day app had taught me only that morning – '*surreptitious* trail of clues.' I paused, trying to gauge whether I'd impressed him with my big-wordiness. 'It's all there, but you don't think it's important. Then when you get to the end, you're, like, "Yaass! Queen of Crime!"'

Mr Dunthorpe nodded. 'Christie's a personal fav of mine.' Stifling a yawn, he glanced at his watch. 'Anyway, mustn't keep you. Your parents must be wondering where you've got to.'

Teacher code for *I'm tired – please go*.

I nodded, not wanting to become a nuisance in his eyes. At the threshold, I spun round. 'I love coming to book club, sir. And you're the best teacher I've ever had.'

His cheeks glowed, caught off guard by the compliment. 'Well thank you. But it's students like you who make it what it is.'

Waving, I hurried off. My parents worried like crazy if I was late. Racist attacks, Boyfriends and Rape — an unholy trinity that gave them nightmares. I could understand the first and last. But having a boyfriend didn't belong in there. At least, not the kind I wanted . . .

I pulled out my phone to let Ami know I was on my way. I got an engaged tone. At least once a week, Ami telephoned the village to check in with her sister and get her gossip fix. For a conservative country, it seemed a lot of scandals went down there. Or maybe they were all made up?

Putting my phone away, I jogged home.

The next day, my form sleepwalked through another boring PSCHE lesson. Twenty minutes ago the school's internet went down. That meant Mr Dunthorpe couldn't show us the YouTube videos he'd found to pimp up the boring lesson on 'Britishness'. Like, what did that even mean? The lesson was flopping.

I forced myself to look at the worksheet in front of me.

1. **The Queen has German ancestry. Is she British?**
2. **Do you think Britain is a cohesive society? Give examples to support your answer.**
3. **Explain how important your national identity is to you.**

The only person who seemed all that bothered was Jadwiga. Maybe it had something to do with recently having emigrated from Poland. Dad was forever reminding me about my roots, like he was afraid Britain might swallow me up or something. Yet he'd also tell me with pride that 400,000 Muslims from the Indian subcontinent fought alongside British soldiers in World War Two.

I glanced round the room, seeking inspiration. I had to admit, sometimes it got complicated trying to balance British values with Pakistani ones, especially when racists were always ready to throw words like 'coconut' and 'oreo' at any Asian or black person with a British accent. I guessed if the Queen wasn't any less of a Brit because of her German roots, then neither was I. Feeling an essay coming on, I began writing.

'Psst! Muzna!'

Making sure Mr Dunthorpe wasn't watching, I turned round. It was Malachy.

'You done the maths homework?' he asked, tugging at his topknot.

'Tried it.' I raised an eyebrow. 'Why – didn't you?'

He grimaced, scratching behind an ear. 'I could spin you some bullshit story about how it was my hamster's funeral. But I'd never lie to my best bud, Muzna.'

I smirked. Across the classroom, Jadwiga was interrogating Mr Dunthorpe.

'Match was on last night,' Malachy continued, braces gleaming in his crooked smile. 'You catch it?'

I shook my head. Playing sport was bad enough. Watching it was my idea of hell.

'Went to penalties, yeah? Oh man, I almost shat myself, I'm telling ya! Then Lacazette put one straight in the back of the net.'

I blinked at him. 'That's a good thing, right?'

'Frickin' awesome!' he agreed, punching the air. 'Thing is though, it'd already gone half eleven . . .'

Watching him grovel and squirm was strangely entertaining. But I didn't want to be That Girl, so I chucked my maths book at him. 'I want it back by the end of lunch,' I said, as he hungrily flicked through the pages. 'And now I own your soul.'

He looked up in alarm, then grinned. 'Gotta fight Satan for it first.'

I smiled back. Then I caught Sade watching me through narrowed eyes, and my confidence slipped. Like Cinderella at midnight, I transformed back into Doormat Muzna: afraid to crack jokes or speak until spoken to.

'Mr Dunthorpe?' Sade said.

She was going to snitch on me. I just *knew* it.

'Yes, Sade?' he said, knees popping like corks from having squatted for the last ten minutes. The sad thing was, for all the time he'd spent with Jadwiga, she still didn't look satisfied.

'I was just wondering,' Sade continued, in a disturbingly silky voice. 'Do we have to learn about Britishness cos of all the *Muslim* people in our class?'

'I beg your pardon,' Mr Dunthorpe said, the warning clear in his tone.

The room fell silent.

'Cos if that's it, well, can't the Muslims be sent off to learn about it elsewhere? I mean the rest of us would never even *think* about bombing Britain.'

There were gasps. Not one single person was impressed.

Me? I was so furious, I blasted Sade with the full force of my voice box. 'Oh shut up, Sade! We all know you hate Muslims, but we're as British as fish and chips. Deal with it!'

'Yeah, Sade,' Malachy said, nominating himself as my wingman. 'Lessons like this are to teach people like *you* to stop the hate.'

But Malachy could have sworn at Sade for all it would've mattered. She'd switched to tunnel vision. Too late I realized I'd walked straight into a trap.

'Want beef, baby girl?' Sade asked, tossing aside the Tippex brush she'd been busy painting her nails with. 'Fine. Come get some.' She rocked to her feet, summoning me WWE-style.

My heart dropped. A forgotten memory of my father resurfaced.

'*These people think we are their obedient servants!*' Dad had once ranted, after watching an interview with a right-wing MP. '*Nearly seventy years after the British Raj fell, and the stereotype lives on. You show them you are a Pakistani lioness, Muzna!*'

Egged on by an imaginary dad, I answered the call, brushing aside Sarabi, who clung to my sleeve. Fear was gone. I was *fricking titanium*.

Suddenly Arif's broad back materialized before me, close enough to feel the warmth of his skin on my lips. A human shield – protecting me from being whupassed into the afterlife.

Mr Dunthorpe seized control of the situation in a flash.

'Muzna's right,' he said, freezing everyone in place with the deadly power of his voice. 'No place for bigotry in my classroom. Kindly take yourself off to Ms Moon's office, Sade.'

'You what?' Sade asked, as if dealing with a person with learning difficulties. 'It's called "banter", man. Besides I'm half Nigerian, innit? How can *I* be racist?'

The class erupted with outrage. Stirring the pot was Sade's speciality, and she was on point. In the ensuing madness, Mr Dunthorpe calmly flung open the classroom door.

'Out.' He pointed in case she'd forgotten the way.

Sade marked me with a baleful glare, then disappeared.

A few minutes later the pips sounded, and people flew out of the door.

'Can I have a volunteer to collect the worksheets, please?' Mr Dunthorpe said while typing on his computer. Probably recording the Sade-incident on SIMs. I hoped she got excluded.

'I'll do it,' said Arif.

'Come on, *you*!' said Sarabi, helping me pack my things away. 'Let's get out of here before you start any more fights.'

'Yo!' Arif called, as he collected our worksheets for Mr Dunthorpe.

I looked up.

'You did good, fam.' He made a fist. 'I got you.'

'Thanks,' I said, then fled the room, dragging Sarabi behind me.

CHAPTER 16

'Got the hots for him, haven't you?' said Sarabi, as she ate her packed lunch of *dahi phulki* – an Asian potato salad thing.

'No *Ami*,' I said, in an accent that rivalled Uncle Tanveer's. 'I don't like boys. I'm a good lesbian child.'

A *phulki* shot out of Sarabi's mouth like a bullet, as she tried not to laugh. Under the oak, Tallulah was busy teaching a group of boys how to twerk.

'Come on – don't act like you don't think Arif Malik's *hawt*.'

'Actually, I don't,' Sarabi said primly.

I gripped her wrist. 'She has a pulse! How can she not be bowled over by that much cuteness?'

'Fine. He's hot,' she said begrudgingly. 'That's exactly the problem. His type are all players.'

I bristled. 'And you know this how?'

She studied my expression. 'Look, Muzna – I can see you like him. But let's get real here for a second. Say he's into you too. Then what? Do you become girlfriend-boyfriend? Would your family be OK with that?'

The girl had a point. My parents were so hands-on, I could practically feel my throat being squeezed.

In the distance, one of the boys had dropped his trousers, driving Tallulah and her crew into hysterics. He vibrated his bum cheeks like he'd been struck by lightning. The horrified look on Sarabi's face was priceless. Then one of the teachers on duty chased him off.

*

That night, I lay awake in bed listening to Ami and Dad chatting about some family disaster that was going down in the motherland. Dad was about to make a long-distance call to Lahore, and was begging Ami to stick to the script. Communicating with his side of the family was like a UN peacekeeping mission. I'd get the gory details in the morning, whether I wanted them or not.

I sighed, turning over. My phone was still charging. I reached out to see if Sarabi had left me another message, but she hadn't.

I closed my eyes, stroking Laddu's battle-hardened fur. I thought about the way Arif had thrown himself in front of me in PSCHE. I hugged Laddu tighter, my imagination transforming him into Arif's wandering hand.

CHAPTER 17

The following week, Mr Dunthorpe was on a mission to get us to understand responsibility in romantic relationships. *Awkward!*

My eyes kept drifting over to Arif. I'd look away, only to find them returning to him like homing pigeons. He was *so* beautiful. For his part, he was engaged in a staring competition with a magpie on the window ledge. I spotted the single Skullcandy earphone jammed in his ear and could hear the faint buzz of Stormzy.

Remembering Sarabi, I tore my eyes away from Arif, expecting an earful from my prim and proper mate. But Sarabi had zoned out too. Guess the frank discussion about love was too much for her. With sadness, I realized my parents would have preferred her as their daughter.

'If I get a girl pregnant, yeah?' said Gary. The boy was such an attention-seeker. 'Ain't my fault if the cow wants to keep it, is it? I mean, she should've taken contra-septic pills. Or let me do her up the—'

'Stop right there!' Mr Dunthorpe said. 'Nothing gives you the right to offend others while sharing your opinion. Get your things together and wait outside.'

Gary made no attempt to comply.

'Like any girl would even let him get that close!' mocked a girl from the back row.

'You and your mum didn't seem to mind last night,' he shot back.

The girls at the back began to shout insults.

In two strides, Mr Dunthorpe was towering over Gary. 'Out!'

Any normal person would have gone. When Mr Dunthorpe told you to do something, you did it, whether you wanted to or not. But Gary, as Tallulah had once informed me, was an exclusion just waiting to happen.

Gary got up, squaring up to our tutor. 'Make me,' he said.

Mr Dunthorpe made a grab for his rucksack, but Gary, with quicker reflexes, whipped it out of reach. The surprise move unbalanced Mr Dunthorpe. As he fought to stop himself from face-planting, Mr Dunthorpe's hand flew out, momentarily pressing against Gary's thigh.

'Oh my days!' Gary boomed. 'You touched me!' He included us all in a sweep of his finger. 'You all saw this fag go for my dick!'

'Out!' Mr Dunthorpe repeated, but now his cheeks were going bright red, and his voice was drained of power. I felt so bad for him. It was so obviously an accident. A really, really humiliating one.

'I'm going straight to the principal and telling him you came on to me,' spat Gary, swinging his bag high over his shoulder. 'See ya in prison, Mr *Bum*-thorpe!'

He legged it out the door.

Mr Dunthorpe was *shook*. He kept blinking as his chest fluttered beneath his argyle tank. We all knew why. The media had made it clear that sexual allegations – even fake ones – could end a teacher's career.

'Don't worry, sir!' I said, compelled to speak out. 'Everyone knows Gary's a filthy liar. We've got your back.'

'Tag team.' Malachy said, smacking a fist into his palm. 'Me and Muzna will beat him up for you.'

'Fool's just gassing,' added a boy to my left. 'No way is he going to Dillinger. Trust.'

Everyone agreed.

That's when I noticed Arif looking my way with interest.

As I was tugging my maths textbook out of my locker (*Shove it in deep enough, hope it'll end up in Narnia!*), Sarabi placed her hands over my eyes.

'Guess who!' she said in a gruff voice that I knew was supposed to sound like a boy.

'Hmm, hairy, sweaty man-hands,' I said. 'Now who could that be . . . ?'

She thumped my back.

'Actually it was the smell of curry that gave you away!' I said, earning another playful whack.

'I've got maths now,' I said, hugging my fearsome book as I backed up the hallway. 'Same time, same place?'

'Wait!' she cried. 'My sister's *Anand Karaj* is in a couple of weeks.'

'Anand Karaj?' I repeated. 'That your latest Bollywood husband?'

'No, silly! It's the proper name for a Sikh wedding. Besides, Arjun Kapoor is my forever.' Suddenly she looked sheepish. 'The wedding's probably gonna be super-cheesy, but, um, do you wanna come?'

'Well duh!' I said, clapping with excitement. 'Do I get one of those official invites?'

'Yeah, sort you one out for tomorrow,' she said, looking a bit embarrassed. 'Taran had them printed on textured card. She's only giving them to people that are *definitely* coming.'

'I'm *so* there,' I promised.

'Oh, by the way, it wouldn't be the actual-actual wedding. That's happening a day before at a Gurdwara in Southall. The banquet's the day after. But that's the fun part!'

'Lit!' Malachy said, crashing our party. 'Count me in.' He flashed his metallic smile, bouncing a red-and-black basketball like a yo-yo.

Me and Sarabi exchanged glances.

'Oh come on! I can be just as desi as you two,' he insisted, thrusting his basketball at Sarabi. 'Watch this.' He began bouncing up and down on one foot, while twisting two imaginary light bulbs.

'You're not coming to my sister's wedding,' Sarabi told him sternly.

'Especially after that,' I added.

'Aw, why not? Is it cos I is a white boy?' He placed a hand dramatically over his scrawny chest.

'Yes, Malachy,' I agreed. 'Sarabi's low-key racist for not inviting you to her sister's wedding. Who, by the way, doesn't even know you.'

'Have a good time, girls,' he said with a laugh, dribbling his ball down the corridor. 'Save me a doggy bag, yeah? Some *Rogan Josh*. Safe!'

A creased sheet of paper fell out of my textbook. I picked it up and was surprised to find it was my 'Britishness' worksheet from PSCHE, complete with essay-sized answers. A message was scrawled along the top in pencil.

> *Swiped this for you. <u>Not</u> a worksheet.*
> *It's a test from THEM.*
>
> *A.M.*

Arif Malik? My heart was thrumming.

'What is it?' Sarabi asked.

'Just some old worksheet.' I shoved it back in.

As I settled down in maths, my mind was elsewhere. What did

Arif's message mean? Who was *THEM*? I thought back to our lunchtime conversation in that empty classroom on a wet Wednesday.

Praying . . . big manly feet . . . kuffar . . . PREVENT.

Oh. My. God.

It was a test to see if I was an extremist.

CHAPTER 18

The next day, I was surprised to find a haggard-looking Ms Greenberg sitting in Mr Dunthorpe's chair. She was taking the register. Or at least trying to. No one was actually cooperating with the textiles teacher.

'Sorry I'm late,' I said over the din, quickly sitting down. My eyes automatically cut to the desk by the window. Arif was missing. Then, glancing round, I noticed everyone had ditched the official seating plan to be with their friends. 'Where's Mr Dunthorpe?'

Nobody answered. They looked tired and a little shell-shocked.

'Mr Dunthorpe is otherwise engaged,' Ms Greenberg said cryptically, refusing to meet my eyes.

'The stupid school thinks Dunthorpe's a *paedophile*,' Sade said, irritably. 'Got the sack or summink!'

'What?' I asked in disbelief. I looked at Sarabi for confirmation. She nodded sadly.

'Children, please!' Ms Greenberg said, trying to impose order. 'We mustn't discuss this sort of thing in school!'

'There's got to be some sort of m-mistake . . .' I stammered.

'Gary made good on his promise,' explained Sarabi. 'He reported Mr Dunthorpe to the principal for . . . *you-know-what*. Mr Dillinger had to suspend both of them while they investigate. It's like a rule, or something.'

'That's bullshit!' I said, slamming my hand down on the desk.

'Language, Muzna!' Ms Greenberg snapped, before a paper aeroplane nosedived into her chestnut curls.

'You think our school will be on the news?' one of the boys speculated.

'As the person with the most followers on Instagram, the reporters are gonna want to hear the details from me,' announced a girl, giving herself a second coat of lip gloss.

'How dare you!' I roared, making the girl draw a line of frosted pink across her cheek in surprise.

The class fell silent and stared. Even Ms Greenberg stopped fiddling with the paper plane in her wig.

I swallowed. 'After everything he's done for us. We all saw what happened. We all know Mr Dunthorpe is on the level.'

'Preach!'

I nearly passed out when I saw that voice belonged to Sade. We nodded at each other. A temporary alliance had been formed.

'Everyone's on Mr Dunthorpe's side, and everyone knows Gary's a wanker,' said Alex, stroking her blue bob. 'It'll turn out all right in the end.'

'Are you willing to take that chance?' I said. 'Cos I'm not. I know that without Mr Dunthorpe, I can kiss my English GCSE goodbye.'

'Right, if you children won't stop talking about this, I'm writing your names down and passing on the list to Ms Moon!' Ms Greenberg whinged.

'Dunthorpe's been our tutor since Year Seven,' chimed in a boy. 'We owe him.'

'OK, so what's your plan?' asked Alex.

My cheeks burned. I hadn't thought it through. Injustice was what got Doormat Muzna yapping.

'Doesn't have one!' said the girl with the lip gloss.

Anger flared inside me, and without realizing it, I tapped into the more powerful version of myself.

'I'll set up a petition online, and everyone can sign it,' I said, thinking on my feet. 'I'll also go to Mr Dillinger with the truth.'

In the movie version, everyone would burst into rapturous applause, and I'd crowd-surf into the Falstrum history books. In reality? There was this big, fat, awkward silence.

The pips sounded, ending the vacuum of cringe. I waited outside for Sarabi, going over in my head exactly what I was going to say to Mr Dillinger. Maybe it would do nothing more than get me in trouble. But I couldn't stand by and do *nothing*. Mr Dunthorpe had believed in me when nobody else did.

Suddenly my arm was gripped so tightly, I nearly screamed.

'Set up that petition and send me the link,' Sade instructed. 'I'll forward it to my contacts.'

I nodded, wondering who this was and what she'd done with the real Sade.

'Dunthorpe's all right, innit?' she said, sensing my WTF confusion.

'What was that about?' Sarabi asked, catching the tail end.

'Nothing. Come on. Dunthorpe's counting on us.'

I dragged Sarabi up to the principal's office. With the number of reservations she kept coming up with, I was afraid if we didn't get there fast she'd chicken out.

The principal's secretary looked up from her computer screen. With pore-less caramel skin and lush copper curls, she could've doubled for Zendaya. At any other time I might have taken a moment to feel jealous. But this wasn't any other time.

'Um, hi,' I said, with a little wave.

'We'd like to see Mr Dillinger, please,' added Sarabi.

The lady gave duck face. 'What's this about? Shouldn't you two be in lessons?'

I sensed Sarabi opening her mouth, so I blurted: 'It's a *child-protection issue*.'

My reading obsession meant I'd dipped into plenty of Dad's

social-work magazines. 'Safeguarding' and 'child protection' were like magic words that made teachers sit up and take note. If not, heads rolled.

Shock flashed in her wide-set eyes, before giving me saccharine sympathy. Probably figured I'd been molested. I didn't care. Bigger things were at stake than my non-reputation.

'Just a moment,' she said. She knocked on Mr Dillinger's door and vanished inside. A moment later she reappeared, waving us in.

Me and Sarabi exchanged looks, swallowed almost simultaneously, then stepped over the threshold.

'Hello, young ladies!' Mr Dillinger greeted us kindly, before switching to a more serious tone. 'Now what's this all about? Hmm?'

'I'd like to report a false allegation made by Gary Simmonds about our tutor, Mr Dunthorpe,' I said, trying to remember to breathe.

'Indeed?' the principal said, his body language losing the welcome factor. 'I'm afraid that particular matter is out of my hands.'

'But he didn't do anything!' Sarabi cried. 'I mean, he told Gary to get out for being rude, and Gary threatened to report him for . . . for . . .'

'A bunch of lies,' I interjected.

I laid the facts out for the principal, point by point.

'How can a teacher get suspended for an accident?'

'And how come Gary gets off scot-free?' demanded Sarabi.

'Oh I can assure you nobody is getting off scot-free,' said Dillinger. 'The school has policies in place for dealing with situations like this. Both parties stay at home while the matter is urgently investigated by the school governors.'

'But sir,' I protested. 'With all due respect, how can they possibly investigate the incident when they weren't even there?

I'm telling you, every one of us saw our tutor slip. Gary's complaint was just revenge for being told off.'

'Yes, and as I've told you—'

'The media's always banging on about sexual allegations ending a teacher's career,' I rudely cut in. 'Even when they're false. We couldn't bear for that to happen to Mr Dunthorpe, sir! He's the best teacher we've ever had.'

Mr Dillinger sighed. 'Everyone at Falstrum supports Mr Dunthorpe's excellent track record. You must have more faith in the school system; let it run its course. Now hurry back to your lessons.'

Had that been a sign that we'd get our tutor back? The rumours said Dillinger was going to retire at the end of the year. Did he even care?

'Well we've done everything we could . . .' my mate said, as we headed towards Building B.

'Did we, though?' I said, an idea taking root in my head. 'Dillinger wants to avoid bad publicity for the school so he can retire on a high. Probably gets a juicy bonus for it.'

'So?'

'So we give him exactly what he doesn't want!'

'Oh Muzna,' Sarabi complained, spotting the twinkle in my eye. 'Please tell me you're not going to start burning your bra and invite the local press to film it!'

'No, Sarabi. Burning underwear is *so* last century.' I shook my head. 'What I'm planning will be *epic*!'

At lunchtime, me and Sarabi went to see Ms Winterborne in her art studio. Sarabi was one of her favourites, so she was only too happy to let us use her art supplies to make some Amnesty International banners. Unsupervised, Sarabi and I began painting slogans that had absolutely nothing to do with the human rights organization.

'This is *bad*,' Sarabi said.

I looked up. 'It is a bit. Here.' I handed her a tube of neon paint. 'Can't go wrong with a bit of pink!'

She shook her head, her face a tangle of emotions. 'It's lying! Just you watch. I'm going to end up being reincarnated as something disgusting.'

'Sade's bum?'

'This is serious, Muzna!' she cried.

I put my brush down and gave her a one-armed hug. 'Come on, Sarabi. You said it yourself: Mr Dunthorpe's a good man. He's been wronged. Don't ask me why, but the universe decided it's up to you and me to put things right.' I swallowed, hoping I was making sense. 'Don't you even want to try?'

She didn't reply. But I must have said something right, because she picked up her brush and went back to work.

Our last stop was the ICT suite. I hastily threw together a leaflet in Publisher. Between us, we had just enough print credits for fifty copies.

BRING BACK DUNTHORPE!

We, the students of Falstrum Academy, request the immediate reinstatement of Mr Michael Dunthorpe. Mr Dunthorpe is an <u>outstanding</u> teacher, who gets results every time. A false allegation was made leading to his unfair suspension.
WHAT: Boycott all classes until Mr Dunthorpe is reinstated.
WHEN: Period 5–7 today and every day till our demand is met!

WHERE: School field.
Come join our massive sit-down protest and become
part of Falstrum history!
<u>**DUNthorpe DUN nuttin' wrong!**</u>

Sarabi added an eye-catching emoji border.

'Emojinal blackmail,' I said. 'Yaaaassss.'

'*Massive* sit-down?' she queried.

'We will be, hon,' I replied, feeding off my own nervous energy. 'All for a good cause, eh?'

'You keep telling yourself that . . .' Sarabi said, her eyes full of misgivings.

Our fliers were snapped up like celebrity nudes. Text messages went pinging back and forth, and we even got #BringBackDunthorpe trending thanks to a celebrity who unexpectedly took up our cause and retweeted for us. Within a short space of time, word got out in a big way.

By two o'clock, the school field was *teeming* with students. Half the school must have turned up. Whether it was out of loyalty to Mr Dunthorpe or an excuse to bunk, I wasn't sure. A couple of boys grabbed one of our banners and danced about demanding Mr Dunthorpe be taken off 'death row'. Alex and her mates waved an eye-catching placard with a focus on LGBT rights. Five girls were performing one of Drake's songs, having changed the lyrics to something about Mr Dunthorpe's betrayal at the hands of 'lying hoes'. Everyone seemed to have warped the message to fit their own agenda. But it didn't matter – they were *here*.

I caught myself trying to spot Arif in the crowd. Still hadn't turned up. His attendance was all over the place. I hoped things were OK at home.

Then I saw Mr Dillinger, and my insides shrivelled. He scurried across the playground like Saruman the White, flanked by a couple of senior orcs.

'OK, I'm gone!' yelped a boy, starting a crowd panic.

'Hold your positions!' I shouted, jumping on to a tree stump.

Sarabi looked up at me in surprise. The bottom dropped out of my stomach. Who the hell did I think I was?

But it didn't matter. I had about three seconds to rally everyone behind Mr Dunthorpe before the whole thing fell apart and I probably got excluded.

'An innocent man's career is at stake!' I hollered. 'Mr Dunthorpe is the best teacher this school has ever known. It's not right that some fool should be allowed to take him away from us!'

'Hear, hear!' said a girl I vaguely recognized. Then it came to me. Amie: the girl who'd taken me up to my tutor on the very first day. I threw her a grateful smile. It was all the encouragement she needed.

'Bring back Dunthorpe!' Amie sang, punctuating the words with little punches. 'Bring back Dunthorpe!'

'BRING BACK DUNTHORPE! BRING BACK DUNTHORPE!' the crowd chanted back.

Sarabi nudged me and smiled. We joined in, adding our own fists to the air.

Amie's chant went viral. And by that I mean it just kept growing and growing until it seemed like the very foundations of the school started to tremble.

The principal and senior teachers arrived looking flustered. We chanted even louder. Power-tripping for sure, but all for a good cause. Mr Dillinger suddenly spotted me and Sarabi, and moved in for the kill.

'I suppose you two are behind this debacle?' he said, waving one of the leaflets in our faces.

My life flashed before my eyes.

'No!' boomed Amie, linking her arm with mine. 'We're all in this *together*. Give us back our teacher. He didn't do nothing dirty, and you know it! You bung all the worst kids in his class cos he's the only one that can handle 'em!'

I could have hugged Amie. She spoke words I'd never dare to. The chanting began again, increasing in intensity. Mr Dillinger glanced wearily at his colleagues, who were muttering, shaking their heads. Just then a news van pulled up by the school gates. Guess that celebrity retweet had really pulled in the big guns.

'All right! You've made your point!' shouted Mr Dillinger, while one of the senior teachers went to tell the news crews to clear off. Dillinger might have had one foot in the grave, but the old guy still had a decent pair of lungs on him. The chanting subsided. 'If you'd like to help Mr Dunthorpe, then I will need your complete cooperation.'

Some students cheered; others told them to shut up and listen. It took another twenty seconds for Mr Dillinger to regain our attention.

'You are all to return to your lessons immediately and to behave sensibly . . .'

This demand was met with jeers. You couldn't just pull the plug when people got themselves this worked up. Water cannons were invented for a reason.

'. . . while we attempt to expedite Mr Dunthorpe's return,' finished Dillinger.

'Shut up and do it!' Amie said in a voice like a foghorn. 'Otherwise we'll never get Dunthorpe back!'

With reluctance, people began drifting back to class.

I ran up to Amie. 'Thanks, hon!' I said, hugging her like mad. 'If you hadn't come through for us when you did, I would've passed out.'

'Your idea,' she said, smiling. 'Besides, I weren't letting them

Tory bastards take Dunthorpe away. He should be running this friggin' school!'

'Well done, Muzna!' someone shouted, thumping my back.

'Yeah, got some wicked selfies!' said another.

I looked around for Sarabi. There she was, holding the door of Building C wide open with an even wider grin on her face. I went over, and we exchanged high-fives and burst out laughing. A teacher hushed us from her classroom door. It only made us laugh harder.

Mr Dillinger was true to his word. The very next day, we got Mr Dunthorpe back, cheering him like a celeb as he walked through the door. He blushed profusely, but we knew he was touched. It was out of mad respect for the guy that we simmered down quickly to listen to him.

'I've been told I'm not allowed to discuss it, but, well, you've made me the *happiest* teacher in Britain!' He held up a large tub of Quality Street. 'My little way of saying thanks.'

More cheers. Couldn't go wrong with chocolate.

'What happened to Gary?' Malachy asked. He was miffed he'd missed the whole thing through flu.

Mr Dunthorpe just shrugged. He was way too professional to divulge a thing like that. Word on the street was that Gary had been shipped off to the local PRU. Good riddance. Dillinger had come good.

Mr Dunthorpe came over to Sarabi and me last. 'Thank you,' he whispered, his eyes full of meaning.

I felt myself blush. He backed off immediately. That's why I liked him so much. Mr Dunthorpe understood us way better than any other adult ever had.

CHAPTER 19

'Ami,' I said, skewering an onion on the steel spikes of a holder to chop it. Ami had got it down at the pound shop, and it was worth its weight in gold. 'Would it be OK if I bought one of those ready-made suits off the internet? For my mate's wedding, I mean.'

Ami was in the lounge. You could still have a conversation, since everything was open plan. I'd stuck Ami in the recliner, having smeared a ninety-nine-pence mud pack over her face and placed a couple of slices of cucumber over her eyes. Much as I liked to pamper Ami, I'm not gonna lie: there was an ulterior motive here.

Ami lifted up a slice of cucumber to shoot me a reproachful look. 'When you already have a beautiful shalwar suit Kulsoom tailored to your *exact* measurements?'

OK, now I was going to lie. 'You're right, Ami. That suit is beautiful.' I suppressed a shudder. 'Better save it for an actual family wedding, eh? And let me go to this one in a cheap—Ow!' The onion spat in my eye. Was God punishing me for my lies? They *were* becoming a bit of a habit . . .

Ami replaced the cucumber slice over her eye and sank back into her trance. 'And how much is this "internet suit", huh?'

'Thirty quid,' I replied. Honestly I had no clue, but it sounded about right. The green abomination Auntie Kulsoom had created belonged in the London Dungeon, right next to the torture rack and the iron maiden. No way could I face Sarabi dressed like that.

'Are you mad? Do you not realize your daddy has become a servant?'

'Ami . . .' I whined. 'I'll pay for it out of my own money, OK? Please. I promise I won't get anything shameless.'

'I'll ask your father,' she relented.

It was the second-best response I could have hoped for. Just one level below an outright *yes*. Dad was always so exhausted from work, he was unlikely to make a fuss. Especially since Ami would be on chaperone duty.

Tuesday morning, we were herded into the hall for the weekly assembly. A couple of chancers from my tutor group tried to sit with their mates from other classes. Bad call. The year curriculum coordinator blasted them in front of the entire school.

Just as I was about to sit next to Sarabi, I got told to fill a gap from a previous line. Sarabi made Sad Face, complete with finger tear. I shrugged. But my disappointment was short-lived.

'Careful, fam,' Arif said as I was about to sit down next to him. 'These chairs been designed by that psycho from the *Saw* movies.'

I laughed. The YCC shot me down with a finger to her lips. It was true though: the chairs were bum-blisteringly bad. As she moved off – Malachy firmly in her crosshairs – Arif pushed a stick of Juicy Fruit into my palm. A hush fell over us as Mr Dillinger's bald pate rose above the lectern like a giant speckled egg.

'Good morning, ladies and gentlemen,' he said. 'You've seen the posters around school, and it's been mentioned in your lessons. Just in case you've been living under a rock for the past week, we are *proudly* celebrating Black History Month here at Falstrum.'

There were whoops of joy and stamping feet. 'Black Lives Matter!' someone shouted. A ripple of laughter travelled through the rows.

'If there is any silliness today,' Mr Dillinger said, shutting us down with a savage tone, 'mark my words, I will have your parents in school.'

The senior teachers backed him up with their best glares.

'So without further ado, I welcome . . . er . . . *Latisha* to the stage,' he said, hobbling back to his seat.

People clapped and cheered as a tall girl with a beautiful smile stepped forward. You could tell she was a nice person just from her vibes.

'Good morning and welcome to our assembly. For those of you who don't know me, my name's Lati*fah*.' The irony seemed lost on Mr Dillinger. 'Everyone involved worked so hard putting this assembly together. So sit back and relax as we BHM you, Falstrum style!'

The stage faded to dark before spotlights descended on a couple of boys.

'My mum says Black History Month is dumb!' said the first boy. 'There's no White History Month. There's no Gay History Month.'

'What you on about?' said his mate. 'Every month's White History Month.'

People cracked up. Even Mr Dillinger smiled.

'This is dope!' whispered Arif, his fruity breath giving my ear chills.

'You never heard of LGBT Pride Month? June's where it's at,' said the second boy.

'For real? Guess Mum's a tool then.'

'I ain't saying nothing. I seen your mum. She gimme licks!'

Laughter swept through the hall.

'So what's this Black History Month about anyway?' asked the first boy.

His mate gave an exaggerated shrug. His acting was on point.

'Boys, I'm so glad you asked,' Latifah said, as she placed her hands on their shoulders. 'Now listen up while I break it down.'

The boys dapped then, raising microphones to their lips, began to beatbox. Latifah bobbed her head a few times, then started to rap:

Now this is our history, Time to get woke.
Black Power be born. Ceiling got broke.
Movements for improvements, Not for amusements.
People get stoked. This ain't no joke!

Media bo jangling: Guns and crime,
Slang and gangs, RnB and grime.
Illusion and confusion, Blasting through delusion.
'Member the time, when Little Rock'd Nine?

Wisdom and Passion will free your soul.
Sports and Music? What the dilly, yo?
Doctors and Teachers, Scientists and Preachers.
Know thyself! Achieve dem goal!

Senior teachers be white; All the cleaners be black.
Security guards Asian, Yo wassup wi' dat?
I know I'm a queen, cuz my daddy told me so.
I ain't no gangsta rapper, Addict. Yo!

Police brutality, insanity. Messed-up mentality.
Diagnosis of psychosis, Crazy-ass reality.
Don't say 'immigrant'. You goddamn ignorant!
Think you own air? You crazy-ass militant!

Yo! I have a dream where race be dead.
No black, no white: We all bleed red.
Christian, Muslim, Hindu or Jew.
It ain't about 'I' and it ain't about 'you'.

> *It ain't about melanin or who you know.*
> *Cain & Abel, big labels. Actin' all ghetto.*
> *Opportunity, community. Seeking out unity.*
> *Whatever yo' past, You still my bro.*

Latifah pierced the air with her fingertips like an Amazon warrior. The rap was fire.

> *Now my rap is done, I'mma hit the quan!*

The crowd went wild as she bust out the viral dance craze. The boys mimicked her like shadows, bringing an extra dimension to the act. I'd never been to a live concert, but I couldn't imagine it topping this. The energy in the hall was *electric*.

'Peace out!' Latifah dropped her microphone, blasting us with raw feedback.

Everyone was mad applauding, whooping up a storm.

'Look at them,' Arif said, narrowing his eyes.

I didn't know who he meant until he nodded in the direction of the senior teachers. They looked a little stunned, like they were still trying to figure it out. But Dillinger and Mr Dunthorpe were clapping like homies.

After the amazing opening, the assembly became the gift that just kept giving. Poems, comedy sketches, and a couple of YouTube videos projected on to the massive screen about people of colour who'd broken glass ceilings. First up was Jessica Watkins: an African-American astronaut. She was so *smart*, I was low-key fangirling, even though the idea of going into space gave me PMS. The other success story featured a Sri Lankan self-made millionaire. Someone booed and shouted 'You ain't black, bruv!' The voice belonged to Sade.

There was mad love for the assembly. Latifah was a certified genius. She and her talented crew got a standing ovation that even the ear-splitting pips couldn't drown out.

'Latifah's Muslim. Did you know that?' Arif asked.

I shook my head.

'Yeah, Nigerian sister. Man, is she gonna get it.'

'How do you mean?' I asked.

'Girl just pointed out how the *kuffar* like to keep us in our place: "Senior teachers all white. All the cleaners be black."'

I blinked. Now he mentioned it, that was exactly how it had been at every school I'd ever gone to.

CHAPTER 20

'This is great stuff, Muzna!' Mr Dunthorpe said, tapping my discursive essay.

Out of the window, the sky appeared the colour of a bruise. I'd had to stay late to discuss my work with Mr Dunthorpe as he'd had an A-Level class to teach first.

'Then why have you scribbled all over it in red pen?' I whined.

I'd poured my heart and soul into that essay. Weeks and weeks of researching, sifting through evidence, correcting my grammar, pimping my vocab. And for what? To have my hard work graffitied?

'Oh, don't feel discouraged,' he said, flapping an elegant hand like a fly swatter. 'I'll let you into a secret: teachers *hate* marking. And *dialogue marking* is surely the bane of every teacher's existence. I only put notes all over yours because it deserved the extra attention.'

'Really?' I turned hopeful eyes to him.

'Muzna, it was *so* good, I let my partner have a read of it. Hope you don't mind,' he added, looking slightly sketchy. 'He's a journo. And let me tell you, he called you a "talent in the making".'

'Seriously?!'

'I think,' he said, stubble crackling like electricity beneath his nails, 'you'd make a terrific journalist.'

'I don't want to be a journalist,' I told him honestly. 'I mean it's flattering and all. But, from as early as I can remember, writing stories has always been my number one.'

'A novelist?' he said, stroking the back of his head. 'There'll be fierce competition. But why not? You've certainly got talent. All we need to do is nurture it.'

'I want to write books about people like me,' I said, wringing my hands. 'Don't get me wrong, I love reading literally *everything*. I just wish there were more stories where the main character was a Muslim . . .' Acid whooshed up my nose, making my eyes water. 'Is that bad?'

He chuckled. Then realizing I was dead serious, he shook his head. 'No, of course not. That would be like having books with only male characters, or always writing straight romances. Representation is incredibly important.'

Dunthorpe was woke. He understood.

CHAPTER 21

The day of Sarabi's sister's wedding finally arrived. Even though Ami had a what-not-to-do list as long as her *dupatta*, I was determined to kick back and have some fun.

I'd picked up a two-in-one hair straightener/curling tong at Lidl for a tenner, and was trying my luck with it. Back and forth my eyes flitted, between the mirror and the laptop screen, comparing and adjusting, adjusting and comparing. Gigi Hadid looked like a total goddess. Me? Not even. Still, the look I achieved was loads better than my usual frizzy mess.

Next, I stripped naked and stared at myself in the full-length mirror. Big mistake. Especially after eyeballing Gigi online. Stretchmarks, pot belly and cellulite. Who would ever want to have sex with *that*? Maybe one day I'd grow into my body. And if not, turning out the lights would always be an option, right?

A sudden breeze brought me out in goose bumps. Turning away from the mirror, I started to get dressed.

'What's all this make-up, shake-up?' Ami asked, summing up my appearance with a sweep of her hand.

'It's a wedding, Ami. And I'm only wearing a *tiny* bit,' I said.

'If that's your *bit*, I'd hate to see your lot!' She gave a single derisive cackle. 'Go wash it all off or I'm not taking you there.'

'But we're already late! Please, Ami! Don't be like that!' I pleaded.

'I'm not about to let my only daughter make her daddy the laughing stock of the community. We are respectable

Muslims, Muchi! *Izzat* is everything.'

I hated the way 'Honour' was always chucked in my face to stop me from having any fun. Dad had a criminal record, for crying out loud, and Ami was an illiterate stay-at-home mum. What was honourable about that? Believing they were good Muslims was the biggest joke of all. The only time they visited the mosque was at Eid, and the only time they remembered Allah was to look down on others. I wanted to tell Ami exactly what I thought of their stupid *izzat*. But though my confidence was definitely on the rise at school, it wasn't happening at home.

I dragged myself upstairs and removed the slap. Not only was I lumbered with being a 'Plain Zaynab', but trying to make myself look even half decent was now a crime. Frustration gripped my jaw as I scoured my face with a make-up wipe. All my careful contouring reduced to a rainbow of smears in the mirror in front of me . . .

An idea popped into my head. Sneaky and dishonest? Probably. But was it my fault if Ami was being so unreasonable? Every go-to cosmetic I owned went straight into my bag. The moment we arrived at the banquet hall, Muzna Saleem would be making an emergency pit stop at the bathroom.

Rajput Hall was a proper amazing venue, if you ignored the fact that it was opposite a plaza of hardware stores.

From the moment me and Ami entered beneath the Roman-style portico, with its tall white pillars and floral hanging baskets, I felt like we'd been transported to some magical fantasy land. The air smelt warmly of jasmine and spice, and I could hear a sitar being played in the background. A rich pallet of red, gold and cream pervaded everything. It was the world of the Maharajas and Maharanis; the Mughal emperors and their queens.

Ushers in matching velvet jackets directed us to the dining

hall. Up on the stage, decorative palms grew out of mirror-mosaic pots that sparkled and gleamed. In the centre stood a majestic golden throne.

'Why haven't the men been separated from the women?' my mother asked in audible disgust.

I tried to hush her, but it was too late. One of the other guests had heard.

'I know,' agreed a plump Sikh woman in a bright orange *kurta*. 'Shameless! This is the fashion – copy Bollywood actors. As if those druggies were anything to look up to.'

Ami broke out in a smile. United in disapproval, she and the lady were soon nattering away like old friends. My cue to go tart myself up.

Standing before the large mirror in the bathroom, I gazed at my beautiful black-and-blue shalwar suit, bursting with pride. A real steal at £29.99. But everything north of it was a disaster. My face needed some serious TLC.

Tying my *dupatta* round my head like a bandana, I lined up my cosmetics, and prepared for battle. Keeping it subtle was key, otherwise Ami would burst a lung, screaming at me in front of the entire British Asian community. Rose-pink lip gloss, eyeliner, and a shimmer of blush – my magic potion for turning Ugly into Acceptable. Finally, I released my hair, letting it spill over my shoulders in a thick black curtain.

'Wow, you look desi-sexy!'

I spun round in alarm, wondering what a boy was doing in the ladies' loos. Sarabi grinned at me like a Cheshire cat. Clearly she'd been working on her boy-voice.

'Don't do that to me!' I placed a hand on my heart. 'Oh Sarabi, you look amazing!'

My mate was dressed in a brocade suit of yellow, purple and cerise. She could have been a bride herself. She hid her smile behind a decorated hand.

'Glitter *mehndi*?!' I grabbed her wrist, mesmerized by the intricate micro-designs on her skin. 'You did this yourself?'

She nodded.

'Shut. Up.' I was gobsmacked. 'Where'd you even get this?'

'I made it. Just add glitter to hair gel, bung it in a cone, and you're ready to go. Want me to do you some day?'

'A thousand times YES!'

'Look at us!' she said, gesturing at the mirror. 'Miss Pakistan and Miss India – together at last!'

I glanced into the mirror doubtfully. It might have been the lighting or the angle, but we *did* look pretty together.

'Are you thinking what I'm thinking?' I asked.

'Selfie moment!' she squealed.

We grinned insanely into the camera lens, heads pressed together like a thousand other best friends wanting to share the moment. Within seconds she'd uploaded it to her Insta and tagged me.

Back in the hall, I spotted a girl wearing the exact same outfit as Sarabi. A couple of seconds later, I saw another. Had they been on sale?

'Don't look now, hon,' I advised. 'Wannabes at one, two . . . and now ten o'clock!'

Sarabi glanced round and laughed. 'We're all bridesmaids, silly!'

'And here was me thinking Flash Mob.'

'Muzna, I bet you're going to love the Bhangra dancers,' she said. 'There's a world class *dhol* player . . .'

But I'd stopped paying attention. Suddenly the urge to book it back to the bathroom was overwhelming. Had to make sure I hadn't done something dumb like give myself an eyeliner unibrow or tucked my *kameez* into the back of my knickers.

Sarabi followed my gaze.

'Plot twist,' I whispered. 'Arif turns up to the exact same wedding as *me*. What were the odds of that happening?'

'Surprisingly high, actually,' Sarabi said, looking over her shoulder. 'Judging by the turnout, looks like the groom went and invited the entire Ether Downs Asian community. My parents are *so* murdering him.'

There he stood, my super-Arif, killing it in a princely *sherwani*. Holding a glass, he chatted animatedly to a shorter man with a slighter build. An uncle or an older brother, maybe.

'Let's go over and say hello,' I suggested.

Sarabi laughed. 'Forget it. If my parents saw me chatting to a boy, I'd get shipped to India.'

One of the bridesmaids called to Sarabi in Punjabi.

'Don't do anything I wouldn't do,' she said, tapping my nose playfully, then hurried off to join the other bridesmaids.

But I'm not you, I thought, a combination of guilt and defiance gnawing at my heart. *And I think I'm done pretending*.

I ran my fingers through my hair, squeezing out every last bit of volume I could get. Then placing my *dupatta* over my breasts in a 'V', I shyly drifted over, glancing back once to make sure Ami couldn't see me. The man with Arif picked me up on his radar almost immediately. His eyes were utterly black, and there was something hawk-like about him. I considered bailing, but it was too late if I didn't want to end up looking like a psycho chick.

'Hey, Arif,' I said, trying to keep my voice relaxed. Not easy when your heart is doing an impression of a *dhol*.

Arif was turned away, muscular shoulders encased in glistening cream fabric. His brother poked him, then gestured with a tilt of his head.

Arif spun round and gave me a confused look. 'Er, do I know you?'

Oh my God. I needed to abandon this sinking ship before I drowned in my own humiliation.

'It's me, *Muzna*,' I said, my voice becoming high and desperate. 'We're both in Mr Dunthorpe's tutor group . . .'

He blinked in surprise. 'Man, I totally did not recognize you! You look different, innit?' Polar-white teeth appeared in the smile I was obsessed with. Peace was restored to my little universe.

'*Assalaamu alaykum*, sister,' his brother said in a deeply serious tone. 'I am Jameel Malik, Arif's brother.'

I responded with the traditional Islamic greeting. The family resemblance was obvious, but it was like I was looking at a photo and its negative. Jameel spoke in an affected London accent, and his eyes never settled on anything for long. Almost as if everything fell short of his expectations.

'You know, a pretty girl like you should be covering up her beauty with a hijab. This –' he made a global hand gesture over me – 'does not please Allah. Look at my idiot brother here, drooling over you.'

'Don't be calling me idiot, *yaar*!' Arif said good-humouredly, fists drawn in a boxer's stance.

I flushed deeply. Taking in the simple white *thobe*, Islamic skullcap and long beard, it was obvious Arif's brother was the devout type. Should have factored that in before making my move. Trying to make amends now, I flung my *dupatta* over my head.

'Well . . . see you, Monday,' I mumbled.

'Nah, man,' Arif said. 'I ain't doing school Monday. Got a conference to go to with this one.' He flicked his chin at Jameel.

'Oh, that's nice,' I said uncertainly.

'Hey, sister,' Jameel said, as if an idea had just occurred to him. 'Would you, by any chance, like to come? It's a conference for Muslims. You could bring your brothers too.'

'Don't have any. Brothers, I mean. I'm an only child.' I glanced back furtively, making sure Ami wasn't on the prowl.

'*Mash'Allah*,' Jameel said, a faint smile forming on his thin lips. 'Allah gives to whom He will. Some couples remain childless throughout their lives. Your parents are truly blessed to have you.'

The compliment made me smile. 'But I would *like* to come . . . I mean, if that's OK?'

'You sure?' Arif asked sceptically. 'Not gonna lie: these things can be *dry*.'

'Pay no attention to this foolish sibling of mine,' Jameel said. 'If you want to improve your *deen*, then of course we'll take you. The pursuit of knowledge is sacred, and in certain cases the rules can be bypassed and whatnot.' He ruminated for a second, his purple lips disappearing inside his bushy beard. 'Tell me, sister, are your parents religious Muslims?'

'Not especially,' I said, torn between loyalty to my parents and being honest. 'They don't pray or fast.'

'That is indeed a shame,' he said, as if I'd just told him one of my relatives had passed away. It made me blush.

'Where is this conference?' I asked, hoping for somewhere glamorous.

'Not far. Wallingham Islamic Centre. Perhaps I could pick you up from school. Do your parents drop you off in the mornings?'

'Dad does.'

'OK, so when the coast is clear, make a U-turn and come straight back out. We'll be waiting for you in my white Micra at the top of the road, near the chippy.'

'Sure, OK!' I said. 'Um . . . should I give you my number?' This was directed to Arif.

'One sec . . .' he said, lifting up his brocade shirt to grab his mobile from an inner pocket. I got a breathtaking glimpse of his happy trail and the V-cut of his lower abs. He stored my number on his gold iPhone. My parents could only afford to buy me a Samsung; the kind Boudicca probably had.

'Well, see you Monday!' I said, giving a girly wave.

I floated away on a cloud of joy. All too soon I was sitting opposite my mum again. In the time I'd been gone, Ami had made three new friends. They were chatting away happily like a brood of clucking hens. I wished I could've inherited Ami's 'social butterfly' gene. She gave me a nod, letting me know she was glad I'd come back.

Then suddenly there was a loud bang. Everyone jumped, and at least two girls screamed out.

A man in a bright pink turban rolled a feral 'R' on his tongue. The *dhol* was struck a second time, sounding like a clap of thunder. In came the Bhangra group, hopping and dancing. Everyone cheered. Even Ami clapped her hands in time with the music, a huge smile on her face. The colourful group made their way along the aisle, encouraging audience participation, and growing in number.

'Don't they look like fresh flowers in a stream?!' Ami said, really getting into the spirit of things.

I was glad she was enjoying herself, but if she got up and started dancing – especially in front of Arif and Jameel – I swore I'd die of shame. *Speaking of which* . . .

I extended my neck like an ostrich, hungry for another delicious glimpse. A churning sea of bodies blocked my view, before an opening appeared. Arif was dancing. Not like Malachy, but *proper* Bhangra moves that got my heart racing. A karate chop struck the back of his neck making me gasp. Jameel glared at his little brother, not looking the least bit amused.

The rest of the wedding party passed in a blur. There were highlights: dapper groom, beautiful bride, Sarabi doing bridesmaid-y things, delicious grub. But nothing that could break the spell woven over my mind. All I could think about was next Monday and bunking off to go to a conference with Arif (and his brother). It may not have been an ideal first date – or a *date* of any kind, if you wanted to get technical – but it was a start. *Go me!*

CHAPTER 22

All through the weekend I was bursting to tell someone about my upcoming road trip with Arif. But there was no one. Keeping it from Sarabi was the worst. Totally necessary, though, if I didn't want to be guilt-tripped out of it. She had Boy-phobia in a way that would impress any conservative Asian parent.

Every time I thought about Arif's beautiful smile, those thick eyelashes, or that short flash of his ripped abs, my blood fizzed like a shook-up can of Monster. If only there was some way I could make him fall madly in love with me . . . No pill I could swallow, no app I could download. Love was old school. It only happened if the elements were right.

That didn't mean there weren't things I could do to help the process along. Like ditching the conference was a no-brainer. Who ever heard of two people falling in love at a religious gathering? Major mood killer. OK, what next? I drew a blank. I tried to remember what books had taught me. Characters found some common ground . . . said or did something incredibly touching . . . stared longingly into each other's eyes, then . . . kissed?

Me kiss Arif Malik?!

I giggled like a tickled lunatic before a horrible idea struck me. *What if I'm crap at it?*

In a flash I had my trusty laptop open, surfing the YouTubian waters for a kissing tutorial. Steamy preview images cluttered the entire left side of the screen. My eyes darted nervously back and forth between the screen and my bedroom door.

If my parents caught me . . .

I hit PLAY.

Watching the demonstration, I tried to convince myself that kissing was no big deal. Sure, it was kind of cringe when people puckered up in public places, and you totally wished they'd get a room already, so why was guilt twisting round my throat? Was it because I was afraid of God or my parents? Suddenly the actors on the screen transformed into me and Arif, kissing up a storm. My head started to spin faster and faster and faster. I needed air. Now.

'Where are you going?' Ami asked, looking up from the glossy aubergines she was chopping up.

'Thought I'd take the washing in,' I lied, palms stickier than a snail's belly.

'You are a good girl, Muchi. And when you come back, you would definitely be my favourite child if you also help me chop up the *baingan*.'

Hate to break it to you, Ami, I thought, *but your daughter is actually Slutty McSketington . . .*

Outside in the garden, I inhaled deeply, tilting my face up to the sky. The fresh scent of fabric conditioner drifted towards me as the clothes stirred on the rotary airer. A bird sang high in the apple tree, drawing my attention. Would Uncle Tanveer let me pick apples in the summer? Would we even be here by then? I didn't think anyone let their brother and his family live above their two-star restaurant forever. The thought was depressing. Everything in the apartment was shiny and new. The thought of going back to our junk-shop way of living filled me with sadness.

If only I could have Arif over . . .

Ridiculous. My parents were never going to allow me to have a boyfriend, or even a friend who was a boy. But sooner or later they'd find out I wasn't the daughter they thought they had.

Then what? A shiver ran down my spine remembering how they'd treated Salma.

As I began to take the clothes down, tossing them into the old laundry basket, my discursive essay floated to the front of my mind. Using high school to figure out who you are instead of rolling with the cool crowd. Shouldn't that message apply at home too? Like, why was becoming the person my parents wanted me to be more important than finding my own place in the world?

I frowned, frustration burning in my gut. It was cruel to bring me up in Britain, make me go to school with British kids, then expect me to act like a girl from back home. Outside of having brown skin, speaking the language, and half-heartedly cheering the cricket team on with Dad, I had no real idea of what it meant to be Pakistani. I mean, how could I?

Maybe going to the conference was a bad idea.

Or maybe it was the *best* idea?

Either way, getting closer to Arif was worth every risk.

'Muchi, you're very quiet tonight,' Dad said with a note of concern.

My family sat in front of the TV watching an incredibly corny Pakistani drama serial. Uncle Tanveer's place had Sky Digital, and my parents were maxing out with a vengeance.

'I'm just tired,' I said, faking a yawn.

> Thx 4 da invite
> Me n Ami had a BLAST!!!

> No worries hon. Thx 4 comin!

Next to her words Sarabi had put every wedding/party emoji known to Teenage Girl.

I smiled.

'Have you finished all your homework?' Dad asked. 'I've been so busy with my job, I haven't really had a chance to ask you how you're getting on with your studies.'

'That's OK, Dad,' I said, stuffing my phone in a pocket. 'Yes, I've finished my homework. And you were right – everything's *so* much better here than it was at Rigsby. My English teacher thinks I'm *brilliant*. He said I could become a professional writer if—'

'What about maths and science?' He cut me off, his eyes somehow managing to look both threatening and worried at the same time.

'Doing well in those too, of course,' I muttered gloomily.

'Did you hear that, Parveen? Our little doctor is doing well.' Dad relaxed and snuggled up to Ami, pleased that the world hadn't turned on him while he'd been waiting hand and foot on the diners downstairs.

On TV, the hero of the drama – a twenty-something with hair from the 90s – was yelling at his father, while his mother looked distraught, ringing her hands. The family were fighting over the son's choice of bride. Apparently the guy had been dating the maid in secret, but the family's honour was at stake.

Oh grow a pair! I wanted to yell at Mr 90s Hair.

Glancing back at Ami and Dad, I was surprised by how upset they seemed for the lovers. It made me sick that they could be so liberal when it came to TV, but would never give their own flesh and blood the same freedom.

CHAPTER 23

By Monday my nerves had got the better of me. I had to call the whole thing off.

I glanced up at the clock and saw that I had about half an hour before Dad expected me to be sitting in the car. Bunking off was next-level bad – was I really up to the challenge? I had accomplices, but while I trusted Arif with my life, I didn't know his brother from Adam.

I rubbed my stomach, trying to disperse the acid build-up of nerves. It suddenly occurred to me that turning up with 'nude' hair was going to make the worst impression. I slapped my forehead, wondering how I could let something so basic slip my mind.

'Get your shit together!' I hissed at myself.

Rummaging through my drawers, I found a green scarf with a bit of gold embroidery on it. Of course, I couldn't leave the house wearing it – not with my parents' hatred of all things hijab. They were like faith Goldilocks: not too religious, not too agnostic, but ferociously clinging to 'somewhere in the middle'. I stashed the scarf away in my school bag before hitting the bathroom again.

'So much fog in Lahore today!' Dad said as we were stuck in traffic, about a mile from school. 'Life has been brought to a complete standstill there. Can you imagine it?'

I was startled by a rapping on the window. It was Malachy grinning from ear to ear, a Marvel Superheroes helmet strapped to his skull. 'Hey, Muzna! Hey, Mr Saleem!' He saluted Dad then cycled off, lanky legs churning like pistons.

'Who was that?' Dad asked, appalled.

'Just some boy from school.' I went rigid, feeling Dad's eyes scanning me like a human polygraph. If I wasn't careful, Dad would end up thinking Malachy and I were dating. The idea was *bare jokes*.

'Keep away from him,' Dad concluded. 'I know his sort.'

Malachy didn't have a bad bone in his skinny body. I hated the way Dad judged people so quickly. Was he really that different from the racists and bigots he hated so much?

We made a little headway before the lights turned red again.

'I know living above a restaurant, even one as renowned as Uncle's, is not ideal,' Dad said in a softer tone. 'At least we are not homeless people, *beyta*. Soon I'll get a better job, and we can get our lives back on track. Don't worry, all your hopes and dreams will come true because you are a good girl.'

I peered suspiciously over at him silhouetted against the paper-white sky. Did he mean it?

'I *will* pay your medical college tuition fees,' he vowed, striking his finger on the steering wheel like a gavel. 'Even if I have to sell one of my kidneys to do it. This I swear!' My anger went kamikaze and suddenly the guilt I'd felt for planning to bunk off school went up in smoke. Every time my parents blabbered on about the huge sacrifices they were making to help me become a doctor, I felt like throwing myself off a cliff. Ami and Dad would *never* change, but it was *my* life, and I was going to make the most of it.

As the Micra sped towards Wallingham, I unzipped my bag and pulled out my scarf. Feeling slightly embarrassed, I wound it round my head in an approximation of a hijab. I caught Jameel's dark eyes watching me in the rear-view mirror and felt myself flush. Instantly his eyes were back on the road.

About five minutes later he said, 'You did well to wear hijab, sister. But really, you should aim to wear it twenty-four seven.'

'Even to bed?' Arif asked, with a cheeky grin.

Jameel asked Allah for strength to 'tolerate such foolish brothers'. Arif turned round and winked at me.

'My parents won't let me . . .' I told him honestly.

'It is good that you show your parents respect by following their wishes. But know this: there is no obedience in disobedience.' Jameel paused, gauging if I'd got it. 'Tell her what it means, Arif. And if one more foolish utterance escapes your lips, by Allah I will stop the car and kick you out. Then you can find your own way to the mosque.'

'Sorry!' Arif said, blushing. 'OK, so what big bro here is saying is this: if Allah has commanded you to do something, and your parents are like "no way", you still have to do it, innit? Cos Allah's the Big Boss of the Universe.'

'OK,' I said quietly.

My parents freaking out wasn't the only factor here. *I* didn't fancy becoming a hijabi either after all the news stories I'd read about Muslim women getting their scarves ripped off or being spat at. One Muslim woman in a burkini had even been forced to take off extra layers of clothing by police, and with the whole world watching, just because she wanted to cover up on a beach. Why would anyone want to put themselves through *that*?

Jameel shoehorned into a gap between a BMW and a Fiat in a side street close to the mosque. A subtle change came over him as he turned off the engine. His eyes were more alert; his movements sharper.

'Do you wish to become a true Muslima?' he asked, turning to me.

'But I am—'

'I'm not talking about only visiting the mosque at Eid, or

praying to Allah as if he were Santa,' he replied, shaking his head. 'I mean *true* Islam, without addition or subtraction. That which was revealed to the Prophet Muhammad, peace be upon him.'

Truth be told, my parents' version of the faith *had* always bugged me. Yes, we were Muslims, but sometimes I wondered if Dad didn't just make up the rules as he went along. Like, one time he said it was OK to buy burgers from McDonald's, speak Allah's name over them, and – hey presto! – they became halal. Then Mickey-D's raised their prices, and the trick mysteriously stopped working.

'I want to be a proper Muslim,' I said solemnly.

He gave a thin smile. 'Then may Allah accept it of you. You are going to hear many things today. Perhaps you will be a little shocked, since the West has conditioned you in how to think. I pray your heart and mind are opened. I pray for you, as I pray for my brother.'

'Thank you,' I said meekly, glancing across at Arif. His large eyes looked sad for a second, but then he blinked, and gave me the cutest smile.

'Follow me,' Jameel said, exiting the car.

He led us through a side gate to a small building beside the mosque. Jameel rang the doorbell. After a moment, a crack appeared, and a single eyeball glared out at us. Then the door was thrown open, and a man in a flowing white gown and a biker jacket hugged Jameel. The guy wore a large white turban on his head, from which coils of oily dark hair escaped.

He invited us into a darkened hallway, leading us forward to a small front room. Several sheets had been spread across the floor. Twelve men sat on them, patiently waiting for the talk to begin. A settee had been pulled away from the far wall, which was functioning as a screen. Behind it sat three women in full-length gowns. One peered out at me from the letterbox slit in her niqab.

The corners of her eyes were crinkling, and I realized she was smiling at me. The women scooched up so I could join them in the gap behind the sofa.

'You'll be OK, yeah?' Arif asked, peering over the sofa.

The women grumbled. He quickly apologized, then perched on the armrest of a chair instead, honouring the rules of segregation.

An older woman, with wispy grey hair peeking out from under her hijab, went round with a tray of appetizers. She'd made the cutest samosas, each folded like a little envelope of yumminess.

'No thanks, auntie-ji,' I said.

She stroked my cheek, before moving on.

The room grew warmer and noisier as more and more people arrived. A claustrophobic pressure began to build up in my chest, making me nauseous. Suddenly a giant man with a ginger beard and a turban entered, *salaam*ing everyone in a booming voice. A hungry grin was strapped to his face, maniacal blue eyes searching for a spot to crash. People hurried to make space where there'd been none to start with. Once settled, the man-mountain told everyone that he used to play lead guitar in a Christian rock band before his call to Islam.

'You are a convert, brother?' a man in a skullcap asked.

'*Revert*,' the giant corrected in a thick Yorkshire accent. 'We're all born Muslim, my brother.'

He then launched into a story about how he'd gone to a mosque one night and several witnesses had seen him glow every time he bowed before Allah. Arif turned and gave me a 'WTF?!' look. I almost giggled.

It was a huge relief when the Arabic prayer began, ending the noisy conversations. An English translation followed. Various men, including Jameel, began to talk about the poor state of Muslims all over the world and the many wars waged against them.

'Palestine, Bosnia, Chechnya, Iraq, Afghanistan, Syria!' Jameel intoned, poking holes in the air. 'How many more before we wake up? Make no mistake, this is the systematic destruction of the Muslims. The obliteration of Islam! It is happening, my brothers and sisters. It is real. And when they have destroyed those abroad, they will come for you!'

As the meeting dragged on, I found myself wishing I'd stayed at school. Even a maths class would have been more interesting than this. Plus one of the men had feet that could scare the stripes off a skunk. I wished someone would tell him to go wash them.

Stifling a yawn that brought tears to my eyes, I noticed Arif trying to get my attention. He was cutting his eyes to the door and jerking his chin. Was he signalling for me to leave? Whether he was or not, I'd hit rock bottom. Either I got fresh air now, or I'd be sick down the back of the caretaker's sofa. I slipped out as discreetly as I could. Scurrying through the hallway, I grabbed the door knob and twisted frantically. But my moist fingers just kept slipping. Suddenly a large ivory hand reached over and flung open the door.

Stumbling outside, I greedily sucked endless fresh air into my lungs. The harsh light of day nearly blinded me. But *man* was it good to be out in the open again.

'Phwoar! Bit stuffy in there, weren't it?' Arif said.

'When your brother said it was a conference, I never pictured thirty of us packed in some caretaker's poky front room.'

'Sorry,' he said, giving Guilty Puppy Face. 'Know what? We should take off; hit up Chessington. It ain't that far.'

'What, seriously?' I asked. Theme parks and religion were chalk and cheese.

He shrugged. 'Place is dead. They talk big about Muslims suffering all over the world. But talk is cheap.'

I shuddered. 'Your brother scares me.' I bit my lip, wondering if I'd gone too far in accusing a pious man of being a bit spooky.

Arif threw back his head and laughed. 'Jamjamz is solid, man. Just a bit boring. He was studying computer science at King's before he chucked it all in. Got a higher calling, or summat.' He stared into the distance, shaking his head.

'What did your parents say?' I asked, knowing mine would go into meltdown if I dropped out.

'Not much. They're dead.'

I'd screwed up. What could I say to patch things over?

'Dad died out in Pakistan,' he said. 'So Mum came over to Bolton to live with her brother. Back then, Jamjamz was about thirteen, and I were in nappies.' He licked his lips. 'Then cancer took Mum away, and Jameel went uni. And I was all alone. Alone with my uncle.' The muscles on the sides of his jaw rippled, and his eyes were two stars hidden beneath heavy brows. With both parents dead before he'd even started school, Arif had every reason to be angry.

'I'm so sorry,' I said, nervously reaching out and patting his shoulder.

He flinched.

'What?'

'Nah, nothing.' He gave a surprised laugh. 'Just them in there, right?' he said, jerking his head back at the caretaker's house. 'They'd go proper mental if they saw us touching.'

He was right. Only that morning, Dad got IDS (irritable dad syndrome) from Malachy just *waving* at me. If my parents caught me and Arif chatting like this, I'd never hear the end of it.

'Are you very religious, then?' I asked, as we strolled down a cul-de-sac.

'Asking me if I'm a fundamentalist?' He winked.

'Are you?' I challenged.

'All I'm saying is I put the FUN in FUN-damentalist.' He drew his thick eyebrows together thoughtfully. 'And I reckon Jameel's got the MENTAL part covered.'

We both burst out laughing, and it felt great to be sharing something with him in private. Uncharted waters, for sure, but that just added to my excitement.

Arif drew his fingers through his quiff. 'Reckon we should be heading back if we want a ride home. They never meet for long, and it's a different place every time.' He rolled his eyes.

'What? Why?'

He gave me a look. 'You know how it is, fam. People see a pack of Muslims meeting up and start getting funny ideas. Next thing you know, the cops are making arrests.' His upper lip curled into a snarl. 'First it was black people; now it's the Muslims.'

'We can change it!' I said. 'If we're united.'

He gave me a thoughtful look. 'Tough though, innit? Black man commits a crime, people say he's a gangbanger. If it's a Muslim, he's a—'

'Terrorist,' I interrupted.

He nodded. 'But if it's a white guy, he gets called a "lone wolf", and suddenly it's all about mental health issues.'

I stared at his brooding profile. Not only was Arif eye candy, he was brain candy too. A man who was all kinds of provocative.

As we headed back to the mosque, I saw a large gang of youths rock up on bikes and scooters, and my stomach dropped. They were all wearing polos or beanies with a special crest on them, like they went to the same school. Only that couldn't be right. Most of them were in their early twenties.

Even as I looked on, someone lit a firework and lobbed it over the fence. It struck one of the caretaker's windows and exploded with the sound of a shotgun, rattling the pane.

'Get in!' shouted a teenager, already lighting another.

Arif swore under his breath. Suddenly he was sprinting straight for the gang, leaving me frozen with fear.

The congregation flooded out of the caretaker's house, ants fleeing a burning nest. Islamophobic chants filled the air as a second volley of fireworks was launched. To my shock, one yob unzipped his shorts and sent a jet of urine splattering through the bars. Some of the younger gang members had brought eggs and tomatoes in carrier bags. They began throwing them like water balloons, cheering every time a target was hit. An overripe tomato exploded smack-bang in the face of the lady wearing the niqab.

A Muslim woman had just been humiliated. There was going to be a fight.

CHAPTER 24

The way I saw it, I had two options: join Arif on the battleground, or duck and run.

I found myself tearing after him, adrenaline spiking my blood. Some of the Muslim men had armed themselves with brooms and spades and were coming out to meet the gang head-on. Arif had already nabbed a stocky man covered in tattoos, preventing him from launching his lighted rocket.

'Throw fireworks at a woman, would ya?' Arif sneered in his face. 'Let's see how *you* like it, mate!'

Arif's knuckles stood out like bullets, driving Tattoo Guy's hand back towards his face. Tattoo Guy swore, thrashing about like a mad man as the rocket spat sparks on to his quivering cheeks. He threw a left hook. Big mistake. Arif snagged his second arm and jerked it back with an audible pop. The man howled in pain and began to sob, snot dribbling freely into his gaping mouth.

'Arif, let him go!' I shouted, watching in horror as the fuse shrank.

All around us tempers flared and blows were exchanged. It was bedlam. And instead of going to school, I'd ended up in the middle of it.

'Arif!' I cried again, fear draining my voice. But he ignored me. I had to do something. Had to try, or Arif would end up with a criminal record, and this guy would end up in A&E.

I thrust an arm between them and yanked the firework with all my might. It slipped through my fingers, flipping end-over-end . . .

Kaboom!

A tinny ringing pierced my ears as electrified snowflakes scattered in every direction. My heart pounded wildly in my chest, rocked by thoughts of what might have happened.

The roar of sirens filled the air, growing louder by the minute.

Everything was dropped as car doors were slammed and bikes and scooters snatched up off the ground. There was a mad frenzy to get the hell out of dodge.

'Come on, you two!' barked Jameel.

Arif's eyes drilled into mine, and my heart sank. I'd disappointed him. He grabbed my arm and hauled me towards the white Micra. As we piled in, I was surprised to find the lady in the niqab sitting beside me. She was still sobbing.

'Belts on!' commanded Jameel. 'Everybody hold tight!'

I fumbled with my seatbelt, just as three men burst out of the mosque, shaking angry fists at us. Jameel floored it and the car lurched forward. A second slower, and I might have head-butted the back of Arif's seat; had blood gushing down my chin. As Jameel began whipping in and out of lanes, I found myself comforting the woman beside me.

'Don't worry, sister,' I said. 'You're going to be all right. Tomato washes out. Thank Allah it wasn't a firework, eh?'

'Bloody Britain First!' Arif roared, slamming his fist down on the dashboard.

Was that them? I wondered in awe. The far-right group came up in the news every now and then, but you never imagined knocking heads with them in real life.

'Why are we running away?' I asked. 'Shouldn't we stick around to report them to the police?'

'No, sister,' Jameel said firmly, eyes locked on the road ahead. 'Your faith in the British police is misplaced. There is no justice for Muslims, except from Muslims.'

Thirty minutes later, Jameel and Arif dropped me off on the Broadway. I watched the Micra vanish into traffic. My heart was still racing, my fists clenched tighter than lumps of coal. I walked home in a daze.

CHAPTER 25

The next day, Mr Dunthorpe handed me and Arif letters to give to our parents asking them to explain why we'd been absent. My heart dropped. I'd never skipped a day of school before. Worriedly I looked across at Arif. He winked, and – just like that – my fears melted away. Of course it was no big deal. I'd seen tons of people get these letters before, sometimes weekly.

Yesterday we had shared something special. It had ended in chaos and fear, and I'd seen a side of the world I'd have been a *lot* happier not knowing about. But in the space before the violence, there'd been warmth and understanding. Maybe I was way off base, but I was actually starting to think Arif wanted to be more than friends.

'Where were you?' demanded Sarabi, with eyes like saucers.

'You know I was with Arif,' I replied, trying not to smirk. 'Oh, don't give me Mum Face. It's not like I've ever bunked off school before.'

'I'm worried about you, Muzna. First you start hanging out with boys; then you start skipping school. What next? Hmm? Sneaking off to get an abortion?'

Her words shot me down. 'OK,' I said, my eyes growing moist. 'First off, it's not "boys" – just Arif. Second, I was at a *religious* gathering. And third, "abortion"? Really?'

Sarabi dropped her eyes, ashamed. 'OK, I'm sorry. That part was out of order. But promise me you'll never do anything like it again!'

I wanted to ask her who the hell she thought she was – my mother? But the better part of me knew she was just trying to be a good friend. I sighed and nodded.

'What sort of a place is a religious gathering for a first date, anyway?' she asked, pacified.

'We're Muslims, Sarabi. We do things differently.'

'Muslims and Sikhs are not that different, in spite of what our parents might say. Anyway,' she said, relaxing a little, 'did you hear that Tallulah's dumped her boyfriend?'

'Which one?' I asked, pretending to care.

'Shh!' Sarabi said, giggling. 'Matt – the tall one that looks like that guy off *X Factor*. You know, with the dimples?'

'Oh,' I said. 'What'd he do?'

'Well, I wasn't there, but . . .' Sarabi said reluctantly, throwing nervous little looks over her shoulders.

'But?'

'*Well*, there was a party at one of their houses, and apparently Matt got drunk and took a different girl upstairs for *you-know-what*.'

Wow. Sarabi couldn't even say the word 'sex'. Why did our parents do this to us? Did they want us to be traumatized on our wedding nights?

'And,' she continued, 'someone told Tallulah. So she stormed upstairs to see if it was true. You'll never believe this! When she caught him, Matt said he thought the girl he was . . .'

'Screwing.'

'Yes, that,' she said, pointing. 'He said he thought she was *Tallulah*!'

'No way!'

'So Tallulah snaps a photo of them for revenge. Now it's gone viral!'

'Blow a day off school, and miss all the drama, huh?' I said.

*

On a gloomy Tuesday that threatened to rain down buckets, but couldn't work up to anything more than a drizzle, my RS teacher asked me if I could run an errand for her. She'd left our worksheets on the photocopier again. Since I'd been made to sit next to a regular fart machine, I was happy to go. Just for the oxygen.

Coming out of Building A, I decided to cut across the muddy field to get to Building D. Lost in thought, I ended up smack-bang in the middle of a violent game of rugby: mud flying, boys charging, testosterone pumping — I noped out of there FAST. Then something caught my eye.

Arif was standing on the sidelines in his rugby kit chatting to Tallulah.

I stared at them, puzzled. Only then did Sarabi's ominous words come back to haunt me: *Tallulah broke up with Matt*. Little Miss Perfect was a free agent. Arif was hands down the best-looking boy at Falstrum. Why had I not seen this coming?

Even as tears sprang to my eyes, my treacherous feet carried me closer. I had to know the truth, even if it killed me. The blustery wind worked in my favour, carrying their voices towards me, while masking the sound of my own shoes squelching in the mud.

'Oh, come on,' Tallulah drawled. Her newly done ombré hair flapped like satin in the wind. 'It's this weekend. You know, you're not allowed to refuse a girl on her birthday.' She pouted, flaunting those sexy bee-stung lips of hers.

'Nah, parties ain't my thing, fam,' Arif replied, wiping sweat off his brow.

She pressed her palm to his left pec. 'Then tell me what is . . .' she purred. Her hand slid down his torso, caressing every contour.

It felt like she'd hooked a crowbar under my ribs and was trying to rip out my heart.

Arif caught her hand as it passed the checkpoint of his navel. Suddenly our eyes met, and I froze – a rabbit in the headlights; a perv at the window.

'*She* is,' he said. Tossing her hand away like trash, he jogged towards me, leaving Tallulah stunned.

Was the matrix glitching? Could any straight guy say no to that succubus?

As Arif closed the gap between us, all tall and handsome, my eyes were drawn to the rippling muscles in his hairy legs.

'*Assalaamu alaykum*,' he said, flashing his heroic smile.

My heart grew wings seconds before a wave of hatred hit me like a truck. I glanced back to see Tallulah blasting me with high-octane evils. Even Arif felt them.

'We're Muslims, innit?' he told her with a wink.

The bee-stung lips retracted into a hyphen. Without another word, she stormed off. Arif chuckled loudly, but I was bricking it. I'd beaten the Queen Bee in a game of love. Tallulah and her massive fandom would *never* forgive it.

'What you doing here, then?' Arif asked, scratching his sweaty chest. 'Come to check me out in my PE kit?' He gave me a wink that made my body tingle.

'N-no. Running an errand for my disorganized RS teacher . . . Oh crap!' It was insane how quickly I forgot things when I was around Arif. 'Laters!'

'Message me tonight!' he called.

'Er . . . OK!'

CHAPTER 26

'Go on. Have a read of this,' Arif said, waving a rolled-up newspaper at me. Dust motes shimmered like glitter in the hazy sunlight.

He'd texted me the night before, asking if I could help out with some geography homework. Not my strongest point, but if it meant spending more time with Arif, I was *so* up for it. So here we were, up in the school library: me nose-deep in a stuffy geography textbook; Arif treating a chair like a hammock.

Only now the sexy-doofus was distracting me.

'Trying to finish your homework, here,' I reminded.

Pitching forward, he swiped his geography book from under my pen, and flung it in the general direction of his bag. 'Forget my boring homework.'

'But you'll get detention!' I protested, with growing confusion.

'Nah, man,' he said, placing two newspapers down in front of me. 'Half-done homework ain't the same as not-done homework. This one's from 2015; and this here's 2011.'

Warily, I looked at the article on the left. On 7th January 2015, two brothers had forced their way into the Charlie Hebdo offices in Paris and started shooting. It was supposed to be payback for publishing a cartoon mocking the Prophet Muhammad; it ended up making 1.8 billion of us look bad. The journalist wasn't shy about using phrases like 'Islamist barbarians' and 'savages from another time'.

I felt sick to the pit of my stomach. Why did these people have to grab the headlines and make their own religion look bad? It was almost like they were bred in an evil factory somewhere.

I shuddered, pushing the article away.

'Now take a look at this one,' he said gently.

The second article was about a white Norwegian man who had bombed a government building killing eight people. He'd then driven down to a summer camp and sprayed sixty-nine people with bullets, most of them teenagers. His beef? Along with a load of other crazy ideas, Muslim immigration. The guy claimed to be 'one hundred per cent Christian'.

'Biased reporting,' I said. 'The brothers were "Islamic terrorists", but this guy just gets called crazy. Surely they *all* are to do something like that?'

'Smart lass!' he said. 'Now, look at this.'

'I'm done,' I said, fanning my moist eyes. 'This stuff *really* upsets me.'

'Last one. Promise.' He proffered the paper.

I looked into his eyes and saw exactly how much it meant to him. Steeling myself for one last onslaught of mindless murdering, I took the newspaper.

The final article was a small piece. This time the location was Sehwan, Pakistan. A suicide bomber had blown himself up at a shrine killing ninety people and injuring over three hundred others. It was a *massive* bloodbath, and ISIS had claimed responsibility.

'Oh my God!' I cried. 'Three hundred people? How come I never heard about this?'

His face was hard. 'Simple: no hashtag, no filter, no solidarity,' he said, his eyes hidden in shadow. 'Brown lives don't matter.'

I stared at him, mouth agape.

'Journalists ain't got no shame with their two-cent Islamophobic reporting!' Arif scowled, stuffing the newspapers back in his bag. 'Terrorism kills more Muslims than any other group – but the papers don't want to tell us that. I didn't choose the terrorist life; the terrorist life chose me . . .'

'Maybe I can help fix this,' I said.

'Eh? How do you mean?' he asked.

I cringed, realizing I'd vanished up my own bum. 'I-I want to be a novelist some day.' A finger crept to the corner of my mouth. I quickly folded my arms, banishing my childish gesture.

'What, writing books and that?' he asked absently.

I nodded, then filled him in on my lifelong ambition.

'Think about it,' I added. 'If people had some Muslim heroes to look up to, there'd be public outrage every time the media came up with this crap.' I shot a dirty look in the general direction of the newspapers.

'Yeah?' He looked interested.

'We're that shady *Other*,' I went on. 'The group you're allowed to hate on because we're "terrorists" or "benefits scroungers". People don't get to see us as anything else. Soon they'll even forget we're people.'

He cracked his knuckles.

'Wait!' I said, in the middle of a brainwave. 'What if part of the problem is that we don't put ourselves out there enough? Like, let's say you're really good at – I dunno – skateboarding.'

He raised an eyebrow.

'Just go with it,' I pleaded.

Obediently his eyebrow dropped back into place.

'So you're this skateboarding genius, right? But your parents want you to be a doctor,' I continued, not entirely sure where I was going with this. 'But cos you've had it drilled into you that "parents know best", you waste your life trying to become a doctor. Then one day you fail and end up on *Benefits Street*. Or worse: a criminal.'

'Damn.'

I nodded. 'But, like, if someone had believed in you, you might've taken skateboarding to the next level.'

'How?' he said, trying not to laugh.

'Worked your way up.' I flapped my hands, trying to get him to use his imagination. 'I'm not saying you'd be saving lives. But you might go on to become a world champion skateboarder and end up with your own line of skateboards or PlayStation games.' I shrugged. 'Good for you. *Awesome* for Muslims. Cos suddenly, hey! We're not just terrorists any more. We're also skateboarders.' I punched the air. 'Represent!'

I saw the glimmer in his eyes. 'It's not even that. I know your parents are proper desi, but plenty of people's folks are OK with 'em trying their hand at all sorts. So either we're all failing, or Muslim success stories are being hidden from the general public.'

I considered this. 'Don't make things easy for ourselves though, do we?'

'How'd you mean?'

'As a community. I mean, everybody's so busy watching everybody else, instead of minding their own and just letting people live.'

This made him chuckle.

'And don't get me started on forced marriages, honour killings, child brides, FGM, witchcraft—'

Arif sat up sharply, sliding his leg off the table. 'Whoa. That ain't Islam, fam. That's *culture*. Messed-up traditions people pass down to their kids.'

I stared at him, thinking of my own parents. 'What, even honour killings?' I asked.

'Course. The Prophet married off his own cousin to an ex-slave. Back then, that was proper dishonourable. People are ignorant, fam. Believe what they want to believe.'

'You learned Islam from Jameel,' I said. 'How can you be sure it's the right version?'

'Cos Jameel's me brother.'

A suffocating silence followed. Arif was super-protective of his brother, which I totally did not get. Jameel was like the anti-brother: cold and distant. But what did I know? I was an only child.

'So, you wanna gimme a peek?' His voice was soft, the awkwardness dismissed.

'Huh?'

'You know. At one of your stories,' he said, rubbing his hands together.

I hugged myself and shook my head. 'You're not gonna like them. They're from before you clued me in on the difference between Islam and culture.'

'I'll love 'em. C'mon, stop playing hard to get.' He caught my wrist. Our eyes met and I blushed.

Writing stories was like the most personal thing you could ever do. It didn't work unless you laid your soul bare. I didn't want Arif to think of me as part of the problem. I wanted him to see me as a slayer of Islamophobia and ignorance.

But maybe it was more important for him to see me as I was.

I pulled out my phone and thumbed through the files. Each story was another piece of the Muzna Puzzle. About ten times more revealing than any cringe family photo album.

'The Burning Bride?' he read, squinting at my phone. 'Mad ting. Heard it happens in some villages back home.'

Arif was a slow reader. I tried not to smile, watching his lips move faintly as he journeyed from paragraph to paragraph. A couple of times he shifted about, trying to get more comfortable, but he stuck with it to the end.

'What do you think?' I asked, sweating bullets. 'I was in Year

Nine. Just saying. And I totally didn't know any better . . .'

'You wrote this?' he asked, doubtfully. 'Raa, some day you're gonna be bigger than Dickens or whatever his name was.' His smile dropped, eyes widening. 'Aw Muz, what you crying for, bae?' Strong hands gripped my trembling shoulders.

'I dunno.' I sobbed. 'I thought you'd be mad.'

'Mad? Don't be daft! Your story is about bad traditions.' He brushed his beard. 'Guess you could always add a bit on to make it clear it ain't some "Muslim problem".'

I nodded enthusiastically. 'Definitely.'

'But those people in your story. Feel like I've met 'em before!'

'Nobody gets me, Arif.' I sniffed. 'But I'm starting to think you do.'

'Course I get you, dummy!' he said, chuckling. 'You got the heart of a poet, innit?'

I stared at him, laughing and crying and nodding all at the same time – God, I must have looked *fugly*. Feeling a lot braver, I said, 'Can I share a quote? It's one of my favourites.'

'Knock yourself out.' He closed his eyes, pointing his goatee at the ceiling.

Taking a deep breath, I recited. '*I have spread my dreams under your feet. Tread softly because you tread on my dreams.*'

His eyes sprang open. 'You make that up?'

'I wish! It's Yeats. This *amazing* Irish poet.'

'Dude had talent,' he said, rubbing his jaw. 'Allah is the most merciful. Think about it, yeah? He even puts beautiful thoughts in the dirty minds of the *kuffar*.'

I froze.

Was that how the *kuffar* saw us too – *dirty*? I glanced over at his bag, the vision triggering memories of old news stories. *Beheader, paedophile, terrorist.* With a sinking feeling, I began to think that they probably did.

*

Half-term couldn't have arrived sooner. We were completely burned out from the intense revision sessions each lesson had warped into. Every teacher acted like their subject was the only one that counted. The terrifying dragon that was our GCSEs – the legend we'd been warned about since Year 9 – was finally casting its mighty shadow over the horizon. I felt sick with worry. But Arif told me Allah had a plan. With Him in control of the universe, we had nothing to worry about.

I regularly texted with Arif throughout the break. At first, only short, shy messages; but later, longer, emoji-filled ones. But no matter how much I wanted to, I could never get myself to add the kissing face. So I waited, hoping he'd do it first. Never happened. Boo! Still, messaging each other at midnight was fun. Almost like being in bed *together*.

Then on Wednesday, Sarabi rained on my parade like a monsoon of misery.

'We never do anything fun any more!' she complained over the phone, as I lay back on my bed, picturing Arif looking HAWT in his rugby kit.

'Well what do you want us to do?' I asked.

'I just want us to *hang*. You know? Like we used to. And for you to actually *be* there.'

'Hmm?'

'See what I mean? You're not even listening!'

'Don't be dumb, Sarabi. Of course I'm listening.'

'Is that why you don't like me any more?' she said, her voice loaded with emotion. 'Because you think I'm dumb and immature?'

Sarabi was a good mate, for sure. But for a while now, I'd felt like she was holding me back. Her opinions were my parents' opinions, or close enough. She was the way I *should* have been, which only made me hate myself. I couldn't deal with negative emotions on top of all the exam stress.

'No, of course not. You're my best mate.' Why did that sound so fake?

'Then let's do something together!' she pleaded. 'Like old times.'

'You wanna see that new Arjun Kapoor movie at the Odeon?'

'What? Really?' she asked.

Sarabi was like a little girl in a teenager's body. This was how our parents wanted us to be until we got married. I remembered Ami getting upset when I'd told her that playing with Barbies just wasn't doing it for me any more after getting busted by Salma. She wept actual tears. I was *thirteen*.

'Sure,' I said. 'Can you text me the details?'

'Done!' she said instantly. 'I promise you won't regret this. The critics are calling it his best performance yet. And I swear Spice FM has the soundtrack on repeat!'

A couple of hours of eye-gouging torture for Sarabi? Anything for a mate.

The movie grated on me worse than steel claws on a blackboard. It was just one camp dance number after another. How on earth could Sarabi find this stuff exciting? Every twenty minutes, almost like clockwork, she'd look across at me with this dopey grin on her face. I'd smile and nod, pretending like I was having a good time. But I wasn't. The struggle was real.

After a while, I started getting annoyed with Sarabi, which made me feel worse. Guilt added to the shopping list of negativity I was experiencing. Pretty soon I'd end up crying.

That did it. I needed air.

'Back in a sec,' I whispered, heading for the toilets.

Out in the lobby, I stood undecided. Part of me wanted to get the hell out of there. But the better part knew Sarabi would never forgive me if I did. I glanced at my watch. Fifteen minutes more to go.

'I can do this,' I told myself, turning back.

Something exploded on the back of my head, chilling my brain, sending ice crystals skittering down my back. I yelped, spinning round to confront who ever had thrown their drink at me.

Tallulah stood victorious. Not one drop of shame or remorse touched that pretty face of hers. Lackeys flanked her, left and right, tearing me apart with hateful eyes. All three looked like they'd taken five from filming a music video just to come and assault me.

'That's for embarrassing me,' Tallulah said.

'What are you talking about?' I shrieked – a human soda fountain, leaking all over the floor.

'Ugh! How dare you act like it was nothing. Arif was *mine*,' she said, slicing the air with a manicured nail. 'But you just had to come over all Rihanna and twerk that fat, FAT booty at him, didn't you? There are words for girls like *you*.'

'Skank!' agreed one friend.

'Hoe!' chipped in the other.

'Are you insane?' I asked, scooping sticky fluid out of my eyes. 'You do realize none of that actually happened, right?'

'So you're denying you and Arif are an item?' Tallulah asked, tossing back her glossy curls.

'What? I n-never said that . . .' I stammered, backing into a cardboard cut-out of Chris Pratt.

At a nod from Tallulah, her minions uncapped frothy lattes and prepared to hurl them like grenades.

'Muzna, if you didn't want to watch the movie, why didn't you just—' Sarabi stopped in her tracks, taking in the scene with eyes like frogspawn.

'Don't you dare fling those cups at my friend!' she shouted, whipping out her phone. 'I'm filming everything. If you don't get lost, this video clip's going straight to the police.'

A lackey took a step towards Sarabi.

'Don't even. It's set to instant cloud backup!' Sarabi warned her.

I could have hugged my mate. Why on earth was she putting her neck out for a friend who didn't even treat her right?

'You need to take a long, hard look at yourself in the mirror, Muzna,' Tallulah said scowling. 'You're a fat, ugly bitch. How long do you really think you'll be able to hold on to Arif?' She flashed her eyes meaningfully, then stalked off. Her friends gave menacing hair-flicks, then flounced after her.

'Muzna, are you OK?' Sarabi asked, patting my face with a napkin. 'You poor thing! Come on – let's get you cleaned up in the loos.'

CHAPTER 27

'Muzna, *beyta*, hand me the *imli* sauce, please.'

'Huh?'

'*Imli* sauce!' Dad's voice was like a brick through my window of thoughts.

'Sorry,' I said, managing to knock over the bottle. The fruity-spice scent hovered in the air. 'Sorry!' I repeated, mopping up the mess with tissues.

'*Beyta*, are boys bothering you?'

'No!' I said defensively, before realizing Dad was shooting in the dark.

'Stay away from boys,' he warned, drizzling *imli* sauce over his golden pakoras. 'Thank God we got you away from that immoral Salma before she spoilt you.'

'I . . . was thinking about Dadi-ji,' I lied. 'I hope she gets better soon.'

My father's sick mum had been the furthest thing from my mind. I'd never even met the woman. The incident at the Odeon kept playing over and over in my head, slowly driving me into paranoia. I was half expecting Tallulah and her friends to break into our apartment packing machine guns. *Brap, brap, brap!*

Ami stroked my cheek with the back of her hand. 'Don't worry, Muchi. Dadi-ji will get better. She's pulled through worse.'

'It's different this time, Parveen!' Dad said, eyes ablaze. 'She's older and weaker, and the doctors are worried that if she doesn't get better soon, her body will just give up.'

'I'll pray for her,' I said, trying to reassure him.

'What good are prayers?' he demanded. 'Allah doesn't give a shit one way or the other!'

I looked over at Ami in shock. She gave a small shake of her head, instructing me to zip it.

Dad wilted until I was afraid he'd dunk his head in his bowl of curry. Abruptly he got up and left the table. A few minutes later, the apartment door slammed, and he was gone.

'Ami, is it really that bad?' I asked. 'Do you think Dadi-ji might die?'

Ami sighed, mopping up the *imli* sauce on her plate with a fluffy piece of naan bread. 'Yes, *beyta*. And when that happens, we will have to drop everything and go to Pakistan.'

'What?!' I cried in horror. 'I have school. My GCSEs are a couple of months away!'

'Death is more important than gee-see-ees!' she chided. 'Growing up in this country, you are ignorant of what things are like back home. The moment Dadi-ji becomes the beloved of Allah, there will be a violent grab for the wealth and property she leaves behind. In Pakistan, you cannot trust even your brothers and sisters! They would sooner put a hex on you than let you take your rightful inheritance.'

She stroked her chin, in a calculating way. 'No, Muchi. With our financial situation in tatters, making sure we get that money will be our number one priority.'

I stared, open-mouthed.

All my life, my parents had coaxed, bullied and threatened me into believing that becoming a doctor was my sole mission in life. That I owed it to them for the love and care they'd showered on me. Yet here was Ami telling me to drop everything I'd worked so hard for. *WTF?*

Imagining my Well of Calm, and diving in, I decided Ami was just being silly. She didn't understand how you couldn't just start and stop an education whenever you fancied. But Dad got it. He'd never take me out of school just to attend a funeral abroad. Dad was many things, but irresponsible wasn't one of them.

But if my parents *ever* found out about Arif, all bets would be off. The only thing more important than having a doctor daughter was having a daughter who hadn't been tainted by a boyfriend.

At 10 p.m. my phone rang. It was Arif.

'What's up? It's kind of late . . .' I said.

'Is it?' He sounded tired, almost weary. 'Oh, crap. Gotta go *Isha* in a bit.'

Isha was the last of the five daily prayers. Jameel always dragged Arif along to the mosque to perform the night prayer in congregation.

'You already prayed?' he asked.

'No, not yet.' I sighed. 'To be honest, Arif, I don't actually pray.'

Awkward silence.

'You need to pray, Muz,' he eventually said. 'It's hard at first, course it is. Like in that famous Malcolm X quote.'

'What quote?' Wasn't Malcolm X just a badass version of Martin Luther King?

'Just a sec,' he said. I heard rustling, as if he was rifling through a book. 'Got it. OK, you listening, Muz?'

'All ears.'

'OK, here it is,' he said, and began to read. '*For evil to bend its knees, admitting its guilt, to implore the forgiveness of God, is the hardest thing in the world. It's easy for me to see and to say that now. But then, when I was the personification of evil, I was going through it. Again, again, I would force myself back down into the praying-to-Allah posture.*'

'Wow,' I said, lost for words.

'Yeah, he was saying, like, how the knees are arrogant and don't want to humble themselves before Allah. But once you start, once you put in that little bit of effort, it's like Allah holds your hand, and you're never alone again . . .'

There was a pause on the line.

'Hey, I gotta go now, yeah? I want you to pray *Isha* tonight, babe. Will you do that for me?' he asked.

'Absolutely,' I promised. But truthfully . . . I wasn't feeling it. I didn't even know why. Maybe my knees had an attitude problem?

'And tomorrow, we can go Chessington or Thorpe Park, if you fancy. You up for it?' I could almost hear the smile in his voice.

'*Insh'Allah*,' I said, trying to score brownie points.

'K. Text you laters, Muz.'

I flopped on to my bed, my mind racing a million miles an hour. Tomorrow Arif and I would go on a proper date. Selfie Heaven. MuzRif – the cutest couple ever. Well . . . I was just *me*, but Arif was cute enough for the both of us.

I got up to pray, before running into major setbacks. I actually didn't know *how*. I paced up and down, feeling *dirty*, wanting to put things right. Asking my parents was out. They'd automatically think I'd joined ISIS. We didn't own any Islamic books either . . .

The answer came to me in a flash. YouTube. Some good soul was bound to have uploaded a prayer tutorial. I reached for my laptop.

CHAPTER 28

The next morning, I woke up to pray *Fajr* in inky dark. The tutorials I'd watched made it clear that the prayer needed to be performed before sunrise. I dozily crept into my bathroom to make ablution, wincing from the ice-cold jet of water. Drying myself off, I pulled out my scarf, and wound it round my head.

That's when I heard footsteps. *Someone was coming.*

Swinging into action, I launched myself at the door, slipping the bolt into place. My nerves jangled, and I held my breath. A few seconds later, the kitchen tap squeaked, and I heard the rush of water. Whoever was out there was just thirsty.

Having to hide an innocent thing like prayer from your parents was messed up. *This isn't a home*, I thought. *It's a prison camp.*

I cleared my head. If I was going to pray, I had to let go of all negative thoughts and feelings. Anger was supposed to come from Satan, and he was the enemy.

A few minutes later, when I'd finished *salaam*ing the angels, I felt a deep sense of peace descend on me. There was something about following a tradition that was hundreds of years old; it made you feel *connected*. Something bigger than your parents or governments or any power of earth. I doubted I could keep it up – praying five times a day was a *huge* ask – but in that moment, I was proud of my little achievement.

Stashing away my makeshift prayer mat and hijab at the back of my wardrobe, I turned my attention to my looks.

You're a fat, ugly bitch. How long do you really think you'll be able to hold on to Arif?

I'd never be able to look as flawless as Tallulah. There wasn't a beauty hack under the sun that could do that for me. But I could be the best version of *myself*.

My fingers hovered over the cosmetics I'd laid out. Arif was a religious guy. Not in the intense way of his brother, but he played by the rules. Going overboard with make-up could be a deal-breaker. He cared about what I was like on the inside. Still, couldn't go wrong with a bit of strawberry lip balm and a smidge of eyeliner, right?

I dressed myself in a cute stripy top and diamanté studded jeans. My stomach was still bigger than it had any right to be, but the top I chose helped disguise that. I glanced at the clock and baulked. Still two hours to kill before my train left. So, reluctantly, I pulled out a maths paper and my calculator, and settled down for a slog of exam practice. I saw it as a trade-off – doing some maths to cancel out the haram of going on this date.

'I'm off now, Ami,' I called, bouncing towards the door. Even the crap grade 4 I'd scored on the practice paper couldn't squash my excitement.

Ami had her feet up on the recliner, darning a pair of Dad's old socks. Ever since he'd had to wait on tables, Dad got through socks super-quickly. She was listening to an Urdu programme on the radio. The host was inviting listeners to dial in their opinions on whether elderly Asian parents should live in care homes or with their children. Ami kept saying 'Leh!' every time she disagreed. I pitied the fool who tried to put Ami in a care home.

'Where to?' she asked.

'Thorpe Park?' I said, hoping to jog her memory. 'With Sarabi. Remember?'

She nodded. 'Have you eaten your breakfast?'

'I'll pick something up on the way.'

'Be careful, *beyta*,' she said. 'There are all sorts of pickpockets out there. And you know English people are worried about terrorists. Make sure no one knows you're Muslim.'

I went over and gave Ami a big hug, hoping it made up a bit for the whopper of a lie I'd just told.

I hiked up the station slope towards the platform. The jitters were back with a vengeance. I couldn't believe I was finally going on an actual date with Arif Malik. I had butterflies. I had palpitations. Had Ami ever felt this way about Dad? Doubtful. Their marriage had been arranged (though no force on earth could've made my feisty Ami marry against her will).

I spotted him standing on the platform staring at his phone. Looking up, his eyes locked on to mine, and I got chills. A cheeky Bolton grin spread across his face, then he bounded over, pecs bouncing beneath his black T-shirt like slabs of beef.

'Got you a gift,' he said, holding out a small carrier bag.

Inside was a black hijab, embroidered in satin and studded with Swarovski crystals.

'Do you like it?' he asked, biting his lip.

'Yeah,' I managed after a slightly awkward pause.

'Gonna put it on, then?'

I felt a rush of anger. He was trying to *change* me. Get me to cover up like a 'proper' Muslim girl. He wanted me . . .

All to himself?

My anger faded. I knew *I* didn't want to share him with anyone else, least of all that thirsty cow Tallulah. In fact, I didn't even want to share him with Jameel. Hesitantly I used the mirrored window of the station office to wrap the hijab round my head. Three attempts later, I almost had it looking half decent. Arif waited patiently, handing me a cute jewelled scarf pin at the end to hold it in place.

'Could ask my brother's wife to teach you how to do it fancier, if you want?' he offered.

Jameel had a wife? I wondered how any woman could put up with that stick-in-the-mud.

'You calling this a disaster?' I asked, pointing at my head.

'Nah, babe. You look peng. It's just that she can do these nice patterns and stuff, like scoubidous.'

'Scoubidous?' I grinned, remembering the craze from way-back-when.

Long before there were fidget spinners, homemade slime, or even loom bands, scoubidous had ruled the world. Colourful plastic string, knotted together to make charms and bracelets. Not even boys had been able to resist the siren call.

'Were *you* into scoubidous?' I said.

'Me? Nah – got clumsy hands.' He held up his large veiny hands.

'I love your hands.' The words slipped out.

His fair cheeks went pink, reminding me of fresh roses. Then holding his hands out to me he said, 'Take 'em. They're yours.'

We stared into each other's eyes till I was convinced something was going to happen. Thing is, we were Pakistanis. Kissing was illegal.

'This is us,' he said, seconds before the blast of dust from the approaching train struck, ruffling my hijab in the slipstream.

Once on board, we found comfortable seats facing each other. The train pulled out of the station, and sunlight strobed between buildings as we rattled along. I blinked, my world suddenly filled with glowing green halos, my heart bursting with more joy than I could ever remember feeling.

CHAPTER 29

We got off at Staines. As me and Arif walked towards the theme park, I was still having pinch-yourself moments. His large hand found mine, and enveloped it. Male skin on female skin. I think I actually gasped.

'Is this OK?' He lifted our entwined hands, eyebrows enquiring.

Throwing caution to the wind, I nodded. There was always a chance someone might spot us, but since I was wearing a bling hijab, I doubted I'd get recognised.

'Nah, man – *massive* queues!' Arif groaned as we entered through the tall blue gates. 'Come on, Muz – get a wiggle on, before it gets any more packed.'

He bolted towards the shortest queue, leaving me to stare at my empty hand. How lonely it felt without his pressed against it. I hurried after him.

'Two tickets, for me and wifey,' Arif told the dour-looking man in the window, making me flush with pleasure.

'So what you wanna do first?' he asked, handing me the brochure.

I unfolded it and scanned the rides. When I'd been in Year 6, I hadn't been allowed to go on the school trip to Thorpe Park. I chalked it up to my parents not being able to afford it or being afraid I'd get killed. Now I reckoned *boys* had been the reason. Yep, even ten-year-old boys had penises and therefore posed a serious threat to my safety.

Dad had pulled out all the stops to segregate me. And now

here I was, with my very own boyfriend, determined to have the time of my life.

'I hear Swarm's pretty good,' I said with a shrug.

'Yeah, Swarm's wicked. Saw too. Last time I came, yeah, loads of people puked their guts out. Had to stop the ride a full ten minutes while they sent in cleaners to mop up the vomit.'

Watching him talk was fun. Waving his hands, waggling his eyebrows, shifting from foot to foot, and sometimes even winking. He really didn't give a crap what anybody else thought of him, and it made him about ten times sexier. Me? Hiding my feelings under a self-conscious act had passed from habit into DNA. Maybe being with Arif would help me become a normal person. I *really* wanted that.

'. . . That's what I wanna do,' he finished, eyes sparkling.

'What? Saw?' I asked, having zoned out as I'd been studying him.

'Nah, clean up people's vomit.' He bopped me on the head, 'Course I mean Saw, dummy!'

Saw it was. Strapped to our seats, submitting to the will of a maniacal killer puppet, the ride dragged us towards the sky. A horrible clicking sound ratcheted up the tension as we approached the top. The long pause at the highest point gave my stomach enough time to shrink to the size of a peanut. Then without warning, the train tipped over, falling into darkness. The near-vertical drop made me hysterical. Within seconds we were wrenched back into daylight, pupils constricting from shock, before plunging sickeningly towards the ground again.

I screamed and screamed without shame. Arif whooped and cheered his way through the whole thing. Watching him, fearless and brave, made me love him even more. *If we're going to die*, I thought, *then at least we'll be together*. Heer Ranjha – that's who we were. The classic Punjabi romantics Dad used to watch with a tear in his eye.

*

Later, Arif came back from the cafe clutching a large bag of rainbow-coloured candyfloss, and immediately sensed something was wrong.

''Sup, Muz?' he said, plonking himself down on the bench beside me. The ferns behind us whickered in the breeze.

I shook my head. He waited me out.

'Just imagining my dad turning up,' I said, trying to bring my heart rate down. I was trying to enjoy the moment, but I just couldn't help thinking about what would happen. 'If he caught me, he'd . . .' I shook my head. He'd lost it over Salma. This would be terminal.

Arif chuckled. 'Dad'd tear me a new one, innit?' He put on an exaggerated Pakistani accent. 'Vaat you doin' vith my daarter? *Badmaash!* I yaar battam kick aall the vay to Lahore!'

I smacked him. 'My Dad does *not* talk like that!'

'Made you laugh, though, eh?' he retorted, ripping open the bag. He broke off a wisp of finely spun sugar and popped it in my mouth. It melted instantly, becoming strawberry syrup on my tongue.

'Jamjamz is just the same,' he admitted, pushing candyfloss into his mouth like he was stuffing a quilt. 'Sometimes I think he finds *everything* haram.'

'Halal' and 'Haram': 'The Allowed' and 'The Forbidden'. It was all supposed to be black and white. But really there was a valley of grey between the two. Me and Arif were somewhere in that valley right now.

'Jameel seems OK,' I lied, as a man in a zombie costume shambled into view. He paused to wriggle his fingers at me and mumble something about my brains.

'Piss off, mate,' Arif said.

The zombie gnashed its teeth, made angry fists, then shuffled after a girl in a short skirt.

'Gotta go bathroom,' Arif announced, hopping off the bench. 'Be right back.'

'What if there's a zombie apocalypse while you're gone?'

'Fam, there's a zombie apocalypse every day. That's what the *kuffar* are: cruel, mindless zombies.'

He dusted off the back of his jeans. It was difficult not to ogle his bubble butt as he headed off to the gents. Was there any part of him that wasn't utterly gorgeous?

A rippling breeze carried the sound of screaming as a rollercoaster corkscrewed high into the cloudless sky. I smiled, happily gobbling up the rest of the candyfloss, not thinking about my thunder thighs even once.

A ringtone went off. I checked, but it wasn't my phone. Arif's iPhone buzzed across the wooden slats like a giant golden bumblebee. Must have slipped out of his pocket. As I tried to stop it from diving off the end, I saw a picture of a girl on the screen. Photographed in front of a school mural, I recognized the look in her eye. Love.

'Massive queues everywhere today!' Arif crashed on to the bench, sending shockwaves along the slats.

'Who's Hajra?' I asked, brandishing his phone at him.

He glanced at the image, and sucked in his cheeks. 'Checking my messages now?'

'N-no,' I stammered, feeling ashamed, but not enough to back down. 'You left your phone, and it kept going off. Who is she?'

The guilt on his face was unmistakable. But something hovered just under it that was harder to read.

'Look, Muzna,' he said, scooting right along the bench till I could feel the warmth from his thigh against mine. 'I weren't always a good Muslim, yeah?' He pointed at the phone. 'Her-in-the-pic was my girlfriend for a bit. Only she kept pressuring me for sex. So I broke up with her.'

'Then why's she calling you now?'

'Some people!' He drew a circle in the air near his temple. 'Girl went *mad*. Started stalking me online and everything. So I blocked her. Then, when she found a new boyfriend, I thought it were the end of it.' He looked at his phone. 'Guess I was wrong, eh?'

'Oh,' I said, trying to let that sink in. 'I'm really sorry . . .' I felt bad for having doubted him. My low self-esteem was messing things up AGAIN.

'Oh yeah, you're proper evil, Muz,' he said, wrapping an arm around me. 'How dare you care about me.'

I beamed at him, wondering how I'd ever managed to end up with someone so wonderful. It had to be a blip in the universe. If boyfriends were haram, Arif was the exception. After all, he was helping me to become a better Muslim. I just hoped God saw it that way too.

PART 4

FALSTRUM ACADEMY: SUMMER TERM

CHAPTER 30

'Muzna! Is it true?'

Amie clung to me in the corridor, staring excitedly into my eyes.

'Why? What've you heard?' I asked, amused and a little confused.

'Only that you and Arif Malik are going out!'

I blushed, then nodded.

Amie drew me into a tight, girly hug. 'You guys are so friggin' cute. Invite me to the wedding, OK?'

'What? *That* and Arif are dating?' said a brawny girl, overhearing our conversation. 'That's like Beauty and the Beast in reverse!'

My head started to spin. Everyone was going to think the same thing whenever they saw us together. DUFFs didn't date studs. What had I let myself in for?

'Piss off!' snarled Amie. 'Muzna's got a lot more going for her than you have. Just cos you've shagged half the football team, don't make you into some kind of beauty queen.'

I'd heard those rumours too. But how could they be about *this* girl? I checked myself, realizing I was a hypocrite for judging her by her looks.

The girl flipped us off.

'Don't worry about people like that,' Amie said, adjusting my hijab as if I was her kid and she was preparing me for a school photo. 'Not gonna lie: Arif's hot. So they're all gonna be well jel.' She spotted one of her friends and waved. 'Anyway, see you later!'

I was still trying to get over the fact that jealousy would now be an issue, when Mr Dunthorpe came round the corner.

'Hi, Muzna!'

'Oh hi, Mr Dunthorpe!' I said. 'Cool tan. Go anywhere special?'

'South of France, actually.' He blushed through his newly bronzed skin, flustered by my quick observation. Then he made one of his own, as I caught him glancing at my hijab. I wondered if he was going to say something. In the end he only smiled and continued on towards our tutor base, saying he was pleased Dadi-ji had pulled through when I mentioned her illness.

On entering the classroom, my eyes cut directly to the window seat. Empty. An irrational panic unfurled in my chest. I couldn't cope without Arif. Not now that I'd gone all hijabi. Not now that people knew we were a thing. To make matters worse, Sarabi was also MIA.

Sade spotted my hijab and executed an over-the-top double take. 'There goes the school,' she said, banging her head against the table.

'Welcome back, everyone!' Mr Dunthorpe said to a chorus of groans. 'Let's help one another make this our *best* term yet.'

At break-time, I got a text from Sarabi: The sad emoji with a thermometer in its mouth. That explained where she was, at least. I tried Arif a few times, but his phone kept going straight to voicemail. I didn't leave a message.

Without Arif or Sarabi, I was incredibly lonely. I was so irrelevant, that even wearing a hijab for the first time in school failed to draw any attention, other than Sade's bitchy comment. I took refuge in the refectory, nursing a Radnor Fizz and a triple-chocolate muffin I'd picked up at Greggs. It was comfort food of the worst kind: fattening *and* expensive. Staring at it made me want to burst into tears.

Another loud reunion – this one right behind me – made me start. Friends squealed like banshees, telling each other how 'totally insane' their holidays had been. For one moment, I wished I had their life. Then I recalled Arif's comment about people being like zombies, guided by evil.

The refectory was noisier than usual. Every window displayed why. Rain poured out of a fractured sky, falling in sheets. Grabbing my muffin, I got up, deciding that standing in a downpour was better than being ignored in a crowd. Just then, a girl slid on to the bench opposite.

'Hey, Muzna!' she said. 'Can I join you?'

It was Latifah. The brains behind the Black History Month assembly that had won rave reviews and a thick slice of the controversy-pie.

'Sure,' I said, honoured that she even knew my name. Like Tallulah, she moved in popular circles. But unlike Tallulah, no one had a bad word to say against her.

'I really like your hijab, by the way,' Latifah said, rubbing the fabric between her fingers. 'Quality! You get it from Dubai?'

I grinned, about to tell her the name of the little Islamic store on the high street, when Sade interrupted.

'Run for your life,' she told Latifah. 'Else you'll be blowing yourself up in the name of Allah.'

'Do you have any idea how ignorant that sounds?' Latifah said, cutting Sade some major side-eye.

Sade blinked. Not the reaction she'd been expecting.

'Easy,' Sade said. 'Just looking out for a sistah, yeah? Don't wanna end up all *Muslim*, do you?'

'I'm black, Muslim, and proud,' Latifah said, her smile daring Sade to criticize her.

Sade gawped like her systems were crashing. 'I got to you too late!' she spluttered dramatically, then walked off, shaking her head.

I chuckled. 'Should've filmed that. "Latifah shuts down Islamophobe!" Would've broken the internet.'

She slapped the air. 'Girl's just ignorant. I kinda get it.'

'You're kidding, right?'

'You don't know, do you?' Her eyes narrowed as she leaned forward.

'Nope. Completely bafs,' I admitted.

She dropped her voice, forcing me to draw closer till our heads almost touched. 'Sade's dad fought in Iraq. Twice. A year later, her dad comes home with PTSD. Takes to sleeping with a kitchen knife under his pillow. Keeps mistaking his family for "the enemy". Imagine what that's like.'

I swallowed, picturing Sade waking up her father only to have him pull a knife on her.

'Happened one too many times, so he hung himself,' she added, sombrely. 'Guess who found the body.'

'Oh no!' I said, covering my mouth with both hands. '*That*'s why Sade hates us?'

Latifah nodded. 'Blames Muslims for her father's death. Now her mum's working two jobs just to make ends meet. That leaves Sade to raise her little brother.'

'But British Muslims had nothing to do with what went down in Iraq!' I protested.

'Like I said, Sade's ignorant and hurting. Girl needs someone to blame. So the media points the finger, and off she goes.'

'Yeah, well, Iraq and Syria are a hot mess now,' I said. 'Everybody lost.'

Latifah sighed. 'Adults screw things up. Let's hope Generation Z finds a better way.' She looked hungrily at my muffin, so I broke off a piece for her. 'Thanks. Anyway, I've gotta help Ms Simcox with her assembly.'

'Bet you've had them queuing up ever since you slayed with bee-aitch-em,' I said, smiling.

Latifah grimaced. 'Don't believe everything you read in the papers. Certain people got a little salty about some of my rhymes.'

I watched her vanish into the crowd, leaving me to think about Sade's dad. She'd been a complete cow to me and mine for the longest time. But she'd had her reasons. It was an explanation, not an excuse.

CHAPTER 31

'Why were you wearing a silly hijab when you came home from school?' demanded my mum for the second time at the dinner table.

I sighed. I'd been wearing my hijab at school for the past three weeks, always careful to remove it before I got home. Today it had just slipped my mind. *Dayyum*.

'I told you,' I said, trying to be patient with her. 'It's part of Islam, and I *want* to do it.' Arif may have got me into it, but wearing my hijab was between me and God and nobody else.

'It's not part of *our* Islam,' Dad said, flashing his eyes. 'The veil is metaphorical. God doesn't want us staring at each other like pieces of meat. Only extremist idiots take verses from the Qur'an literally!'

Dad's attitude stank. In his own way, he was just as extreme with his 'moderate views'. I was old enough to find my own path to God.

'I don't understand,' I protested. 'How does me wearing a hijab even affect you?'

'It affects our whole family,' he spluttered, his face turning aubergine. 'Thugs will follow you here and burn down the bloody restaurant!'

Overreacting, as usual. When it suited him, he'd complain about being treated unfairly. Then he'd turn around and do the exact same thing to Muslims with stricter beliefs. This had to end now.

'Look, it's *my* choice, and I'm going to cover my hair whether you like it or not!' I yelled. 'I've let you two run my life for the past fifteen years. You won't even let me choose my own career! I don't want to be a bloody doctor!'

The air was shot through with an electric charge. You could almost hear the crackle. A resounding slap from Ami brought me down to earth with a bump.

'Don't you raise your voice in your father's presence!' she boomed.

My eye watered; my cheek buzzed. So much needed to be said.

I quietly got up and locked myself in my room. With trembling hands I fumbled for my phone. Arif answered on the second ring.

''Sup, Muz? You all right?' he said.

I was shaking so hard, I could barely speak.

'Hello? Hello?' he said, before I burst into gut-wrenching sobs. 'Aw, Muzna. Don't cry, babe. Come on, tell us what happened.'

I told him everything in jerky, incoherent sentences. He sighed. I could imagine his long nostrils flaring.

'Jameel once told me that when a person wants to bring themselves closer to Allah, Satan puts obstacles in their path,' he said softly.

'They're my parents, Arif!' I cried. 'They aren't "obstacles", and they've got nothing to do with Satan.'

'Look, Muz, all I'm saying is Satan poisons people's hearts so they disobey God. With your parents beating on you for trying to please Allah, whose side do you think they fall on?'

CHAPTER 32

I tipped my head to Jameel. Arif had convinced me his brother was very well informed when it came to sharia law. For every problem that existed, Allah also created the solution. Only the law of God could set me free.

'Her parents don't want her wearing hijab,' Arif told Jameel. 'Mum slapped her; Dad threatened her. We wanna know what Allah would want her to do.'

'Would you like a piece of baklava?' Jameel asked, as if I'd come to join him for tea.

I passed.

'Hmm,' he said, folding his hands, thoughtfully tapping his lips with the V of his index fingers. 'I advise you to make prayer to Allah that He open their hearts and guide them to His way.'

'That's not going to work!' I almost shouted. 'All my life they've made choices for me. But now they're banning me from the five daily prayers and wearing my hijab.'

'Does your father pray?' Jameel asked.

'No. I told you at the wedding. Remember?' But clearly he didn't.

'Well then,' he said, interlacing his fingers like swords. 'He is *not* a Muslim, and therefore you do not have to follow him.' His verdict stunned me. 'I suggest you keep a low profile for a while. Hide your religious convictions from your parents until Allah provides you with a way out of your misery.'

'What way?' I asked. How could a girl restrict herself to prayer alone and expect God to do all the heavy lifting? Surely He gave us a brain and a body for a reason.

'One way would be marriage,' he said, pensively combing his beard.

'Bro, she's only fifteen,' Arif said quickly.

His brother glared at him. 'She has passed the age of puberty. She is fit for marriage. And what is more,' Jameel said, eyes flashing beneath knitted eyebrows, 'by enjoying one another's company, you two are displeasing Allah. No wonder you are in this terrible mess. The only way for you to make halal what is haram is to marry each other!'

Mind. Officially. Blown.

CHAPTER 33

'But in spite of all the laws and measures taken in Britain today, unfortunately prejudice lives on,' said Mr Dunthorpe.

Leaning back against his desk, he continued to flip through presentation slides that looked like they'd been put together by a five-year-old. The teacher in charge of the PSCHE curriculum was super-lazy. Rumour had it she'd only got the job because she was sleeping with Principal Dillinger. That was just wrong – the guy was practically a *corpse*.

'Examples include racism, sexism, homophobia, Islamophobia, trans—'

'Innit!' said Arif, snapping his fingers. 'How come other religions aren't getting slated, eh? Just Islam. What's *that* about?'

Mr Dunthorpe paused to consider Arif's question. 'Well, what do you think the reason might be?'

Sade reckoned she had the answer. 'Uh – maybe cos people are fed up with Muslims going round driving cars into crowds or knifin 'em in the name of Allah?'

'Those idiots weren't even proper Muslims, though.' Arif said irritably. 'Probably smackheads and alcoholics too.'

'And?' Sade retorted. 'Muslims get up to all sorts too, you know—'

'But not all of us do,' a quiet girl interrupted.

Sade stood up. 'You got something to say, baby girl?'

'OK, OK – you've all got points to make,' Mr Dunthorpe told her. 'Can anyone else think of a *sensible* answer?'

Malachy put his hand up. 'I think the government *wants* it to happen. Cos every time, yeah, government be like: this person was known to the po-po.' He threw his hands in the air. 'So why didn't they stop him, then? I'm telling you, it's well shegged!'

'Perhaps,' Mr Dunthorpe said, 'the authorities didn't think the attackers posed a credible threat?'

He saw my hand hovering and invited me to speak.

I gulped, conscious of being the only hijabi in the classroom. 'No one hates ISIS more than Muslims do.'

Sade cackled.

'They kill people, we get blamed,' I explained, refusing to be intimidated. 'Then haters feel justified taking it out on us. And the media keeps giving ISIS all the publicity it wants.'

'Good point, Muzna,' he replied.

'There's something like a billion Muslims in the UK—' began Alex, zhushing her blue hair.

'Just under three million, actually,' Mr Dunthorpe corrected.

She accepted this with a wave of her hand. 'So how can the police keep an eye on all of them?'

'But that's like saying all Muslims are terrorists. Newsflash: we're not!' I snapped.

'It's in the Qur'an though, innit?' countered Sade. '*Thou shalt kill all non-believers*, or summink.'

'So? It's in the Bible too,' retorted Alex. 'Let's ban all religions; then we can finally have world peace.'

'Do that, and *watch*,' Arif said, anger in his eyes.

'Hey!' Mr Dunthorpe said. 'If you want to threaten people, you can get out.'

'How is that threatening, though?' I said, clamouring to my boyfriend's defence. 'Arif means there'll be riots up and down the country because people won't be told what they can and can't believe in!'

Mr Dunthorpe's cheeks pinked.

'I see,' he said quietly. 'If that's the case, I apologize to Arif. But I do need to steer us back to what this lesson's about, otherwise we'll never meet the objectives. Now, let's talk about *generalization*.'

'Aw,' complained Sade, splitting her face with a grin. 'Just when it was starting to get a bit interesting!'

Arif gave me a nod, making a solidarity fist. Pride unexpectedly swelled in my chest. I felt like an Islamic Warrior Woman fighting for God.

At lunchtime, Arif and I headed straight for the school gates.

'Muzna!' Sarabi called after us.

No one wants to get busted when they're trying to sneak off. Unhappily I turned round to face her.

'Did you forget our lunch date?' she said with a slightly manic smile, casting quizzical looks Arif's way.

'Meet you at the chippy,' he said, taking off.

'Muzna!' Sarabi said, gripping my arms like she thought I might blow away in the wind. 'You're going to bunk off with *him* again, aren't you? Aren't you?!'

'Yes!' I said, pulling her hands off me. 'You're not my mother, Sarabi.'

'And if I was?' Her eyes were glassy, defiant. 'Would you listen to me then?'

I gave her a hateful look. Was she threatening to snake me out?

'Look, I'm already late,' I said, turning away. 'You don't understand – I'm just going to a lecture at a uni. Totally educational.'

'Muzna, stop!' she pleaded, screwing her face up. I could tell she didn't want to be having this conversation. But like a lemming throwing itself off a cliff, she pushed on. 'These meetings are *changing* you. We both know Arif was threatening Alex in class.

So why on earth did you turn it around on Mr Dunthorpe? Not cool, Muzna. Not cool!'

Forced to confront my actions, shame eroded my pride. I'd been rude to the nicest teacher I knew. Me and Arif hadn't done Islam any favours either.

'Look, I've got to go,' I said, gently squeezing her hand. I walked out of the school gates without looking back.

CHAPTER 34

Arif was waiting outside Mr Fryer with a large bag of chips. I helped myself.

'Have to walk and eat if we're gonna make the train,' he said.

I broke into a trot as we headed towards the station. Why were my legs so short? Two of my steps equalled one of his.

'What'd that girl want?' he asked.

'Sarabi? Oh nothing. She was just worried,' I replied.

'She's a disbeliever. You can't trust her,' he said, almost casually.

'Sarabi's been, like, my best mate since we moved here!'

'Yeah, but now you know better,' he said, flinging a burned chip away. 'Look at me. I used to have *kuffar* girlfriends and chase after the *duniya* . . . Won't catch me doing that crap now. Gotta keep our souls pure for Allah.'

Duniya – that was Arabic for the 'material world'.

'Why did you threaten Alex?' I asked.

'Didn't you hear her? "Ban all religions." If those aren't the words of Satan, I don't know what are.'

'Yeah, but you're not winning any votes by attacking people's views, are you?' I said. 'It's like with discursive essays: strong arguments; gentle words.'

'Leave it, man!' he said, irritably. 'Nobody cares anyway. Alex can clap back like a pro.'

We walked in silence for a while before he apologized.

'I ain't like you and Jameel.'

I frowned. 'How exactly are me and your brother the same?'

'You both got the gift of the gab. I just get angry and start swearing, me,' he said, in a quiet voice. 'Plus I owe you both. You saved me from going crazy at school. Jameel saved me from my uncle.'

I opened and closed my mouth like a fish. 'Was your uncle strict?'

Arif was silent till I thought he wouldn't answer. He handed me the bag of chips and cleared his throat. 'Man was *violent*. Hurt me every opportunity he got. Got worse when Jameel went uni.'

I touched his arm. He flinched then glanced down at my hand and smiled sadly.

'So when my brother came home one day and said I could live with him instead, it was literally the answer to my prayers.'

For the first time ever, I understood his mad devotion to his brother. We walked the rest of the way in silence.

We were in central London by one o'clock. The lecture was being held in the prayer room at a top university. Stashing blazers and ties in our bags, we entered the premises, stealthily camouflaged among a loud group of students. Arif looked like a man anyway, so he totally blended in. Actually a bit too well. One thirsty-looking woman stared at him like he was a juicy steak. Sure, it was annoying, but I could deal with it. After all, *I* was the one Arif had chosen to share another spiritual experience with.

As I followed him through the bowels of the historic building, I imagined myself studying English in a place like it. With Arif by my side, anything seemed possible. Maybe we could study together? He had a gift for all things computer; uni would shape that talent. If we both worked hard enough, it would be the ultimate flip-off to those shameful stats about British Pakistanis (and Bengalis) being right at the bottom of the poverty ladder. Uni was still two years away. Plenty of time to bring Arif round to my way of thinking.

The guest speaker was an old Indian man wearing a red-and-white checked *keffiyeh* over a skullcap.

'Poor thing, shivering up there on that platform,' I muttered.

'He's not cold,' said the sister next to me, smiling. 'He's got Parkinson's. It's a disease of the brain that gives you the shakes. Nerve cells in the *substantia nigra* start dying off, which puts dopamine on the slide.' She shook my hand. 'Khadijah. First-year medical student, by the way.'

'Muzna,' I said, smiling. 'I have no idea what you just said there, but my parents would *love* having you as a daughter.' I frowned. 'Though they'd probably barbecue your hijab.'

She laughed. 'Your parents must be worried by all the attacks on sisters. So, what you studying?'

I shrank. 'I'm still at school, really. But if I get the grades, I'd like to read English. I want to be an author.'

'Check you out!' she said. 'I *love* YA books. You working on anything at the minute?'

I nodded. 'I'm writing something about a boy who has these suspicions that his best friend is being taken abroad for, you know, FGM. Thing is, he secretly fancies her, but he knows her parents are strict, so it's never gonna happen. Then one night he does some research and – bombshell! – he finds out FGM isn't even Islamic. So what does he do next?'

'Raa, man! That is deep. You sure you're still at school?'

My heart did a happy dance.

'You, uh, gonna have a doctor character in the mix?' she asked.

I nodded. 'Most definitely. She'll be a hijabi called Khadijah.'

Her eyes widened. 'Oh my days! If I saw my name in a book, I would literally *die*. So naming my first born after you!'

I flushed. 'Muzna's a boring name . . .'

Khadijah glanced at her phone, thumbing the screen. 'OK, here we go. Muzna means "the cloud that brings the rain". Sounds like the *perfect* name for a writer.'

I smiled, touching her arm.

'Hey, my mosque is doing this "hot meals for the homeless" thing on Saturday,' she said. 'Some proper desi cooking going down. Wanna help?'

Did she even need to ask? We exchanged numbers.

'Good lecture, weren't it?' Arif said, as we waited on the darkened platform in the dusty tube station. I'd read somewhere we were breathing in the same dust as the Victorians. Gross.

'I guess,' I said, struggling with my conscience. 'But some of the stuff he came out with, I'm pretty sure it's not *legal*.'

Khadijah had walked out halfway through. Wish I'd had the guts to do the same.

Arif chuckled. 'Yeah, some of it was a bit full-on. At one point I thought he was calling for jihad on the Houses of Parliament!'

'It's not funny,' I chided, making sure he'd not been heard. 'It scares me! Being a Muslim in Britain is tough enough without people like him making us look like a pack of terrorists.'

'Hey, one man's terrorist is another man's freedom fighter,' he said, shrugging. 'Just saying.'

He reached out and tucked a stray lock of hair back inside my hijab. His tenderness caught me off guard, made me forget all about the speaker's ugly ideas. We stared at each other. His Adam's apple bobbed twice, then he leaned in closer.

The moment our lips touched, a deep warmth spread through me. For the first time in my life, I felt the earth move, and I held on to him for dear life. Just as I was getting used to the salty taste of his mouth, the softness of his warm lips, he pulled back sharply.

'Sorry!' he said, wiping his lips like they were covered in poison. '*Astaghfirullah*!'

'It's OK,' I said, stroking his arm. 'I was totally into it.'

Saturday rolled around, and I was on board the number 43 to Ginsby Mosque. I'd texted Khadijah, letting her know I was on my way. She'd hit me back with a whole row of happy emojis.

I'd lied to my parents. They didn't want me mixing with other Muslims, so I'd said I was going clothes shopping instead. 'Don't buy anything that isn't on sale!' Ami had warned. 'And don't buy me any presents.'

Ami found fault with everything I ever got her. Even on those rare occasions when she actually liked a gift, she'd ask how much it cost, then order me to take it back. She wasn't being mean. Ami had grown up in a poor village and believed in saving for a rainy day.

The dome of Ginsby Mosque rose into view like a great golden sun. I jumped off the bus and skipped along to the gates. Inside the forecourt, two navy blue minibuses were parked. *Ginsby Mosque Minibus* was stencilled in white letters on their sides, and beneath it: *Keeping It Halal Since 1988!*

A man carrying a crate of mangoes tottered towards the minibus. The crate was so large, he could barely see where he was going.

I cleared my throat. 'Excuse me, brother . . .'

'Just a sec,' he said, fishing for his keys while trying to keep the crate steady. He poked blindly at the paintwork.

'Here, let me,' I said, taking his keys and unlocking the door.

He grunted, hefting the crate into the back. 'Gotta be careful with mangoes,' he said, rosy-cheeked and sweaty. 'Worse than eggs, and nobody wants mango omelette.'

I nodded.

'So what can I do you for?' He took out a hanky and mopped his brow.

'I'm looking for Khadijah,' I said. 'She invited me down to help out.'

But he wasn't listening any more. Another large man had swallowed him up in a bear hug. I gave them some space, until I reckoned I'd been forgotten.

'Uh, do either of you know where I can find Khadijah?' I interrupted.

'Check the kitchen,' the first man said.

'S'what you always do, you big fatty!' said the bear-hugger.

'Shut up, man! I got big bones, innit? Like Dwayne Johnson.'

I left them bromancing.

Inside, the rich smells of curry wafted about as I threaded through the corridors, navigating towards the kitchen by my nose. I pushed open the door and a wave of heat shimmered over me. A woman had lifted the lid off a hissing saucepan, and clouds of steam flocked to the ceiling.

'Oh my days! Someone turn the fan up! Now!'

I recognized that voice. Twisting the dial on the extractor fan, I headed towards its owner, as steam was sucked out of the air.

'*Salaams*, Khadijah!' I said.

'Oh, Muzna. Glad you could make it!' The first-year med student hugged me, kissing me on both cheeks.

'No worries,' I said, smiling. 'So where do you want me?' There were seven women chopping and mixing and cooking. I was getting that 'spare wheel' vibe.

'Bless you – there's tons of stuff that needs doing. You any good with pakoras?'

'Course,' I said. 'It's in the genes, right?'

'Well, even if it wasn't,' said a girl bent over a silicone chopping board, 'you'll be one hundred per cent desi-fied once we've spliced you and spiced you.'

Everyone laughed. Never in my wildest dreams did I figure I'd get to hang out with uni students. Even their jokes were smart.

Once I'd prepared it, I carried the mustard-coloured pakora mix over to Khadijah, trailing the fresh scents of coriander, cumin and green chilli. She stared intently into a pan, bubbling and brewing with oil.

'Typical,' I said, glancing round the kitchen. 'Leave the women to do all the cooking.'

'Now that's where you're wrong,' Khadijah said, surprising me. 'It's action stations over in the boys' kitchen. They're baking stacks of naans, and roti and paratha. Trust me, we got the better deal. All that baking's going to chap their faces and frazzle their beards.'

Experimentally, she dropped a dollop of pakora mix into the pan. A frenzy of bubbles enveloped it, and she reduced the heat.

'You left the talk early,' I said.

'Little help here,' she said, ladling scoopfuls of mixture into the oil as fast as she could. It was essential to get this part done quickly if you wanted evenly cooked pakoras. I quickly mucked in.

Once the pan was full, she wiped her hands on a sheet of kitchen roll and turned to face me. 'Yeah. Thought it was going to be about Islam. You'd never think to look at him, but that old guy was filled with more misinformation than a Wiki page. A *dangerous* Wiki page.'

'He was only saying what he believed.' I wondered why I was defending the dude. I'd been equally shocked by the stuff he'd been spewing.

'The Prophet warned us about people like him. He said, "Those who go to extremes are doomed." Said it *three times*! And who was he speaking to? *Muslims*.' Her eyes flew wide. 'No!' she wailed, yanking the fryer basket out of the pan. 'Now I've gone and cremated the pakoras.'

'Extremist frying,' I said. 'Better turn you over to the police.'

She threw her head back and laughed. 'You're funny, sister. I like you.'

Dumping the burned pakoras in the bin, we started over.

With supplies loaded into the minibuses, we drove over to Pilchard Head's Community Centre. It was a single-storey building with large windows, brown bricks and green rails.

A lady with a Cleopatra bob and a string of pearls trotted down the metal ramp to greet us.

'Glad you could make it,' she chirruped. 'They're really looking forward to meeting you.'

As we walked into the centre, the old people looked up, and conversations were aborted. I felt my cheeks burn. Did they see us as 'undesirables'?

'Good morning, respected elders,' said a mosque representative in a bright red hijab with an unwavering smile. 'We're volunteers from Ginsby Mosque. Lunch is on us.'

'Yeah, hope you like Indian food,' said a tall man with a crocheted skullcap and a blue Berghaus jacket.

'Oooh, I like a good curry!' said an old man, rubbing his hands together. 'Spicier the better, I sez.'

Lunch was served, and we were asked to go mingle. I foisted myself on a frail lady with powdery skin and deep-set eyes. The silver pendant round her neck told me her name was Doris. I watched her cutting her Bhuna chicken into thin little strips.

'How is it?' I asked, filling Doris's glass. I was shaking so much, the tablecloth took a good soaking.

'Hang on!' she snapped, stabbing her food with a fork. 'Haven't had a bite to eat yet, have I?'

I blushed, sopping up the spill with a napkin.

'Delicious, dear,' she finally announced, her eyes growing misty. 'You could win wars with food like this.'

I smiled. 'Make curry, not war. If only.'

'Dreams beget ideas,' Doris said. 'Ideas beget solutions. Not every time, mind. But if you don't dream, then what's the whole flipping point, eh?'

I smiled. I was doing so much of it, my poor cheeks felt like concrete.

'You studying for O Levels, are you?' she asked, taking a sip from her glass.

'GCSEs, yes. I want to be a writer.'

Her rheumy eyes lit up. 'Will you be writing whodunnits like Agatha Christie? She's my favourite.'

'Mine too!' I said, bouncing in my seat. 'But she was on another level. The plots, the characters. Man, there's only one Agatha Christie.'

'Saw her once, I did,' Doris said importantly, wiping her chin with a serviette.

'No way!'

She frowned, transporting herself back to the moment. 'I was a young thing then. Ms Christie had written a play for the West End. Come down to make sure it was done proper. You couldn't afford to buy a ticket, not with prices like that. But we queued for hours, hoping for a glimpse of our Queen of Crime. Was murder on me legs, though, I can tell you! Probably why I've ended up with rheum-ee-tism.' Doris made a clucking sound, then rested her jaw between fanned fingers. 'Worth it, though. I can see her now. Ms Christie in her brown fur coat, stood before me, dripping with diamonds!'

'Wow. I can't believe you actually saw her,' I said, imagining the moment slightly speeded up and in sepia.

'You're different,' she said, frowning at me.

'Am I?' I stiffened, suddenly conscious of every one of my flaws.

'Yes. Most girls your age are into their *X Factor* and boys and all this dressing up. When I first saw you people, I was a little frightened, I'll admit. You know, with everything that's on the telly nowadays. But having a good ol' chinwag has warmed me heart. God bless you, dearie.'

'Can I get a hug?' I asked foolishly, getting emotional.

'Go on then!' she said. 'But careful with me bones, mind. Haven't had a hug in years.'

My mouth dropped open. 'Don't your family visit you?'

'My husband passed away ten years ago. It was the cancer that got him in the end, though his drinking couldn't've helped. Never had any children.'

I hugged her with everything I had. 'But you've got your books,' I said. Books had been my lifeline when I was too scared to live in the real world.

She nodded, eyes flickering like she was watching archive footage of everything that might have been. 'Ye-es . . . Got my books, I have.'

Her eyes suddenly darted to mine, as her hand formed a claw round my wrist. 'Don't you go spending your whole life writing, dear! Books can't give you a hug or tell you how much they love you. You find someone, you hear? Someone to share your life with. That's what it's all about.'

Later that afternoon, we distributed gift bags. Each plastic bag contained useful items for the summer: sunglasses, a puzzle book, a stay-cool thermos, a digital thermometer, and a book about who to call in an emergency. Meeting the old people had really touched me. They were white and they were old, but nothing like I'd feared. If there'd been any prejudice in their hearts, I honestly hadn't seen it.

I realized with shame that some of Dad's suspicions about white people had rubbed off on me. Dad grew up in Pakistan, had made Britain his home, but for some reason wanted to keep it out of his house. He'd been a great social worker. I'd seen the cards and messages clients had given him to know this was true. But maybe he secretly believed his history was better than theirs. Maybe that was behind his need for me to turn out to be this 'perfect Pakistani girl'?

I couldn't be someone's symbol. Not even for Dad.

'You all right?' Khadijah asked, handing me a tissue.

'Yes. No. It's just . . . What you guys did for these people today was really sweet.'

'It's what being a Muslim is about. Not the crazy stuff that gets reported.' She kissed my cheeks. 'Thanks for helping out, sis.'

CHAPTER 35

I sat mesmerized, barely aware of the tears streaming down my cheeks as the video clip came to an end.

'Your *nafs* is pure,' Jameel concluded.

It was the last day of the Easter break, and Jameel had invited me and two other girls round to a Sisters' Circle. After having spent nearly every day of the holidays either studying or hanging out with Arif, I kind of felt obliged to go. Besides, saying no to Jameel was impossible. The guy made you feel like you were saying no to Allah.

He'd just shown us a video about the situation in Syria. How Assad's westernized government had murdered his own people for protesting against his evil dictatorship. No method of execution was off limits. Even *children* weren't spared. The graphic footage made my stomach turn. Blistered skin, melted flesh, burst eyeballs. Like something out of a torture-porn movie.

The girl next to me was having a full-on panic attack. I rubbed her back, trying to calm her down. Jameel quickly fetched a glass of water. In the end, I had to hold it to her lips, as her hands wouldn't quit shaking.

'It is indeed disturbing, my sisters,' Jameel said. 'And each and every Muslim, male and female, has a responsibility to try to change it. The messenger of Allah, peace be upon him, said, "Whosoever of you sees an evil, let him change it with his hand; and if he is not able to do so, then let him change it with his tongue; and if he is not able to do so, then with his heart – and that is the *weakest* of faith."'

It made me so angry at the West for arming Assad's regime. Bombs were dropped mercilessly on Syria, pounding it to useless rubble. Survivors fled for their lives, crossing deserts and seas to escape, only to have doors slammed in their faces and tabloids calling them 'cockroaches' and 'criminals'. Muslim refugees were not welcome.

'It's genocide,' Jameel said, catching my eye. 'The West want to obliterate the Believers from the face of the earth.'

I shuddered. It was a scary idea, but I didn't see how it could be true.

'The video I showed you is not permitted to exist on the web,' Jameel went on, strutting about like a rooster. 'Only through special software was I able to gain access to the unpoliced Dark Web.'

'What's that?' asked the Moroccan girl on my left.

'An intelligent question,' he replied, tipping his head to her. 'Did you know that normally we only have access to seventeen per cent of the internet? The rest is not indexed by standard search engines. The unbelievers use the Dark Web to sell drugs, child pornography, weapons, and for cheating husbands and wives to hire hitmen to murder one another. Imagine: we are being forced to put our spiritual education among the depraved filth of the dregs of society!'

'May Allah destroy their faces!' the girl shouted.

Jameel nodded. 'But, my sisters, the situation is far worse than you can imagine. As you increase in *deen*, your unbelieving teachers will start to notice. Their hearts are ruled by Satan, and your spiritual commitment to Allah will cause them to beat their breasts and throw dust on their heads. Why is it that you should see Heaven, when it is certainly Hell that awaits them?'

I broke out in goose bumps.

Jameel shook a finger above his head. 'You may find yourselves reported under a draconian initiative called the "Prevent Duty".

Channel officers – the government's counter-terrorism police – may bother you. Do not worry if this should happen. Yes, they will try to label you as a "radical" or an "extremist", but nothing will stick if you follow my three golden rules.

'One: act as if you have no idea what they are talking about. Two: remind them it is a basic Human Right to practise any faith according to UN convention. Three: do not mention anyone as having inspired you. The *kuffar* do not mind us acting alone, but the idea of us working together aggrieves them. It reminds them of a time when the glorious caliphate – the Muslim superpower – ruled the world, and smote evil wherever it existed.'

My insides shrivelled. I didn't want to get reported. I'd never been in trouble at school for anything. My parents would hit the roof.

Jameel turned back to his laptop. 'Now, let us listen to this beautiful *nasheed* and be inspired by our great brothers and sisters who refuse to practise a watered-down version of their faith. Truly Heaven is their final abode!'

He played another video, this one in crystal-clear HD. It looked just like a Hollywood production. A man sang over the images in Arabic. Though I didn't understand the words, it sounded beautiful and sad. There was a montage of different wars and the suffering they brought. Interwoven were scenes of American and British troops shooting guns and firing rockets, knocking down houses with rampaging tanks, and dropping bombs on a civilian population. There were scenes of injured children screaming for their mothers as an aerial bombardment ripped their world apart. There were images of animals being maimed, clutching on to life even as it was torn from their broken bodies.

Just when the violence became unbearable, the camera panned, revealing five men in black turbans riding heroically towards the camera. Beneath them, glossy stallions charged, raising plumes of desert dust. The singer's voice rose, soaring and defiant. The five Muslim warriors unsheathed glittering swords that hummed as they were pointed to the sky. A startling close-up showed verses of the Qur'an engraved into the mirrored surface of a blade.

We heard their war cry before the scene faded to black.

The final shot, accompanied by the haunting echo of the *nasheed* singer, was of a small child pointing at an American soldier lying on a mound of tiny skeletons. The soldier was begging for mercy as he bled out through multiple wounds. The solemn child shook his head then walked away, vanishing like a ghost. The soldier's body spontaneously erupted into flames.

There wasn't a dry eye left in the room.

As I glided towards the front door clutching my school bag, dazed by what I'd seen, Jameel called after me. I turned round.

'What's this?' He plucked my novel out of my bag.

The image on the jacket was of a couple caught in a clinch on the stern of a ship. I flushed.

'We have to read it for Book Club,' I said quickly. 'We're doing crime fiction.'

Jameel glared disapprovingly at the couple. 'This is nothing but lies,' he said, tossing the book back into my bag. 'Writers of fiction are among the worst of people.'

The bottom dropped out of my stomach.

'But reading broadens your mind, right? It's a good thing,' I countered, getting annoyed.

'When the Author of all Knowledge has already provided you with superior reading material, you choose to read *this*?' The expression on his face said it all. The book was porn.

'I told you, it's for Book Clu—'

'Have you learned the Qur'an off by heart?' His eyes skewered me.

'N-no . . .'

'Study one page every night before going to bed. That will be better for you.' He narrowed his eyes. 'Ah, but I know how you teenagers are – always looking for short cuts and what not. Very well.' He marched over to a side table and picked up a booklet. 'Powerful and moving quotes – read carefully. There will be a quiz.'

I stared at the words before me. Four sheets of printed A4, stapled together – extracts from the Qur'an, as selected by Jameel.

O Prophet! Fight the kuffar and be unyielding to them; and their abode is Hell, and evil is the destination.

I swallowed. Suddenly my throat felt studded with drawing pins. The words seemed kind of harsh and unforgiving. I supposed life had never been a walk in the park, either. Was this just how life was supposed to be? Had growing up in the West made me into a wimp?

I glanced at the book Mr Dunthorpe had given us to read before next week. Jameel had banned fiction. And if stories were haram, a holy spear had just been driven straight through the middle of my lifelong ambition.

'Stoppit!' I hissed quietly to myself. Arif loved my writing. So did Khadijah. And they were both Muslim.

I pressed my forehead to the cool glass of the window. Two builders covered in dust and blobs of white paint swaggered up the street, waving cans of beer, sharing a joke. Someone's granny crept along, pausing every now and then to lean on her walking stick and blink at the world in surprise. And a super-mum babbled into her mobile while pushing a buggy loaded with shopping bags up the street.

Were each of these people nothing more than logs-on-legs heading for the fires of Hell? And what about people I knew, like Malachy, Amie, Dr Agyemang, Mr Dunthorpe and sweet old Doris? The ones who'd helped me or inspired me or made me believe I was more than a quiet little mouse who had nothing to offer the world.

Did Allah hate them? My parents too?

I tugged my hair, breath whistling between my teeth like a hurricane through a graveyard.

Slamming myself down in front of my laptop, I opened up a browser. If I was going to become a good Muslim, the rules had got to make sense in my head. Arif never questioned anything Jameel told him. But I couldn't be like that. I was confused and I needed answers. So I punched keys, hit ENTER, and dived in.

A page loaded with a complete translation of *Surah at-Tawbah*, and the differences leaped out at me. The verse I was looking at spoke of 'unbelievers and hypocrites'. But Jameel's booklet bunged them altogether under the term '*kuffar*'. I frowned. Did it matter? The notes that went with the translation reckoned it did. The verse was about a specific time in history when a peace treaty had been violated in Makkah: a time of war, not everyday life. The online translation also used the phrase 'strive hard against', while the printout said 'fight'. One sounded like a battle of minds; the other, a call to arms.

Still not convinced, I scrolled down to the comments section, and found the usual mix of praise and hate. But then I spotted a flame war happening between a Christian and a Muslim, each accusing the other's holy book of being the more violent. As evidence, someone had quoted from the Old Testament, 1 Samuel 15:3.

*Now go and smite Amalek, and utterly destroy all that they
have, and spare them not; but slay both man and woman,
infant and suckling, ox and sheep, camel and ass.*

My brain was a knob of butter scudding across the surface of a
hot frying pan. Alex, from my tutor group, materialized in my
mind as I recalled her words in PSCHE: *Let's ban all religions; then
we can have world peace.*

Did God – the Most Merciful – want us all to kill each other?

'And don't forget your final version will be due next Friday!' Mr
Dunthorpe said.

He'd got us packed away before the end of the lesson. He was
one of the few teachers who actually bothered. Most just made us
late, getting us into trouble with our next teacher.

'Muzna, do you have a minute?' he asked, as the pips rang out.

'Yes, sir?' I said, adjusting my hijab. Next up was maths with
Mr Evans, who was going through a messy divorce. Somewhere
along the line, he'd discovered we made good punch bags. 'You
have poor emotional intelligence!' he'd rant, or 'Let's see how
cocky you are when you're back next year doing resits!' Needless
to say, dodging a verbal battering was fine by me.

'How come we don't see you at Book Club any more?'
Dunthorpe folded his arms, pouting comically. 'Thought I was
your favourite teacher.'

I managed a small smile. 'I've been busy with . . . stuff.'

'With Arif,' he filled in.

'I'm sorry, and that's your business *how*?'

My tone surprised us both.

He held my glare with his placid green eyes. 'It becomes my
business when your hitherto perfect academic record starts to slide.
Your friends are worried about you. *I'm* worried about you.'

I saw red. 'Yeah? Well you can tell Sarabi, from me, that I don't need friends who stab me in the back and are jealous because I have a boyfriend!'

'Whoa!' he said, raising his hands. 'No one is jealous, OK? We're just a bit concerned, that's all.' He sighed, shaking his head. 'You used to be the perfect student, open-minded and inquisitive. Now it's like the shutters are down and you've made up your mind about all there is to know.'

'Guess I finally realized how the world works,' I said. 'I'm not going to be breaking through the glass ceiling any time soon, am I?' I counted on my fingers. 'Muslim. Female. Pakistani. Too many crimes for any employer, don't you think?'

'Then challenge them,' he said. 'Make them see beyond the superficial. When I said you have talent, I meant it. A talent that *demands* to be noticed.'

I swallowed. Jameel had warned me about the tricks of the *kuffar*. But this was Mr Dunthorpe. All you had to do was look him in the eye to see sincerity.

My tutor folded his hands like a preacher. 'I'm not for one second trying to play down the challenges people of colour face. It's not fair, and something needs be done about it. But you see, Muzna, the perfect answer to silence the bigots is someone like YOU.'

My eyes began to water. He really, really cared about me. God, how much I wanted to open up to him and tell him all about Jameel's strange teachings and how I was struggling to find the right thing to do.

Do that, and he'll have no choice but to report you under Prevent, said Jameel's voice in my head.

'I'll try harder,' I said in a shaky voice.

In the end, it was all I could say.

CHAPTER 36

I got a bad feeling the moment the Year 8 kid turned up at our classroom.

'Yes?' said my history teacher with impatience. Her lesson slides wouldn't open. She was not a happy bunny.

Looking like she was going to wet her knickers, the messenger held up a beige slip. Ms Simcox waved her forward. The girl skittered along, cheeks growing redder with every step.

Ms Simcox squinted at the note, then looked directly at me. My heart sank deep inside my chest.

'Muzna Saleem,' she said. 'Ms Pawsey wants to see you in her office.'

'Now you're gonna get it!' said Sade, with brazen delight.

'Allow it!' said Malachy, getting involved for no reason. 'Ms Pawsey's on everyone's case cos of results and that.'

I left them bickering. In my heart I knew Sade was closer to the truth. Ms Pawsey was the deputy principal, after all.

Stomach lurching like a sack of wet oats, I knocked on her door and entered.

'Good morning, Muzna!' she said, brightly. 'How are you, my love?' With a nod she indicated the chair opposite.

Obediently I sat down, sinking into the tender leather. 'Good, thanks,' I replied. Didn't need Jameel to tell me an attack was coming. I could feel it in every pore.

Ms Pawsey was both huge in size and personality, but with strangely tiny hands. My eyes were instantly drawn to the gleaming gel nails on her fingertips.

'New, they are,' she said, fluttering them at me. 'Tenner on the Broadway. Cheap as chips, but it's nice to treat yourself every once in a while.'

She grinned, exposing a mouthful of crooked teeth streaked red with lipstick. Now I was getting piranha vibes.

'What can I do for you, miss?' I asked, wanting to be a million miles away.

'Aw, bless!' She chuckled, completely ignoring my question. 'There's something different about you. Can't quite put my finger on it . . .'

'My hijab,' I said flatly, suppressing an eye-roll.

'That's right!' She snapped her fingers. 'Weren't wearing it last half-term, were you? What's made you change your mind?'

I shrugged. 'Just experimenting, I guess.'

'Lovely! When I was your age – cor dear! – I had this thing about David Bowie, God rest his soul. Dyed my hair bright orange and wore it in a feathered mullet.'

I deadpanned. Didn't sound miles worse than the purple crew cut she was currently rocking. How old was she – sixty?

'So you've decided to make a greater commitment to Islam?'

I shrugged again. 'Is that a problem?'

'Absolutely not. No, no, no. So long as it is *your* decision.'

'No one's forcing me.' I noticed her looking at my balled fists and wrenched them open.

'That right?' She stroked her chin in the way Ami did when she was about to say something cutting. 'Not even, say, Arif Malik?'

I looked lasers at her. But her eyes were impenetrable, like sewage water.

'He's a friend,' I said carefully. 'Malachy and Sarabi are also mates. Why aren't you asking me about them?'

'You're a gentle soul, my love. Arif has a history of intimidating other students into his way of thinking.'

I snorted. 'Well I'm not exactly the easily intimidated type. Besides, the Arif I know is not a manipulator.'

'Well there's evidence on his old school records . . .'

'Then maybe he's changed. Or maybe those records were written by an Islamophobe,' I said pointedly.

She didn't like that. The flicker in her eye followed by a sharp inhalation of breath told me so.

'Teachers deal in facts. There are proper checks and balances in place to ensure that.' Her voice softened. 'So was it Arif's views that inspired you?'

'No!' I said, bubbling over with frustration. 'I'm a writer. I research stuff. I just happened to come across some websites on Islam, and I realized I've been practising it wrong.'

'How so?'

'You wouldn't understand.'

'Try me.'

'My parents mix Islam with Pakistani traditions and random bits of Hinduism.'

'So what parts do they get wrong, in your opinion?'

'Well wearing the hijab, for one. Also praying . . . and fasting. It's all compulsory.'

Her pen zipped across her notebook as if it were a scalpel being raked across my throat.

'Look – Islam is all about being kind to others.' I threw out a hand. 'I volunteered at an old people's community centre just before Easter. We made them lunch and kept them company for a couple of hours.'

She wanted details. Probably thought I was lying. So I told the cow everything I knew about Khadijah's group and their community work.

'Islam's a great religion,' Ms Pawsey agreed, nodding. 'Only there's this nasty movement on the rise trying to waylay young people. I'd hate to see someone as intelligent as you getting exploited.'

I wanted to jump down her throat, tell her that every religion had its share of crazies, so why-oh-why was she singling out Islam? But going nuclear was the last thing I needed. Prevent had been activated for sure. Pawsey was searching for that one false move; that single sliver of evidence to pass me on to the police.

She was getting *nothing* from me.

'Thanks, miss,' I said, 'for looking out for me. But I'm all clued-up on religious psychos. I'm looking for a peaceful life. So are my mates. *All* my mates.'

Ms Pawsey scribbled something down on her pad. Or maybe it was a sketch of me behind bars?

'Aren't we all,' she said. 'Anyway, you hear or see anything a bit daft, you let me know. My door's always open. A community has to look out for its own, and it's my job to safeguard all you wonderful young people.'

I nodded, eagerly rising to my feet. I'd made it all the way to the door before she spoke again.

'Remember, Muzna: someone like you has a bright future ahead of her. Don't let anybody spoil it for you, OK?'

'*Wagwan*, Muz?' Malachy said as I walked into the sunny playground. Cracked me up when he spoke patois. But right then, my sense of humour was DOA.

'Nothing much. Pawsey's being extra,' I grumbled.

He nodded. We stood silently for a while, watching excited little Year 7s crowd round a kid with a radio-controlled drone.

'Man, I hated being in Year Seven,' Malachy said, his sky-blue eyes following the drone flying across the playground. 'Kept missing primary school: playtime, potato painting, and that. Now with the exams coming up, I look at the sevens and wish I was back there again. Little shits don't appreciate what they have.'

'We're going to be all right, Malachy,' I said. 'Everyone goes up a grade from the mocks. Sometimes more.'

'Yeah, but I did crap in the mocks. No college's gonna want one-grade-up-from-a-fail, are they?'

I didn't know what to say. If niceness was a GCSE, he'd come top of the class.

'Probably end up working for my old man at his garage.' He dragged a forearm under his nose. I handed him a tissue. 'Thanks, bruv.'

'Look at it this way. You've got a back-up plan. How many of us can say that?' I said.

His smile was magic for the few seconds it lasted. Then he dropped his eyes.

'What's up?' I asked.

'Nothing. Just . . . you're a good mate, Muz. Don't wanna see you get hurt.'

I laughed. 'Failing GCSEs won't put me on suicide watch.'

'Nah, I mean . . . Look, I'm worried about you and Arif.'

I bristled. Sarabi, Dunthorpe, Pawsey – now Malachy too?

'Hear me out,' he said, reading my expression. 'You know me. I'm Black Lives Matter. I'm Hug-a-Muslim. But, well, my boy Arif went a bit mental in PE.' He licked his lips nervously. 'Missed this shot, right? So Dan opens his stupid gob and says something about Arif being "hopeless as ISIS". Arif went batshit – trust! Started ranting about Dan being a *kafir* and going home in a body bag. Took four of us to drag him off.'

'Sounds like Dan started it.'

'Dan's a wasteman,' he agreed. 'But you should've seen Arif! Can't explain it proper.' He chopped the air in frustration. 'Arif's my G, yeah? But it was like he really wanted to do it.

Like he'd done it before or somethin'.'

'You saying Arif's a terrorist?' I glared at him, lips pursed.

'N-no. I'm just saying . . .' Now he was doing The Robot as he struggled to get the words out. Then his batteries died, and his face went lax. 'Dunno what I'm saying, really. Just wanna protect you, is all.' He flushed beetroot, his voice cracking.

You couldn't get mad at Malachy. He was too hopelessly earnest. 'You worry too much,' I said. 'Everybody's on edge cos of exams. That's the only reason Arif exploded.'

Malachy nodded, but neither one of us was convinced.

CHAPTER 37

Temperatures in London were soaring, with the first wave of GCSE exams set to take place in five weeks. The hall would become the centre of our existence. Endless rows of collapsible desks, prison-guard-style invigilators, and us packed in like battery hens. If the weather held, the stench of BO and cheesy feet would add to the fun.

I sat on a bit of wall staring suspiciously at my cheese and tomato sandwich. A fly landed on it. That decided me. I flung the sandwich in the bin.

'Hey, could you do us a flavour?'

Shading my eyes from the glare of the sun, I gazed up at Arif. A flick of his hand sent sweat splattering to the tarmac, where it sizzled. Today was a scorcher.

'Only if it's of the smoky-bacon variety!' I stuck out my tongue, making him laugh.

'One of Jameel's mates brought Zamzam water back from Makkah. But I got football practice after school, innit? Couldn't deliver a bottle to my uncle, could ya? Lives right next door to Victoria station. You wouldn't hafta go far or nothing.'

'I don't know . . .' After my conversation with Mr Dunthorpe, I was worried stiff about my grades. Enough to spend all of break up in the library designing a new study schedule. He seemed to think I was a shoo-in for uni.

'Oi, *dutty bwoy*! You're needed back in the game, my son!' shouted Malachy, chugging a sports drink. His topknot had come loose, and his sweaty hair hung in his face like Cheestrings.

Arif ignored him. '*Please*, Muz,' he said, putting his hands together and kneeling in the dirt. 'Chuck in a bottle for your family too. Holy water from the holy land. Vampire ever turns up at your door, fill a Super Soaker, and give him what for.' He clutched his throat: a vampire in the throes of death. Hammy as hell, but it did the job and had me in fits.

'Go on then,' I said.

'Get in!' He pumped his fist. 'Only thing is, I don't have it on me. Jamjamz is coming round after school. I'll text him to give it you instead. Safe. You're a life saver!'

He kissed my hand, then ran off back to his game of footie. Arif's smiles were infectious. They gave me face ache in the best possible way.

I leaned against the main gate after school, trying to remember the different types of chemical bond. I *sucked* at chemistry. Plucking out my colour-coded revision cards, I flicked through. *Ionic*, *covalent*, *metallic* – how was I meant to remember this crap?

The white Micra turned in at the top of the road, bringing my street-side revision session to a close. But instead of stopping by the gates like any normal person, Jameel drove further along. I tried not to get angry as I trekked the extra distance. Difficult, since chemistry already had me feeling like a baited grizzly.

The window slid down. '*Assalaamu alaykum*, sister,' he said. 'I have a little time, so I'll drive you down to the station.'

Quietly I got in the back. The AC was turned on full blast, and it was a relief to be out of the heat.

'The bottle is on the seat beside you,' he said, giving the indicator and pulling out. 'Just under that cloth there. Have you found it?'

'Pretty hard to miss!' I said, glaring at the bottle. It was one of those giant five-litre deals from Tesco, complete with reinforced handle. 'Arif said it was a bottle, not a *vat*.'

His face twisted. Whether grimace or smile, the jury was out.

'Generosity is the way of our beloved Prophet,' he replied.

That shut me up. You couldn't argue with the Prophet.

'Why can't *you* deliver it?' I asked, trying to sound curious instead of bolshie.

His black eyes locked on to mine in the rear-view mirror. 'I am speaking at a gathering in Harrow in exactly three-quarters of an hour. But please tell Abdi-Aziz that I will make time to come and see him at the weekend. This is your stop.'

I glanced out of the window. Further up the road stood a line of ticket barriers marking the entrance to the station. I clambered out of the car, struggling with the large bottle.

'It weighs a ton!' I complained, swinging it for emphasis.

His face coloured. 'Be careful with that!'

I flushed. Who the hell did he think he was, shouting at me in public: my dad?

'The handle is not as strong as it looks, my sister,' he added in a mollifying tone. 'It will break if you're not careful, and all your rewards for doing this task would be taken away by Allah.'

I turned away, pulling out my Oyster card. I trudged over to the station, pausing to study the screens overhead displaying arrival and departure times. The next train was due on platform three in seven minutes.

As I rode the train to Victoria, I wondered why Arif and Jameel had that chalk-and-cheese dynamic going on. Was it the large age gap that put them at odds? Or were brothers always like that? I hoped to God Arif didn't grow up to be like Jameel. That would suck.

I was distracted from my thoughts by that creepy feeling you get when people stare. Opposite me sat an old couple, their eyes flitting back and forth between my hijab and the water bottle. *Islamophobes*. Getting nasty looks for wearing my hijab in public was something I was finally getting used to. Irritating as hell, but it didn't hurt like it once had. What was eating them anyway?

Think I'll blow you up with a bottle of H2-Whoa?

The sarcastic smile faded from my lips, my last thought rebounding round my skull. My palms turned slick, and my mouth went dry. Suddenly the walls of the coach ran together like melting ice cream, and the old couple's faces stretched into nightmarish leers. I closed my eyes, telling myself to breathe.

When the driver announced the train was about to terminate and reminded us not to leave anything behind, it was the biggest relief. The second the doors hummed open, I was tearing down the platform. Legs pumping like mad, I dodged commuters, heading straight for the ticket barrier.

'Excuse me!' shouted a station guard.

Busted.

My bladder throbbed, as if I was about to wet myself. I measured the distance to the exit with my eyes. Too far to make a run for it. So I forced myself to turn round.

'Cor, where's the fire?' The bald station guard smiled at me. A tribal tattoo crawled out of his collar, tucking itself behind an ear. 'Dropped this, love.'

My eyes fell on the Oyster card he was holding out. 'Oh . . . thanks!'

I was more relieved than he could ever know.

I sat on the park bench, feeling numb. The five-litre bottle stood at my feet. The park was deserted but for a couple of ducks and a diseased seagull bobbing along on the choppy surface of the lake.

'I've got to know,' I told myself.

Bending down, I pressed the safety buttons on the side of the cap, and unscrewed it. Hesitantly I pitched forward, sniffing. Nothing. Even with my nostrils hovering directly over the mouth of the bottle, there was no incriminating odour.

I placed the lid back on, thoroughly confused. I'd been wrong. Good.

So why couldn't I let it go?

I closed my eyes and tried to recall what my chemistry teacher had taught us. Just like practically every other chemical we ever used in experiments, hydrogen peroxide was boringly colourless and odourless. I remembered being partnered with Malachy, and him claiming his mum kept a bottle of the stuff in her medicine cabinet to disinfect wounds. Thinking he was having a laugh, I asked our teacher if it was true.

'Actually, yes!' Dr Daire said. 'At different concentrations, it can be used for disinfecting, bleaching, promoting plant growth. But it can be also be used as an ingredient in bomb-making.'

We'd all laughed. But I wasn't laughing now.

I stared at the fluid, willing it to give up its secrets. Zamzam or peroxide – water of life, or water of death?

What was wrong with me? Why did I keep looking for terrorism where there was none? Just because Jameel was a devout Muslim who was critical of the West, didn't automatically make him into a crazy militant. Man, I'd been conditioned into becoming an Islamophobe.

But the niggling feeling wouldn't shake.

Then it hit me, the one way I could put the stupid suspicions to rest. I poured out some of the water into the cap. Reaching under my scarf, I pulled out a few strands of hair and dipped them in the liquid.

I'm not sure how long I left the hair in for, but it couldn't have been more than thirty seconds. I pulled out the dripping strands and stared.

'Oh shit . . .' I whispered, my stomach squelching sickeningly. My hair hadn't been bleached blonde. It was ghost white.

I was packing over a gallon of hydrogen peroxide. If I got caught . . .

My first thought was to dump the bottle in the lake. The image of dead ducks floating in a soup of bleached fish shot into my head. Couldn't do it. Life was sacred. Besides, what would I tell Jameel when his contact reported me a no-show?

I considered telling the police. But there was nothing linking the bottle back to Jameel. He'd probably handled the damn thing with gloves. The cops might end up thinking I was a rogue bomber who'd got cold feet and invented some stupid story to protect herself. Especially if Ms Pawsey had listed me under Prevent's 'Most Wanted'.

A boa constrictor clung to my chest as another terrible thought crept into my mind. If I grassed Jameel up, what would Arif say? Wait – was he in on this too? No. Arif was *nothing* like Jameel. He was straightforward and honest. He'd never hurt anyone.

One thing I did know, even through the fog of disbelief and fear, was that I needed to act fast if I wanted to save myself. I lugged the bottle over to a large, gnarly beech tree, carefully positioning it so that it was hidden from oncoming traffic. Next I scanned for CCTV cameras. Thankfully there weren't any; none that I could see, anyway. Trusting myself to fate, I unscrewed the cap, and tipped the bottle over.

Glug, glug, glug. Why was it making so much noise?

Glug, glug, glug. Why was it taking so long?

Sweat dripped down my back like hot syrup. Knowing my luck, someone was going to catch me. I'd end up with my mug on the six o'clock news, and my parents would never live it down.

Once I'd drained it down to a quarter, I set the bottle back upright. The delivery had to go ahead. If Jameel was part of a terrorist cell, my life could depend on it. With a bit of luck, they'd think it was their supplier that had screwed them over, rather than me.

It wasn't a foolproof plan. Not even close. But it was all I had. For the one hundredth time, I made sure there weren't any busybodies about, then dunked the bottle in the lake, this time filling it up.

'Allah!' I muttered, hugging my stomach. 'Please help me!'

I found myself in a derelict street behind the station. Overfilled skips lined the pavements on both sides, vomiting trash, rubble and rotting furniture out on to the street. A fox poked its head out of a hole in a mattress, nearly giving me a heart attack. It made a strangled sound, then vanished.

I rang the doorbell and waited. Nobody came to the door. It was actually a relief. I hurried back down the drive.

'Hello! Hello!'

I turned round to see a skinny man waving at me from an upstairs window. I'd assumed Arif's uncle was a blood relative. But with an aquiline nose and oval face, this guy looked Somali.

'One minute, blease,' the man said, vanishing from the window, only to reappear at the front door a moment later.

He was wearing a grimy vest and *Adventure Time* lounge pants. We *salaam*ed each other.

'This is for you,' I said, holding out the giant bottle. 'From Jameel Malik.'

He laughed. 'You are a good girl, sister,' he said, taking the bottle off my hands as if it weighed nothing. 'Which es-school you go?'

'Falstrum. It's in Ether Downs,' I said, looking over my shoulder, eager to get gone.

'Ah, yes, yes,' he said, leaning in the doorway. 'I work at

Al-Maghrib. You know this es-school?'

I shook my head, but from the name it was clear it was a Muslim one.

'I am caretaker,' he said, prodding his scrawny chest. 'It is good. My children don't bay fees because I'm working there.'

A caretaker.

My chemistry teacher had said peroxide was used for cleaning and disinfecting. In my head, I played back my conversation with Jameel in the car and realized that at no point had he claimed the bottle contained Zamzam water. Maybe Arif had got it all wrong and got me into a panic over nothing?

'May Allah reward you for this!' the man said, drawing me out of my reverie as he pointed at the sky. '*Insh'Allah.*'

I *salaam*ed him and left. I wasn't sure what to think any more. Was Jameel a shady terrorist or just some lazy git who thought I was running a free delivery service? I hiked back to the station, deciding it had to be option two.

Massive relief!

CHAPTER 38

Arif and I walked silently back to the bus stop.

'You didn't have to run out like that,' he said, his tone reproachful.

I flinched at his touch, saw the hurt in his eyes, but couldn't bring myself to apologize.

The meeting he'd brought me to had been held in the basement of a clothes store in Peckham, among dead-eyed mannequins with bleached bone bodies. The moment 'jihad' had been mentioned, I was ready to bolt. But it turned out the speaker was actually talking about a spiritual war. I could get onboard with fighting your inner demons. But the guy switched up fast. He told us jihad also meant firing an AK-47 at the enemies of Islam if the opportunity came around. Unable to control myself, I waved a hand like I was at school, and told him straight that murder was a sin.

'Not if the ones you fight are the children of Satan,' was his comeback. 'Then, my daughter, you are doing the world a favour. Oh ye who believe, do you not use antibiotics to destroy infections? Will you not perform your duty if Heaven is the reward?'

I shuddered from the memory. 'I can't go to these meetings any more,' I told Arif.

'You don't like learning about Islam?' Arif asked with concern.

'I mean the ones about jihad and war,' I said, getting annoyed. Sometimes I felt like he was possessed by Jameel, and it pissed me off. 'I've already had Ms Pawsey on my case.'

'Me too. Woman's a frickin' Nazi, taking all the Muslim kids out of class to interrogate.' He shrugged. 'Don't worry about it, fam.'

But not worrying did nothing for the blot on my conscience.

'Look, maybe Pawsey's a cow. And maybe she's not. Maybe it makes Falstrum look good if we end up with careers instead of being banged up in prison on charges of terrorism.' I took a breath to calm myself. 'But, Arif, if we're going to meetings where we're being told murder gets you into Heaven, then that god-awful woman actually has a point.'

'Don't be daft. You heard the brother saying jihad is like struggling against your dark side.'

'Yeah, right before he broke out the AK-47s,' I reminded him.

He pushed his hands into his pockets, flexing his jaw. 'Look, fam, if I ever fight jihad, it'll be nowhere near Pawsey. England's my country, and I love it.'

'Yeah, well I don't want you fighting. End of.' My vision went hot and blurry. 'Soldiers end up dead, Arif. It's just what happens, whatever side you're on. The people left behind are the ones who really suffer.'

'Don't cry, bae,' he said gently. 'I ain't goin' nowhere. Come on. Let's get some grub in you.'

The Chicken Cottage down the road was packed. Unsavoury men with staring eyes and filthy minds sat in every corner. I wondered why my hijab didn't put them off. Arif ordered us two number 5s off the menu.

'Let's go round mine,' he suggested, glaring at the men.

'Jameel's gonna get all up in our faces again . . .' I moaned.

'See, that's where you're wrong. Jamjamz has headed over to Luton tonight.'

'For real?' I said, instantly cheered up. 'That's, like, *miles* away.'

Why Jameel might be going to Luton was a question that never even crossed my mind.

*

We had the best time at Arif's house, just like in the old days. When had everything become just about religion and war? We joked and laughed, chilling to Tupac, Wizkid and Stormzy like regular teens. At one point, Arif got up and started street dancing like a pro. And when he pulled off a solid backflip, I fell in love with him all over again.

'My brother saw that,' he said, face flushed, chest heaving, 'he'd call me a *batty man*!'

'Psh!' I said, vanquishing the ghost of Jameel with a wave of my hand. 'You could totally win *Britain's Got Talent*.'

'Yeah?' he asked. 'Wanna see me do my Bolton-Bad-Bwoy striptease?' He stood with his legs apart, fingers hovering provocatively over his fly.

I looked away, laughing. 'Right, cos that wouldn't be the least bit haram!'

Kneeling down in front of me, he looked up into my face defiantly. 'It wouldn't be though. Not if we were married.'

He placed his head in my lap. I found myself staring at a poster of Che Guevara on the opposite wall. With a trembling hand, I began to stroke the stubble on the back of his head. I had dreamed about marrying Arif since the moment I'd met him – psychotic, but true. I'd also seen the news reports about Honour Killings. Would my father be prepared to kill his only daughter if she married without his blessing? Dad wasn't a violent man.

Ya think? piped up the facetious voice in my head. *What brought you guys over to Ether Downs in the first place?*

Dad got fired for knocking a client over with a chair.

Had she really attacked him first? I'd never questioned his version of events. But things were different now. I knew the world was an ugly place where every last one of us had the capacity for evil.

'Oh shit, I'm so horny!' Arif cried, blasting my thighs with his furnace like breath.

He leaped to his feet as if whipped by angels. Running hands manically through his hair, he looked away, flushed and frustrated. Then just as suddenly, he clasped my hands, staring into my eyes with an intensity that had me shook. 'Marry me tonight!'

'*What?*'

Nervous excitement danced in his eyes. 'Come on. There's a mosque a couple of blocks away that's open till late. We could do it there!'

'Arif! You don't just get married because you feel . . .' I blushed, my conservative upbringing gagging me.

He went down on one knee, just like in the movies, and my heart burst.

'I know the way I feel about you, Muzna Saleem,' he said, eyes glistening with emotion. 'I love you with all my heart. And I want you to be my wife. Not just for tonight, but forever.'

A sob rose in my throat. To hell with my godless parents and anyone else who stood in our way. Arif was all I would ever need.

CHAPTER 39

I was a bundle of nerves as we approached the mosque. The doors lay wide open.

Don't be surprised if you find a couple of hog heads staring up at you in the morning, I thought sadly.

There had been news stories about local mosques, schools and community centres getting special deliveries of pig meat, vomit, and even poo. It was supposed to be payback. Even if a terror attack happened all the way over in New York City, British Muslims would still get the flak. Revenge attacks happened, or demands were made for public apologies.

'Come on,' Arif said, leading me up the stairs to reception.

'I'm scared,' I said, hating myself for sounding like a whiny child.

'Me too,' he admitted, which sort of made me feel better. He gave my hand a final squeeze then let go. Two unmarried Muslims turning up in the dead of night, holding hands, looked seriously wrong.

The receptionist reminded me of a hardboiled egg in a cosy. I would've placed the guy in his twenties if not for the kinky grey hairs in his cute little boy-beard.

He greeted us, quickly averting his eyes once Arif told him we were looking to get married tonight. It sounded kind of dirty.

'Please take a seat,' the man said, 'and I will see if I can summon one of our Imams to help you. Do you have any witnesses?'

Arif shook his head.

'And where is the girl's guardian?' asked the man.

'My parents aren't Muslim!' I blurted.

'I see,' said the man, with an expression that was impossible to read.

Would he contact my parents and find out I'd lied? Everyone knew everyone in the Asian community, didn't they? But then, I hadn't lied. Not according to Jameel's interpretation of Islam, anyway.

'I'm Jameel Malik's brother,' Arif explained. 'He said if I ever needed to get married, it'd be OK to get it done here.'

I looked up sharply. Why hadn't Arif shared this before?

The change that came over the man was like the biggest switch up ever. 'Ah, brother Jameel! Well why didn't you say so?' he said, grinning so hard you could see his back teeth.

'I just did,' Arif replied.

'Would it be OK for me to contact him?' the man asked, simpering.

'Knock yourself out.'

Every girl dreams of getting her happy-ever-after with a handsome prince. I blame Disney. When I was old enough to realize being Asian wasn't just a 'phase', out went Disney, in came desi. The updated wedding fantasy was similar to the kind Sarabi's sister had enjoyed at Rajput Hall.

My wedding lasted twenty minutes in a poorly lit backroom, conducted by an elderly Imam with a cold, and two witnesses I'd never seen before in my life. It was *horrible*. Just as well Arif wasn't in the mood for chat on the way back. I probably would have thrown up or burst into tears.

I'd gone and made the biggest decision of my life without any of my usual OCD levels of caution. Caught in the moment, all that mattered was removing the millstone of haram from our necks. Little did I know the trade-off would be a big boulder of guilt in my belly.

The moment he closed the front door, Arif began kissing me with the desperation of a hungry beast. This time, there was no restraint. His hands ran over every inch of my body, like he knew no shame. The guilt-boulder vaporized; every nerve ending crackling to life. I knew what was going to happen, craved it just as much as him.

Finally, I would be closer to Arif than Jameel ever could be.

CHAPTER 40

When I finally got home, there was hell to pay.

Of course there was. Story of my life: no pleasure without pain; no carrot without stick. And as long as I lived under his roof, Dad would always be my judge, jury and executioner.

'Where have you been?' Dad bellowed, dragging me into the apartment with both hands as if he thought I'd only come back to do a runner.

'She's been with a boy!' Ami cried, grasping my shoulders. 'I can see it in her eyes!'

Dad pulled Ami off me. 'Well?' he demanded. 'What do you have to say for yourself?'

I blinked, trying to find my voice. 'I was at the mosque.'

Dad's face contorted with rage, eyes flashing like pits of fire. No joke. I honestly wondered whether he was demonically possessed.

'You stupid girl!' he spat, ripping my hijab in two with his bare hands. 'How many times do I have to tell you we are not that sort of Muslim? You think Allah wants to make your life difficult by putting you in harm's way? A Pakistani girl wandering off at night to pray in the mosque!' He shook his head, scandalized by the very idea. 'Do you want someone to dishonour you and leave you in the gutter? Do you want some racist to throw acid in your Pakistani face?'

A snapshot of Arif holding me against his powerful body, flicking his tongue across my throat filled my mind. Then memories of extreme pain. Don't get me wrong: Arif had been thoughtful and tender, but it had *hurt*. Just like our wedding ceremony, sex had turned out to be NOTHING like they made out in books. It was messy and painful. And here I was, feeling vulnerable and confused and sore, and all my stupid parents could do was yell at me.

'No,' I mumbled.

'Besharam!' Ami said, pointing at me. 'Dishonouring your father like that!'

'Parveen, please!' Dad snapped at Ami, before turning his wrath back on me. 'You have dragged our family name through the dirt. I was so worried, I contacted the police. They are out looking for you now. I'm obliged to let them know you've returned.'

As Dad rang up the police, Ami glared at me.

'You may be able to fool your daddy,' she hissed. 'Saleem sees you with the blindness of a loving father. But I see you for what you are.' She poked me in the ribs, making me gasp. 'Who is this boy? Is he Muslim? What will you tell your father when your belly grows fat with your bastard?'

I glared back at Ami. For one self-righteous moment, I felt like breaking it down for her. How my stupid parents with their stupid rules had driven me to desperate measures. How their controlling attitudes meant I could never bring stuff like boyfriends or sex or marriage to them without being threatened with getting shipped off to Pakistan. How my life and my body were my own, and I had every right to do with them as I pleased.

But — most of all — I wanted to tell her how scared and lonely I was feeling. I needed Ami to hug me, not shout at me.

'We will have to take you to Pakistan and get you married quickly,' Ami went on, stroking her chin. 'That way your husband will never know the baby isn't his . . .'

'Oh my God! There is no baby!' I cried. 'I'm not like that. I'm a good girl.'

'No, you're not,' my father said, returning. 'You are just like that accursed Salma.'

A diss more brutal than Ami's slap. Salma had been caught in bed with a boy in somebody else's house. I'd done it by the book and got married. How was that even the same thing?

Except . . . why did I feel so *bad*?

Suddenly I was transported back through time to the dank refectory at Rigsby Academy. Salma was begging me to hear her out. But I'd been warned to keep my distance because she'd slept with a boy and something like that was 'catching'. Had she been feeling the same way I was now – worried, confused, scared? And what had I done to my friend? Turned my back on her, that's what.

Dad shook his head. 'I hoped we'd got you away from that girl's evil influences in time, but I was wrong to blame her. This is what England does to our children. Gives them freedom to disobey their parents and engage in whatever filthy acts they like!'

The doorbell rang. It was the police.

'Are you sure you're going to be OK?' Officer Desirée Sealy asked again, her eyebrows hammocks of sympathy. She was a short, mixed-race lady with honey-coloured eyes and a voice that made me think of coffee.

I nodded. The offer of temporary accommodation was tempting, but I knew my parents' pride would be wounded. In spite of everything, I didn't want to hurt them any more than I already had.

'Well, Ms Saleem,' Officer Paul Redman said, putting away his spiral-bound notepad. 'I think we're all agreed – sneaking off to pray in the middle of the night is unwise at your age. By law, you are a young person and considered vulnerable.' He was tall and powerful with fingerprint freckles and hair like a copper brush.

I nodded apologetically. Easiest way out, I figured.

'How long have you been wearing the hijab?' he asked.

I nettled. How could he even know I was a hijabi? Dad had ripped my hijab up only moments ago. 'Why? What's that got to do with—'

'Two months,' Dad interjected, not realizing I'd worn it for way longer. 'I told her not to wear it. Sends out the wrong sort of message.'

'What made you start wearing it?' Officer Sealy asked, with a curious smile.

I shrugged. 'Dunno. I just thought it'd be nice to try religion for a change.'

'Any of your friends wearing it?'

I shook my head. 'I don't understand what this has to do with me coming home late. I get that I should have told my parents I was going out . . .' I turned accusingly to Officer Redman. 'Wait – you think I'm part of ISIS, don't you?'

His lips formed a grim line.

'Of course we don't,' Sealy said quickly. 'But part of our job is considering all the angles. Child exploitation is a very serious matter.' She folded her hands over her stomach. 'When I was a youngster, there used to be a man down our street who was the very definition of happy. Irie-Stanley everybody called him. Unlike all our parents, he was never stressed, and he'd have these delicious coconut drops for us to try. Couldn't get them in the shops for love nor money.

'It turned out he was lacing his drops with cannabis. Called it the "wisdom weed". Claimed it brought you closer to God. He was *very* convincing. If I'd got carried away, I might've ended up with a lifelong dependency on marijuana.'

I baulked, imagining her having to go through that horrible experience. 'Look, I just wanted to experiment with the hijab to see if it would make any difference to the way people treat me. I don't like ISIS, or whatever they're called. They've got Islam upside down. Killing is totally un-Islamic.'

Dad caught my eye, and a smile flickered on his lips. He was still mad at me, but he liked what I was saying.

Sealy smiled. 'Of course it is. Your daughter's got a smart head on her young shoulders.'

Dad nodded. Ami just looked grim.

'Would you be interested in attending a weekend club for young people like yourself?' Redman said. His strained smile didn't just look fake – it belonged in a horror museum. 'All kinds of cool activities are run at the civic centre. You'd meet other Muslim kids.'

My sixth sense was tingling. I went for broke. 'You're a Channel officer, aren't you?' I turned to my dad. 'Look, Dad – you registered me as a missing person, and they sent anti-terror police!'

'We're exploring every possibility,' Redman said, looking irritated. 'I admit I am part of the counter-terrorism unit, but Officer Sealy is not. It's standard protocol for me to be involved in a case like this. I'm just offering your daughter a safe environment where she can socialize with other young people and develop an immunity to radicalization.'

My father shook his head. 'This is not the sort of help I asked for.'

'Muzna –' Redman turned his attention to me – 'you'd have free access to some terrific opportunities—'

'No thank you!' I said, cutting him off with a cold stare.

'Well, thank you for your time,' Sealy said, giving everyone a bright smile.

They left shortly afterwards. Surely a missing kid with a

'funny'-sounding name wasn't enough to trigger this level of paranoia. It had the stink of Falstrum all over it. Ms My-door-is-always-open Pawsey had reported me to the cops.

What a joke. I was in love with Arif, and the whole world was against us. Even Romeo and Juliet never had it so bad.

'Sorry you had to go through that,' Arif said, after I'd told him about the drama with the police the night before. He offered me another Jammie Dodger.

'I wish I could live with you instead.' I twisted apart the two halves of the biscuit, and licked the filling.

'Yeah, but we can't get legally married without your parents' say-so till you're eighteen.'

I sagged.

'Hey,' he said, lifting my chin so our noses touched. 'I really love you, Muz.'

'I love you too,' I replied, losing myself in his brooding eyes.

'Would you die for us?'

The question made me start. 'Morbid much?'

'But seriously, if my life depended on it, would you?'

'Course I would. Do you even need to ask?'

'Same,' he said, smiling. 'It's how we're supposed to feel about Allah, and the *ummah* too.'

I loved Allah more every day. Why not – he'd given me Arif, right? But it was more than that. My faith gave me the power to defend myself against all the voices that tried to control me. Once upon a time, I'd feared the hijab; now I felt like it was armour.

But loving the ummah . . . loving the *entire* Muslim community . . . ?

'Need to work on that, Muz,' Arif said, reading my expression before kissing my forehead. 'Only way we're going to be together forever is if both of us end up in Heaven. That ain't happening unless we're both *massively* pious.'

'But how?' I said, swallowing the last piece of biscuit. 'How can I love over a billion people I don't even know?! And what about selfish Muslims, or Muslims who commit crimes?'

'I know where you're coming from,' he said, rubbing my arm. 'But you gotta train yourself, yeah? If you start off *pretending*, eventually it'll become real. I'd lay my life down for the ummah, me. Like, if I had a gun, and I saw someone trying to shoot a brother – I'd shoot 'im first. Even knowing that the police'd take me out later, I'd still do it. Otherwise, I'd be questioned in the grave about why I let my brother down.'

I nodded, but I didn't get it. Guns, violence and dying were not things I even wanted to think about.

'Hey, lovely people!'

We looked up as Latifah came towards us beaming like the sun.

''Sup, Latifah?' Arif said, lifting his chin.

'I come bearing gifs,' she said, holding up her tablet. On the screen was a page of animated Lolcats doing all kinds of crazy stuff.

'Look at that one!' Arif said, pointing.

A shaggy ginger cat crashed through a window of the White House, snagging a bowl of jelly as it slid down an extra-long dining table, before dumping it in the president's lap. The president leaped up and jiggled like a mad man with the cat hissing on his head. The camera zoomed in to the president's crotch and went to slow motion. The words 'Make America Gyrate Again' flashed, before the animation looped.

I covered my mouth, laughing. How had they managed to make it look so real?

'So, I'm planning on doing another assembly,' Latifah announced, putting the tablet away.

'Yay!' I said, clapping.

She winked at me. 'And this time, the theme is . . .'

Arif gave her a drum roll.

'Islamic History,' she finished. 'Dun, dun, dun!'

'Oooh,' Arif said, placing a hand over his heart. 'Brave choice, fam.'

She frowned. 'With all the disrespectful nonsense going on in this crazy, crazy world, I think our faith could do with a li'l PR injection.'

'That would be totally amazing,' I said. If anyone could change public opinion at Falstrum, it would probably be someone like Latifah.

'It's time to shake up the idea that all Islam has ever done for the world is oppress women and spread terror.' She shook her head, gold hoop earrings flashing in the sunlight. 'For instance: do you know who set up the world's first university?'

'A Muslim?' I guessed, though I doubted it.

'A sister named Fatima from Africa,' she confirmed, nodding her head. 'Imagine, that bold Muslim woman in ancient times coming up with this revolutionary idea *and* being supported by the masses.'

It blew my mind. 'I'm sold. So what's the favour?' I asked.

She squinted as if defusing a bomb. 'I need a show-stopping poem. And a little bird called Dunthorpe told me you're the Go-To Girl.'

Arif nodded. 'Fam, Muzna's got skills. I seen her stories.'

Seeing my look of horror, she placed a hand on my shoulder. 'Literally all you have to do is tell them how it feels to be a Muslim girl in Britain.'

'I'll write it,' I said. 'But *you* read it out. Your voice is way better than mine.'

Latifah shook her head. 'I don't wear the hijab. Rightly or

wrongly, it's important that it come from *you*.'

I glanced at Arif.

He nodded. 'Think you'd do great, Muz.'

I grinned as my creative juices simmered, ideas bubbling to the surface.

'OK, I'm in. But on one condition.'

Latifah raised an eyebrow. 'Conditions? This one's a regular businesswoman.'

'Let Arif be in your assembly too,' I finished.

Arif's jaw dropped as he sat up in surprise.

Latifah pointed at him. 'This peng ting? Sure, but what's the Arifster going to do?'

I smiled confidently. 'He's going to blow you away with his street dancing. He can do backflips and—'

'Quiet, man!' he said, slapping a hand over my mouth.

'Your secret's out,' Latifah whispered. 'Impress me, and I'll write a special rap to go with it.'

He shook his head.

'Come on, Arif!' I pleaded. I'd seen him dance both Bhangra and street. He *had* this. 'End the year on a high. Just imagine the look on Sade's face.'

He tilted his head sideways, a smile spreading over his lips. Me and Latifah held hands waiting for him to say yes. But suddenly his smile snuffed out.

'I can't. My brother . . .'

'As if he's going to find out!' I snapped.

'Breaking down stereotypes would really help the cause,' Latifah suggested. 'Come on, my man. Say yes. Adding "assembly performance" to your personal statement's going to look seriously impressive.'

'Pleeeeease!' I said, piling on the pressure.

Arif was silent for the longest time. Then he took his phone out. Was he going to text Jameel for permission?

He leaped up. 'OK. I'll show you what I got, but don't blame me if I flop.'

Latifah cried in delight as the intro for 'Juju on That Beat' blared out of his phone.

Arif performed the dance that had gone viral. Slow moves, fast moves, robotic moves, moves of liquid smoothness. He knocked them out, growing in confidence and finesse. Within seconds, a crowd had gathered round and were clapping and bouncing to the beat.

Then the pips went, and teachers broke up our little party. But Arif had smashed it.

'You guys!' gushed Latifah, fanning herself. 'I can't even!'

Arif shrugged off the praise. But the delight in his eyes was unmistakable. Students from every year surged forward to bump fists, pat him on the back, or muss up his hair.

Imagine, I thought, taking in the scene. *Imagine how awesome my Arif could be if Jameel would go away and never come back . . .*

On Thursday, the final pips went, and I beat a hasty retreat. The day had been long and pointless, and I really needed to go home and revise. It wasn't fair – rich kids could afford tutors, so it was no big deal if they ended up with crap teachers. Poor kids like me had no one to turn to but YouTube. I'd subscribed to a channel where a very nice teacher went through past papers. If I ended up with a 6 in maths, I swore I was going to leave her the biggest, cheesiest 'thank you' comment ever.

As I headed towards my locker, I slowed down to a crawl. *I'd recognize that plait anywhere*, I thought. Only now I'd come to think of it as a scorpion's tail. Moving seats in tutor group so she wouldn't have to sit next to me was low-key insulting. But snaking me out to Pawsey? A betrayal like that was against the sisterhood, even if she'd been crazy enough to believe she was saving me from 'radicalization'.

Sarabi chatted happily to Jadwiga. I could imagine the expression on her face: eyes wide; manic grin; slurping away at the excess saliva brought on by two sets of braces. I was actually glad she'd gone and found a replacement mate. Still, what I wouldn't have given for an Invisibility Cloak right about then . . .

As I drew closer, I heard Jadwiga telling Sarabi that Bollywood was big in Poland.

'I go Bollywood dance class every Friday,' Jadwiga revealed. 'Our dance teacher say we can bring friend for free taster session. You wanna come?'

'Me? Seriously?' Sarabi was practically foaming at the mouth.

I speeded up, hoping they were so engrossed in their plan-making, I'd slip by unnoticed.

'Wasn't that your friend?' I heard Jadwiga say.

Then I was out in the fresh air, beelining for the school gates. I'd almost made it too when a husky voice wrapped itself around me, lassoing me to a halt.

Perched on the wall to my left was a petite Asian girl. Only she had to be a figment of my imagination.

'You forgot me?' she said, rising to her feet.

Though the smile was welcoming, the voice was like a paper cut. She looked different. Longer hair dyed silver-grey, and knee-high boots that glistened like tar.

'Oh-em-gee!' I cried, surprised by the lame expression that rolled off my tongue so easily. Hadn't used it in years. 'Salma!' I threw my arms around my original BFF.

'Air hug!' she joked, echoing another crappy line from our childhood together. She smelt like somebody else. Couldn't get Versace down at the pound shop. I'd loved the scent of her cheap mango perfume – it brought back so many happy memories.

And then one seriously awkward one . . .

'Oh man,' I began, feeling my throat tighten. 'An apology is waaaaay overdue.'

'You think?'

I swallowed. 'I thought I'd get found out if I contacted you!' I babbled, eyes watering from shame. 'My parents had me running scared. Then GCSEs got in the way and—'

'Don't sweat it,' she said, making a flippant gesture. 'You moved on; *I* moved on. It's all good.'

Why did hearing that hurt? I'd been the one to turn my back on the friendship.

'Hey, how're things with you and . . .' I tried to catch his name out of the air. 'What's-his-face . . . Tariq?'

'It ended. His mood swings were doing my head in.' Her plum-painted lips curved up in a wicked smile. 'Plus he was nasty-fugly.'

'Regrets?'

She looked at me as if she thought I was mad. 'Hell no! My experience with Tariq gave me Freak Radar. Dodged enough bullets since.' Her voice softened, fingers curling round my wrist. 'Getting kicked out of the Pakistani community was like the best thing *ever*. Once those bastards turn their backs on you, you're free to live your life the way you want.'

I stared at her, dumbfounded. I'd never thought of it like that; I'd always figured you were doomed to walk the earth alone, cursed for the rest of your days.

'Anyway,' she continued, a flurry of acrylic nails and excitement, 'I've been with my current boyfriend going on three months now!'

'Cool.' I wanted to ask her if he was Muslim, but somehow I doubted it.

'Sometimes you gotta kiss a lot of frogs before you find your prince.'

I kept my mouth shut.

'You became a hijabi,' she noted, gazing up at my scarf. 'What's up with that?'

'You wouldn't understand.' How could she if she thought it was OK to go round kissing boys on a quest for The One?

'What I do understand, girlfriend,' she said, leaning in, 'is that your parents are straight-up dictators, and this hijab business is some kind of whacked-out rebellion. You wanna know how I found you? My cousin goes here. Told me about you the day you set foot on Falstrum turf—'

Her phone went off. She ignored it.

'. . . But I figured: give Muzna her space. She'll look you up when she's good and ready.'

For a moment she seemed distant, almost vulnerable. My toes curled with guilt.

'After a while, I gave up and moved on with my life,' she said, sighing. 'Only reason I came back now was for *your* sake. My cousin tells me you've been radicalized by some idiot who knows you got anger in your belly and a shit home life.'

I goggled at her. 'This your idea of a wake-up call? It's cute. Look, I'm gonna be totally honest with you even though you've been super-rude to me. You're right. My parents are dictators. They had no right to end our friendship. And I'm sorry I was too much of a coward to hook up with you once things blew over. But you're wrong about radicalization.' I hooked a finger in my scarf, and tugged. 'I discovered God, not grenades.'

I faltered, remembering the last talk I'd attended. The speaker had been Grenade Central.

'I've got the most amazing man in my life!' I said, switching tack. 'Everyone fancies the pants off him, but he chose *me*. So you see, *girlfriend*, life is better than good!'

If I was gloating, it was only because her sassier-than-thou attitude had provoked it.

'You think Allah wants to separate you from the world?' she asked, worry pushing the sass out of her voice. 'Cos that's what I'm hearing, Muzi. You and this Arif guy live in an Islamic bubble, and that ain't healthy! Especially when you keep bunking to go radicalization meetings.'

'Will you listen to yourself?' I cried. 'I actually feel sorry for you.' For one time in my life, I *refused* to back down. Salma's bossing days were done.

'OK. Why you?' she asked, placing a hand on her hip.

'Excuse me?'

'Think about it. He can have any girl he wants. So why pick you?'

Her words hit harder than a slap. Tears rushed to my eyes.

'Come on, Muzi,' she relented, seeing my hurt. 'Not putting you down or nothing, but you're way too smart for this. What's this guy's agenda?'

'He likes my mind!' I said, ashamed of how lame it sounded outside my head. 'He likes my *deen*.'

My ego was more fragile than sugar glass. I *had* to be right about Arif. Because if I messed up, if I'd got it wrong, it was proof that I needed Ami and Dad to run my life. I couldn't bear that.

'Oh please!' Salma snapped. 'Sixteen-year-old boys aren't cruising for brains and faith. How dumb are you? You're being *used*, Muzna. Face facts and dump his ass.'

I could taste metal at the back of my throat. Could Salma be awakening fears I'd carried around for so long they'd been lost to white noise?

She sighed. 'Guess I've done my duty as an ex-mate. So long, Muzi. Hope this phase you're going through doesn't land you in prison or get you killed.'

'Salma!' I called after her. 'You invite Allah into your life, nothing can ever go wrong again. Trust me. Just give it a try, OK?' I held out my precious little prayer book – a gift from Arif – to make up for abandoning her all those months ago.

Salma stared at the book for a long time. 'Nah, life's good just the way it is.'

And with that, she turned on her heel and sashayed out of the gates.

It was the last time I ever saw her.

CHAPTER 41

'Excuse me, sister,' Jameel said. 'But I must take this call.'

He walked out of the sitting room. I breathed the hugest sigh of relief. It was hot and stuffy, and having him around only made things worse. I'd swung by looking for Arif and ended up with Jameel. If that wasn't bad enough, he'd started lecturing me about my duties as a wife. The man was *bare jarring*.

'A problem?' he said, out in the corridor. 'One minute . . .'

I heard the diminishing sound of footfalls as he ran up the stairs. A few seconds later a bedroom door closed.

I threw open a window to let some air in. Man, was I *parched*. Woody *attar* tickled my nostrils as I passed through the narrow corridor on my way to the kitchen. Suddenly something snagged my sleeve. Alarmed, I cried out.

It was just the handle on the cellar door. I relaxed. The door stood slightly ajar, quivering in a draught. I unhooked my sleeve and was about to close the door when I spotted a blue glow coming from deep inside. I knew it was none of my business, but my sixth sense was pinging.

Glancing upstairs, I made sure Jameel hadn't finished his call, then crossed the threshold, padding softly down the basement stairs. It was dark and humid, and a monotonous hum pervaded the air. Boiler, probably – or ancient electrics. The deeper I went, the stronger the feeling of being a moth drawn to a flame became. But by then, I couldn't be stopped.

A battery of eight laptops were behind the misty blue glow. They were placed four a side on adjacent workbenches. Cables ran between them in an electrical cat's cradle. Other bits of hardware were strewn about, almost carelessly, but their LEDs flickered with life. Some stuff I recognized (webcams, Ethernet hubs, headphones); others, not so much. I knew Jameel was supposed to be a computer guru, but this was like something off a sci-fi show.

I glanced at the screen next to a half-empty crate of disposable phones. An indigo programming box lay open, filled with white lines of code. I recognized a 'loop' and a 'repeat' command, but the rest was next-level programming.

A second screen displayed a map of the London Underground. The cursor hovered over Paddington station, and a small tag, a bit like a Post-it note, lay open. On it was a bad selfie of a guy who looked stoned, with some confusing information next to it:

Dennis Sanders
07 25 B. L. Pl 3 North
4/10
07 40 GMT

Out of the corner of my eye, I spotted something come rushing towards me. Nearly jumping out of my skin, I threw my hands out defensively. At the last second, I caught the hurtling laptop, its cable taut as a cheese cutter against my hip. Somehow I'd got myself tangled up in the network of cables. If I wasn't careful, I'd have every last laptop come crashing down. Eight humpty-dumpties' worth more than my family had in the bank.

My breath whistled between my teeth. Trapped in a Twister game from hell, I contorted my body, desperate to free myself. With enough slack, I was able to push the runaway laptop back on to the bench, and step out of the mess of cables. The motion caused the darkened screen to awake.

A chat box. Time encoded and sent within the last hour.

Cheesy flirtation between a couple of teens.

For one horrible moment, I wondered if Arif was having an online affair. But the profile image was of somebody else. A good-looking guy, for sure, but one I'd never seen before. So who was he?

I spotted an icon on the taskbar called 'Hunters'. Weird. Clicking on it restored the program window to full size. To the left of the screen was a list of boys' names, and beside each one a separate status box. Some were coded 'active'; others as 'dormant'. I clicked on a few of these. Each time, in the right-hand corner of the screen, a window popped open with a profile pic, a tab marked 'gallery', and stats for the boy. I was kind of surprised. Don't get me wrong: I only had eyes for Arif, but each and every one of them was super-cute. Was Jameel secretly running a talent agency for teen male models? Surely he'd consider that haram?

Clicking randomly, I came across a subsection called 'personality', which opened up descriptions of what each user would and wouldn't do. It was the kind of thing I jotted down when creating characters for a new story. A manual for keeping it real.

Are these profiles fake?

As I scrolled through the list, my heart skipped a bit. One of the characters was called 'Kasim Iqbal'. Intense flashbacks of Year 8 summer holidays came flooding back to me, of the time I'd nearly been catfished straight into a body bag.

Heart galloping, I clicked on the link. Every last shred of doubt fell away as I came face-to-face with the image that had nearly destroyed my childhood. Kasim Iqbal: taking a shirtless selfie in a locker-room mirror.

I now had all the pieces of the puzzle. I knew what was going on here. Hunters was grooming software for multiple users. Not a paedophile network, but a *radicalization* one. Lonely girls who would be flattered by the attention of any one of these fit boys. And once she was hooked, what demands would be made of her? Steal Mum's wedding jewellery so it could be used to pay for weapons? Throw away her future to fight 'jihad' in foreign lands?

My brother-in-law was a member of ISIS.

I'd had my suspicions. Had just gone and buried them under a mountain of denial with an icecap of excuses.

'What do you think you are doing?' demanded a voice that was unmistakably angry.

The spider had returned to his lair.

Every hair on my scalp felt like a sharp pinprick. Slowly I turned round to face my nemesis. Jameel had always been a bit scary, but knowing what I knew now, even staying conscious had become a mission.

'The cellar door was open,' I said, trying not to stutter. 'I thought someone had left a light on in here. My parents are always going on about energy prices being too high.'

I scurried up the stairs. But Jameel did not step aside. He'd become a block of granite, barricading the only way out.

'Indeed?' he said.

Every laptop suddenly blue-screened. He'd done something to them. His eyes glistened in the pea soup darkness. I glanced longingly at the partially open cellar door behind him.

Beneath me beckoned the murky depths of the cellar. Fear brought the worst of my imagination to life. One push was all it would take. One push, and Jameel's terrible secret went with me to the grave. A note might surface later, claiming to be from me. Teachers would confirm I'd been unhappy at home. The police already had a report of me running away in the middle of the night. Verdict? Teen suicide. Case closed.

Jameel was part of an organization that had evaded the

combined intelligence agencies of the UK, the US and the EU. What was one mediocre Asian girl to all of that?

Like a clap of thunder, the front door slammed shut, startling us both.

'Yo! Jamjamz! You home, bro?'

Relief crashed over me. 'It's my husband!' I said, nearly pushing Jameel over the edge in my haste to get out.

'Muz, what you doin'?' Arif asked, as I flew into his arms.

'She lost her way,' Jameel replied, emerging from the depths of the cellar, like Dracula rising from his crypt. 'It's a very dark cellar. There might've been an accident.'

'What'd she find? Dead bodies of all your exes?' Arif asked with a cheeky grin.

Jameel shot him a withering look, then his phone went off again. Glancing at the screen, his face became a thunderstorm. 'By Allah, I am surrounded by fools!' he hissed. Then brushing past, he vanished upstairs.

'You shouldn't do that,' I said. 'One of these days he's going to hurt you.'

Arif swallowed. 'At least it'll get me off having to sit my GCSEs.'

Then he was hugging me, cocooning me in his love.

Ignorance is bliss. But I reckon denial makes for a pretty good stand-in. My house of cards was on the verge of collapse.

Arif and I had been radicalized by Jameel. Jameel was in my brain, making me act and react in ways that weren't me. A parasite who'd woven twisted ideologies round both our minds, filling our hearts with suspicion and hate.

I'd swapped the prison of my parents' rules for the prison of Jameel's radical Islam.

Bile filled my mouth remembering the videos I'd watched with other girls in the back room. ISIS propaganda on a 4K screen –

though Jameel had been careful to keep their name out of it. I couldn't believe I'd been so dumb. The material was beyond powerful, really pulled at your heartstrings, watching the terrible injustice your brothers and sisters were facing . . .

Now that I'd snapped out of the hateful trance, I had to shop Jameel to the police. But before I could so that, Arif had to be saved too.

Think he wants saving? asked the imaginary Salma in my head.

In all the time I'd known him, Arif had never once let me down. Good people like that were rarer than gold. Jameel had worked a number on him, for sure, but Arif was totally worth saving. It was going to be tough. Not only had Jameel been poisoning his mind for years and years unchallenged, but he'd also rescued him from a violent uncle. Could I even compete with that kind of hero worship?

Whatever it takes, Arif, I'm going to free you. You were just a kid when your brother started messing with your head. I'll make you see the truth — then we're both taking Jameel down.

CHAPTER 42

Sugarplum Hijabi – a poem by Muzna Saleem – version 1.0

I stand before you, and I am on trial.
Are you offended because of my style?
What do you see – the scarf or the girl?
While you consider, shall I give you a twirl?

Some call it 'rag': a sign of oppression.
Some want to ban it: a sign of aggression.
Your concern has been noted; politely turned down.
I don't need rescuing. This hijab is my crown.

Who is the man who kills in my name?
Commands and demands I commit the same?
He says he's a Muslim. I think he's a liar.
Murder and torture, both sins of the Fire.

So many voices, shouting advice.
'Do this!' 'Say that!' 'Cover your eyes!'
Show me the way, Lord; rescue my soul.
Keeping the faith, Lord; but it's taking its toll.

I scowled at the poem I'd been working on for Latifah's assembly. My mind was all over the place. I couldn't tell whether it was any good or a smouldering pile of bad.

I heard the front door close. Dad was home. I cracked open my bedroom door to eavesdrop.

'Is Muzna OK?' he asked, yawning. He took a load off, feet presumably throbbing from another tough day of waiting on people down in the restaurant.

'Don't ask me about that girl!' Ami snapped. 'I'm nothing to her. All I'm good for is cooking and cleaning.'

'Don't worry, Parveen,' Dad said, rubbing her back. 'Pakistan will fix her. In two years' time, she'll be studying MBBS at King Edward Medical College, and you will forget this ever happened.'

Ami snorted.

'She starts her GCSE exams in three weeks. We'll leave straight after,' Dad promised.

'Tanveer makes you work like a donkey. Each day you're coming home later and later. If that scoundrel tried this with a *gora*, he would take him to court!'

'Hush, darling,' Dad said. 'I won't hear you speak badly of the one who provided a roof over my family's head when I failed in that responsibility.'

Slinking away from the crack in the door, I flopped on to my bed. There it was: the confirmation I had never wanted. The dreaded move to Pakistan – that idle threat that had drifted in and out of my life since I'd been about six years old – was going to happen after all. Cut all ties, wipe the slate clean: the ultimate cultural reboot.

The sad thing was I didn't even care. My mind was consumed by the horror of Jameel being an actual terrorist. I urgently wanted to shut him down, but I'd backed myself into a fricking corner. If I picked up the phone and told the police, Arif would get dragged into it. If I told my parents, in around seven hours I'd be waking up in Lahore. And telling Mr Dunthorpe was ultimately the same thing as telling the police.

All that optimism I'd burned so brightly with yesterday, believing I could take Jameel down and deradicalize Arif, was dying embers.

The red-band headline on the TV screen made me sit up.

BREAKING NEWS: FAILED TUBE BOMBING

I turned up the sound.

> . . . *loss of life and the strategic placement of the bombs would have crippled the London Underground, bringing the entire network to a standstill. It remains unclear whether they were working alone, but Islamic State have claimed responsibility for the attempt via a post on social media. Tonight, all three men are being held in police custody. The prime minister was quick to condemn the attempt and released a defiant message to IS warning them that Britain and her allies would never be cowed.*

I sat on the end of my bed, shaking like a leaf as the full significance of the plans dawned on me. I remembered the tube map on Jameel's laptop. And though the names and faces of the would-be suicide bombers hadn't been released yet, I was certain Dennis Sanders was one of them. I hadn't known it at the time, had got distracted by the whole Kasim Iqbal bombshell, but what I'd been looking at on Jameel's laptop was the blueprint for an actual terror attack.

My stomach churned. I'd sat on crucial information like a fat, selfish bitch. Saving Arif was my only concern. People could have *died*. Dead. Gone forever.

I fell on my side and began to bawl.

*

It was raining heavily by the time the bus pulled up to the stop. Just my luck, I'd left my umbrella back at the library. I clambered on, touching my Oyster to the card reader. I wove through the steaming passengers standing in the aisle. Humidity made the bus stink like old basketballs. 'Sorry,' I muttered, stumbling over somebody's handbag.

I practically crashed into the empty seat next to an old woman. Rain pelted the windows fiercely, reminding me of a time when Dad could afford to use the automatic carwash at the petrol station. Now every Saturday morning, Dad would carry two buckets of water round the back to wash the Vectra by hand.

Guilt sat like a rock in my stomach. I didn't know how to handle the Jameel situation. Every time I thought about it, I felt like I was going to have a panic attack. My life had become a living nightmare. At school, I sat through class after class, dazed and delirious, wishing I could change the past.

I took out my phone and flicked through the new apps Arif had installed. I tapped a *Hadith* one – authentic sayings of the Prophet:

> *The Compassionate has mercy on those who are merciful.*
> *If you show mercy to those who are on the earth, He who*
> *is in Heaven will show mercy to you.*

The old lady next to me shifted, giving a small gasp. One of her legs was epically swollen.

Suddenly a woman with a pixie crop and enough piercings to make her ears look spiral-bound steamrollered her buggy over my foot. I caught the flash of glee in her eye. I tutted, looking down at the muddy pattern of treads left on my shoe.

'What's *her* problem?' asked her friend, mousey-brown hair

pulled so tight her forehead seemed to begin somewhere on the back of her head.

'Why? What'd she say?' demanded the woman with the buggy, rear-ending into a pram. Both kids woke up and started to bawl.

'Gave you a dirty look, din' she.'

I ignored them. The failed tube bombing had everyone on edge. Muslims would just have to ride out the storm.

'Oi!' Pixie Crop said, snapping her fingers inches from my nose. 'Don't give me lip, then act like you're bloody deaf!'

I glanced at the doors, wishing there was some way I could get off the bus without looking like a loser.

'Oi!' the woman repeated, this time actually rapping her knuckles on my forehead.

'Do you mind!' I snapped.

'Hear that, Shizza?' said the woman with the wrap-around forehead. 'Asked you if you mind her coming to your country, taking food out of your kids' mouths, and blowing people up on the tube.'

'Yes, I bloody well do mind!' Shizza screeched, ripping off my hijab. The scarf pin grazed my forehead, drawing blood.

'Give that back!' I yelled, making a grab for it.

Shizza shoved me back down with enough force to send vibrations rocketing through my tailbone. My scarf was thrown out of the open doors.

'Keep it down, back there!' called the bus driver, pulling away from a bus stop.

'Excuse me,' mumbled a man in a Ted Baker suit, brushing past us. Couldn't get away fast enough.

My mind filled with hatred for everyone on the goddamned bus. If I hadn't been a hijabi, I was sure someone would have stood up for me. But no – I deserved everything I got. I *must* be a frigging terrorist. Arif was right. The *kuffar* were cruel.

'I'm calling the police!' I said.

Shizza slapped my hand, sending my phone skittering down the aisle. 'Like hell you are! Don't like it here, go back to Muslamoland!' she roared in my face.

'Hear, hear!' said an old man in a trilby.

Delighted by her newfound fandom, Shizza turned up the heat. 'Gerroff the bus, rag-head. I don't feel comfortable with you around my baby.'

'ISIS cow!' spat her accomplice.

Cornered and humiliated, tears pilled over my cheeks. I knew I was giving them everything they wanted. The satisfaction of completely destroying me. But I was powerless to stop it.

The old lady beside me clasped her walking stick and rose unsteadily to her feet. 'You get off this bus, you vile creatures!' she told the women. 'Harassing this poor girl when she didn't do a thing to you.'

'Oh yeah, that's right!' sneered Shizza, squaring off against the senior. 'Stick up for a Muzzie instead of one of your own.'

The woman drew herself up proudly, 'Young woman, you're *not* one of my own.'

Then something completely unexpected happened. Other passengers gave the old lady a round of applause. 'Off, off, off!' they began chanting at Shizza and her friend. Someone handed me a tissue and asked if I was OK. I dabbed at my eyes as someone else handed me my phone.

'OK – show's over, people!' the driver said, emerging from his compartment.

'And you, driver,' the old lady said, pointing her walking stick at him like a rifle, 'ought to be ashamed of yourself! Allowing the situation to escalate.'

'What the hell was I supposed to do?' he yelled, cords

sticking out of his lobster-pink throat.

'Nuh worry yuhself pickney,' a man in a rasta-cap told me. 'Me flim everyt'ing. When me reach a me yard, me a guh sen police everyt'ing fi dem fi deal wid it. Dem dutty criminal a guh get what's comin' to dem, fi sure.'

Bless him.

Hearing this, Shizza's friend yanked her arm. 'Come on. Let's get the next bus.'

'Yeah, this one's full of traitors and terrorists!' Shizza agreed, nearly giving her baby whiplash as she yanked the buggy. Punching the emergency door-release button, she reversed out of the door. 'You lot are a bunch of wankers. Just wait till there's a filthy Muzzie down at Number Ten!'

My heart stayed in my throat long after the nasty women had been and gone. The old lady twittered gently to me, patting my hand and telling me everything would be all right. 'Thank you,' I said on loop. 'Thank you.'

Britain was my home, and I wasn't about to leave it. Not for those vicious women. Not for my parents either. I was as British as Big Ben. Somewhere along the line, I'd begun to forget that . . .

Jameel and Arif had me believing the world was 'Black and White', 'Good and Evil', 'Muslim and *Kafir*'. But it wasn't that way at all. The brave old lady sitting next to me, who could barely even stand, had reminded me of that. It hadn't mattered to her how I dressed or what god I worshipped. She'd stood up for me all the same.

Outside, the rain went torrential. The English summer had been driven back.

I am Muzna, I thought. *I am the cloud who brings the rain.*

CHAPTER 43

'Got a little present for you.'

I looked at the crystal tumbler in Arif's outstretched hand. It was decorated in cute crimson hearts. Inside sat a golden bear gripping a red satin cushion with 'I <3 U' embroidered in ivory.

'Aw, it's beautiful!' I said, fishing the little bear out of the glass and snuggling it.

I wondered if this was a peace-offering for bailing on Latifah's assembly. I'd read an upbeat version of my poem, had almost cried from the totally unexpected standing ovation I got, but inside I'd felt like a hypocrite. There I was laying down empowerment rhymes, when the truth was I was more messed up than I'd ever been. The assembly would've brought the house down if Arif had performed. But the ghost of Jameel had got to him and spoilt that too.

Guilt blotted out my moment of happiness. I knew I had to do something about Jameel, but fear and confusion had tied me in knots.

'Missed the best part,' Arif said, chuckling. 'Take another look.'

I stared into the empty glass in his palm, before spotting the golden envelope beneath it.

'Thanks, babe,' I whispered.

Instead of a card, like I'd expected, two glossy pieces of paper slipped out. One side had an image of the London skyline at dusk; the other, a barcode.

'Tickets to the Shard!' I gasped. It would have been the perfect half-term gift, just before knuckling down for our finals. But Jameel cast a shadow that seemed to stretch to the ends of the earth. Everything was tainted.

'Only the best for Mrs Arif,' he said, kissing my temple. 'Call it a cut-price honeymoon.' He looked a bit sheepish. 'Some day – when I get a job, yeah – I'm gonna take you on a proper one to Dubai, *insh'Allah*.'

I stared at the tickets.

''Sup?' he asked, finally picking up on my inner meltdown.

It's time, I told myself.

'You know the stuff on the news, about the failed bombing on the London Underground?' I said, placing the gifts on the coffee table.

He nodded, jaw muscles stiffening like elastic. '*Kuffar* giving you a hard time, are they?'

I began to shake my head, then stopped. 'Every time there's another terrorist attack, people strike out at us because they're angry. I mean, there's the extremists, like Britain First, right? But then regular people start jumping on the bandwagon too.'

Arif nodded. 'It's full-on war, Muzna. Has been since the Crusades. They're never gonna rest till Islam gets wiped out.'

'But that's just it!' I exploded, struggling with my emotions. 'It's becoming a self-fulfilling prophecy.'

'Eh? What's one of them?'

'Some Muslims think isolation is the answer. So they build walls, and people start thinking Muslims are stuck-up. Then there's the few whack jobs who believe terrorism is the way to go. But it's *us* – the peaceful majority – who end up taking the flak.'

He knitted his brows. 'You saying we bring the hate on ourselves?'

'No. Not at all. What I'm saying is there are bad guys – extremists, if you like – on *both* sides. They're the ones who keep this stupid war going, while the rest of us suffer.'

He looked at me like I'd told him a joke. 'You all right, Muz? Cos you're starting to sound a bit brainwashed to me.'

'You're the one who's brainwashed!' I exclaimed. 'I love you, Arif, but you need to know your brother is poison. He's changed you. The boy I fell for was happy-go-lucky, and now you're so suspicious. He's radicalized you. He's radicalized *me*. We have to stand up to him, together.'

'How can you say that?' The betrayal in his eyes was savage.

'Uh, because it's true?' I said, swallowing. 'And I can prove it. I can show you Jameel was involved in that failed bombing.'

Arif looked at me in disbelief, blinking like he wasn't even sure how to react. Anger won through. 'It's *haram* to slander a pious man. He's my brother, and I know he can be a bit extra, but he's a better Muslim than either one of us.'

I nodded. 'I used to believe that too. Mostly cos of what you said. But everything I've seen of him has been judgemental and shady. Besides, I wouldn't be saying this stuff unless I had concrete evidence, right?'

Still fuming, he agreed to let me show him what I had. I tried the cellar door. It was locked. 'Who puts a lock on a cellar?'

'Um, the suspicious old lady we bought the house off?'

'We've got to bust it open,' I instructed. 'Quick, before he gets back!'

'Or we could just use this,' he said, grabbing the key off the spice rack.

Within seconds he had the door open. Anger came off him like radiation. But Arif had to know the truth, had to see his brother was not the hero he thought he was. I owed him that. Even if he hated me for it.

The cellar stretched before us like a cauldron of shadows. This time, there was no blue glow to navigate by. For one terrible moment, I wondered if Jameel had shut up shop and moved on.

No, the bastard was*n't* *allowed* to win.

Arif activated the flashlight on his phone, and we descended the rickety steps. I shot over to the workbenches, desperate for Arif to stop hating me and to finally see the truth for himself.

'No!' I cried, beating the empty surface with balled fists.

It was all gone. Nothing remained but a single unplugged laptop.

'Where are the other seven?'

'Downloaded a virus or summat. Sent 'em off to get fixed,' he said.

I remembered the laptops displaying blue screens after Jameel caught me down here. Coincidence or engineered crash?

I booted up the remaining laptop. Dust made me sneeze, adrenaline made me shiver, but determination made me committed. Glowing to life, the laptop prompted for a password.

'What's his password?' I asked, tapping my fingers impatiently.

Arif shrugged. 'How should I know? Snooping ain't my style.'

Ouch. Part of me wanted to say I was sorry, that I'd made a terrible mistake. But that would've been lying. Of course he was going to be angry. In his foolish, trusting eyes, Jameel could do no wrong.

Ultimately, I had to settle for guest status, ignoring the warning telling me several features would be disabled. I double-clicked on the hard drive and scrolled through the files. Nothing but Islamic essays, presentations, and a digital Qur'an with an English translation. Even the browser history had been wiped.

The crafty scumbag must have transferred everything to a safehold.

'Satisfied?' Arif asked frostily.

I looked into his eyes, desperate for him to believe me, even with the lack of physical evidence. I'd never lied to him before.

Surely he could see I was telling the truth now?

'Think you better ask Allah for forgiveness,' he continued, deliberately avoiding eye contact, like the sight of me made him sick. 'Slandering a pious man is like eating meat off a rotting corpse.'

Tears of frustration pricked my eyes. If only I'd thought this through, been smart enough to take pictures on my phone the day I'd stumbled on the incriminating evidence.

'Wait!' I said, going for broke. 'Remember the Zamzam water I was supposed to deliver to Uncle Abdi-Aziz?'

He gave me a withering look. 'Yeah, course.'

'It was hydrogen peroxide!'

He nodded, like this was boring him. 'Yeah, I got it wrong. Uncle Abdi-Aziz is a caretaker at some primary school. Uses it to disinfect the floors or summat.'

It was over. The final nail hammered into my coffin. I'd come in guns blazing, certain I could convince Arif his brother was bad news with tons of evidence. Turned out I had nothing. Jameel had seen to it. Once again I realized how dumb I'd been to think I could go up against an international terrorist. He was a trained professional. I was a nobody.

For a moment I toyed with the idea of telling Arif about Jameel's disgusting 'Kasim Iqbal' scam. But what was the use? With nothing to back it up, he'd just hate me more – if that was even possible.

'Arif . . .' I whispered, reaching out to touch his arm.

He dodged my fingers, and I swallowed, praying I hadn't destroyed the best thing that had ever happened to me.

Arif bounded up the stairs, calling to me impatiently from the postage stamp of light at the very top. I imagined the disappointed look on his face. It made me want to cry.

Despondent, I moved away from the workbench, when I heard

a sharp crack. I raised my foot, wondering what I'd stepped on. Thick shadows swirled round my ankles, like mist on a lake.

'Muz. *Now!*'

'Coming!' I called back, crouching down for a better look. My fingers swept through an inch of grit and grime. Then I hit pay dirt. Pincering something small and flat between my nails, I lifted it up into the lambent glow of the laptop screen. A USB memory stick. Palming it, I hurried up the stairs.

I did *not* sleep well that night. On the one hand, I worried that me and Arif were headed for divorce. On the other, Jameel's illegal activities had me bricking it. Could he be rubbing shoulders with the likes of Abu Bakr al-Baghdadi himself?

I *had* to free Arif from Jameel's influence before it was too late. Whatever it took, whatever the cost to our marriage, it had to happen. Exposing Jameel had become my sacred duty. I was *sure* of it.

I pressed my phone to my ear, my hand moist with sweat. Every beep of the dial tone was a threat, ratcheting and ratcheting up the tension till I could take it no more. I slid my finger towards END CALL.

''Sup, Muz?' came Arif's voice out of my phone. He sounded bored. Had he got over our spat in the cellar?

'I love you.' I sounded like I'd been sucking air out of a helium balloon.

'That it?' he said, confused. 'That why you called me?'

Not by a long shot. I took a deep breath to steady my frazzled nerves. 'I've been thinking about what I saw in Jameel's cellar . . .'

The sharp exhalation pierced my eardrum. 'We talked about this,'

'I can't!' I babbled. 'I can't keep quiet! We *have* to tell the police.'

'You crazy?! The feds'll come round and shoot Jameel. And for what reason? Cos you *think* you saw some stuff?'

'I did see it! I swear!'

'Fam, my brother is innocent. Look, I'll ask him about it in the morning, OK? Bet he's got an explanation that'll even satisfy you.'

He hung up.

I sat on the floor, clasping the dead phone to my ear. If Arif repeated my fears to Jameel, ISIS would come after me – maybe my parents too – and silence us for good.

The ticking of my wall clock split the darkness like an axe.

'Oh God!' I cried, letting my phone clatter to the floor. 'Please, please help me!'

I reached for the memory stick I'd found in the cellar. Moonlight turned the hairline crack in the plastic to liquid silver. It occurred to me that someone as sketchy as Jameel might have left it behind as a red herring. False information to throw me off the scent. Or worse: a virus to infect my hard drive.

My mind conjured up the revulsion in Arif's eyes when I'd called his brother a terrorist. Losing my laptop, I realized, was a risk worth taking.

Snapping on the lights, I slid the memory stick into the USB port of my laptop, waiting for it to be recognized. I was sweating bullets, and my ankles flapped like fish tails. A window popped up asking what I wanted it to do with the portable drive.

'Don't kill my laptop,' I told it. Tensing every muscle in my body, I clicked OPEN.

There were only three files on the drive.

The first was a document in a strange language. Not Arabic, nor anything I'd ever seen before. So I tried Google Translate, but that didn't work either. It had to be some kind of code. Figuring it out was never going to happen. But just before I called time on the window, I spotted a needle in the haystack. A single piece of information I could actually read: **2nd June**. What was so special about this date?

Swallowing thickly, I double-clicked the next document. Nothing happened. The screen just froze, and then the sound of a windstorm came out of my keyboard. I tried to move my cursor but it was jammed. My computer had gone into lockdown. I'd have to wait it out and pray my laptop didn't die.

In the end, the processing lasted a full three minutes, then the massive file was opened. It was a huge PDF, *thousands* of pages long. I scrolled through the contents. Guidance on deleting your 'digital footprint' . . . protocols for contacting other cells . . . and a *massive* section devoted to bomb-making. There was even stuff about military-grade explosives and radioactive payloads.

My mouth went bone dry. There was an actual terrorist manual on my laptop. I could feel the edges of my brain starting to melt. I closed the file, wiping away tears.

Psyching myself up for the final reveal, I clicked on the last file.

Password protected.

'What could possibly be more secret than a flipping *terrorist manual*?' I hissed.

Bad question. I jerked my head, crashing *that* hideous train of thought and killing the demons that rode it. Sometimes, I realized, having a powerful imagination could be a curse.

Even without access to the final file, I was pretty sure there was enough evidence here to put Jameel Malik behind bars. But what did that mean for me and Arif? I'd given up my parents, my mates, even my GCSEs for the man I loved. He was my reason for being. But when the cops came for Jameel, I knew Arif would lose it, and attack them. He as good as told me he'd kill a *kafir* to protect a Muslim, and this was his own flesh and blood we were talking about. The police would likely shoot him too.

A world without Arif wasn't one I wanted to live in. I clutched my belly, tears streaming, looking up at the ceiling, appealing to God for help with this impossible choice.

All the while, the clock continued to tick.

2nd June.

Less than a week away.

Less than a week to break the spell Jameel had cast over Arif's heart and mind.

CHAPTER 44

'You all right, Muz?' Arif asked, as we approached the Shard. 'Thought you were well into it.'

'Totally!' I said, trying to sound bubbly and carefree. Given I'd never managed a decent grade in drama, I was about as convincing as a pig in a wig.

As if to taunt my fractured mind, Arif looked H.O.T. He was rocking an oversized vest – which barely covered his pecs – and rolled-up denim shorts, showing off incredible calves. His hair had been freshly clipped and styled into a cute jagged quiff.

Seeing him look so fly just got me feeling about ten times sadder.

Scooping me up in his strong arms, his fingers twitched across my ribs. 'There! That's the smile we've been waiting for.'

Now my heart was bleeding.

I wish I'd never met you! my mind screamed at him. *How dare you show me what it means to be happy, then have a terrorist for a brother. Why couldn't you have ignored me like every other popular kid? Now I'm just a train wreck heading for a fall.*

Whatever happened now was going to damage me for life.

'That a selfie stick?' I asked Arif, tilting my head to one side as he rummaged in a pocket.

'You tell me!' he said, with a wink. Then holding the handle against his crotch, he extended the pole to full length.

I jabbed him in the stomach, and we both cracked up. Arif was too funny to be part of a terrorist organization. I *must* have got it wrong.

'Here we go!' he said, hugging me close. Cheek to cheek, faces tilted up to the iPhone perched at the top of the selfie stick, he snapped the pic. 'Now for a belfie!' he announced, reaching round and taking a shot of my bum.

'Gonna need 360-degree panorama mode to fit that in!' I said.

His smile dropped. 'Muz, don't say that. You're beautiful, man. OK?' He reached for one of my hands. Placing it on his heart, he folded his large hands over it. 'I love you.'

The queue at the Shard seemed to stretch to infinity. London was experiencing tropical temperatures, and it was pulling in the crowds from China to New Zealand and beyond. Arif acted like a kid at Disneyland. He chatted and joked, barely noticing how quiet I was.

Then finally it was our turn, and we were ushered into a massive glass lift. Arif took pictures of literally *everything*. Honestly, he was worse than the freaking tourists.

Everyone's eyes went straight to the LCD ceiling of the lift. It displayed the four seasons with exciting 3D graphics and special effects. The tour guide had interesting facts on tap, like his brain had been hooked up to some massive database about all things Shard. I watched the numbers roll by on the monitor as we zoomed up the tower. Faster than a rollercoaster, but with none of the drag force. Mind-blowing.

Gripping my hand tightly, Arif bounded up a flight of stairs. In this new section, everything was made of glass. I felt like I was a cloud in the sky, just floating through the air.

The attraction was *amazing*. Round every corner was another thing waiting to steal your breath away. I gasped at the full 360-degree view of everything London had to offer. It was a panorama for the ages.

A second lift spirited us up to the sixty-eighth floor. But this time the experience was lacking. A couple of women in skimpy dresses couldn't take their eyes off Arif. I think they even snapped a picture of his butt when he bent over to pick up his keys. For his part, Arif seemed completely oblivious to the effect he was having on them.

Is he also oblivious to the evil in Jameel's heart, or is he onboard with it?

The view from the top was *supreme*. A network of cables ran through the crystal tower like delicate bones of silver. As I stepped into the glass atrium, I teared up, feeling like I was seeing something not meant for mortal eyes.

Arif wandered over to a machine called a 'Tellscope'. Within seconds he'd figured out how to use it. He was like that. Stick a piece of tech in front of him, old or new, and he'd have it sussed in seconds. He'd added tons of features to my Bronze Age phone.

'Right, I'm off to see Uncle Aqil,' he said. 'Won't be a mo.'

'Your uncle works here?' I asked in surprise.

'Nothing fancy. Security guard, innit?' He tapped the neon-green USB wristband he was wearing. 'Jameel ripped some engineering software for his son or summat. Costs seven hundred pounds in stores. Who's gonna afford that?'

'You seen what's on that flash drive?' I asked, twisting my fingers, afraid of wrecking the mood.

'You kidding? Engineering sounds proper boring!'

Instinct told me the drive was evil in wristband form. So, was Arif fronting, or did he seriously not know what was on the drive? Were he and Jameel partners, or was he just an overly trusting brother? I knew from experience that Jameel deflected difficult questions by saying they showed a 'weakness of faith'. It had shut me up enough times.

But then I'd stumbled on his cellar of terror.

I tilted my face up to Arif, gently stroking his cheekbone, as if committing his face to memory. 'Do what you have to do. Just promise me you'll never let anyone push you around, OK?'

'Eh?' he said, giving me a funny look.

I knew my comment sounded random. But it was my last chance to save him.

'Remember what you said to me?' I said, losing myself in the beauty of his dark eyes. 'If we want to be together forever, we have to please Allah.' I swallowed, fighting back tears. 'Sometimes your family doesn't know what's best for you. Look at me. My parents pinned all their hopes on me becoming a doctor. Never gonna happen. Not with this brain. And all that pressure has made me grow up believing I'm just not good enough.'

'I'm sorry,' he said, squeezing my hand.

I shook my head. 'Thing is, I can't go on blaming them for the rest of my life, can I? At some point we have to take responsibility. We're the ones living our lives, Arif. Not my parents. Not Jameel.'

I looked out at the River Thames glittering in the sun's final encore. A ferry painted like a stick of rock candy chugged along trailing foam.

'Never do anything, unless it feels right in *here*.' I placed my hand over his heart.

He looked down at it thoughtfully, then kissed my forehead. 'That's deep. Thanks.'

There. I'd given it my best shot. Words were all I had – all I'd ever had – and these came straight from the heart. My poor Arif: years of being programmed to follow Jameel's abomination of Islam. Could my words break through?

'Wanna go gift shop?'

'Sure,' I replied, making my smile warm. I had to believe Arif would do the right thing. Because if he didn't, both our lives were over.

*

Up in the gift shop, Arif handed me a twenty-pound note. 'Treat yourself, babe. You deserve it.' He hugged me tightly.

Maybe I was reading too much into it, but there was something final in that hug. And as he stared into my eyes, the mask he'd been wearing all day slipped and I saw how tired and scared he was.

Abruptly, he spun round and ran off.

It was over. Jameel had won the war for Arif's heart.

That night I couldn't get to sleep, no matter how many mugs of warm cocoa I chugged. The date I'd seen on Jameel's memory stick kept flashing in my mind, like a neon sign on a cheap diner.

2nd June! 2nd June!

Three days to get my head sorted. Three days to do the right thing . . .

I tossed and turned like a spin dryer as the hours slipped by. By 1 a.m. I called it quits.

No rest for the wicked! my mind hissed.

'I'm not wicked,' I said aloud. '*I'm not.*'

Bleary-eyed, I traipsed to the bathroom, and made ablution, every motion painful. Then I was standing before God on the prayer mat, offering a voluntary prayer, seeking a way out of the epic mess I had ended up in. After weeks and weeks of it, I was finally cracking under the pressure.

I prostrated myself on the prayer mat and cried my heart out. Right and Wrong; Love and Hate – they'd become so mixed up, I could barely tell them apart. Just what the hell was I supposed to do? If I went to the police, they'd ask why I'd been sitting on the memory stick for so long. If I'd got it all wrong, I might as well be putting a gun to Arif's head. He'd lose Jameel, and his life would be destroyed. How could I do that to someone who had given me confidence, hope and belief in a better tomorrow?

I curled up into a ball, wishing I hadn't shut my parents out of my life. I wanted to hear Ami tell me silly stories about life in a Pakistani village; listen to Dad brag about being the champion kite flyer of Lahore for three years straight. I wanted to tell them I was sorry for not being smart enough to become a doctor, and I was sorry for the number of times I'd lied. But most of all, I was sorry for not being the daughter they'd always wanted.

CHAPTER 45

'I had no choice!' I shrieked in terror.

Darkness.

Silence.

Where was I?

Slowly my bedroom furniture surfaced from the gloom, their familiar shapes comforting. My heart wore knuckledusters as it pounded inside my chest. I'd fallen asleep on the prayer mat and had the worst nightmare ever.

A cloud shifted outside my window, bathing me in milky moonlight. I stared at the crescent moon, so pure and high in the starry sky. Soon dawn would approach and with it my last chance at redemption.

The Compassionate has mercy on those who are merciful, my mind whispered to me. *If you show mercy to those who are on the earth, He who is in Heaven will show mercy to you.*

Fifteen minutes later, I walked out of the apartment.

CHAPTER 46

I stepped into the buttery glow of reception, certain I was going to throw up.

The officer at the counter gave me a wary look. 'Can I help you, miss?'

Suddenly I was a deer caught in the headlights. I longed for the warmth and security of my bed. If I could just hold out till my exams were over, my parents would take me to live in Pakistan. Then I could begin a new life: fresh and blameless.

The phantoms from my nightmare reared before me. Wisps of smoke that were heavier than mountains.

This had to end now.

'I-I'd like to report a terrorist threat,' I croaked. 'There's going to be an attack on London, and I've got details.'

The police officer raised smudged eyebrows. Maybe she thought it was a sick prank? I couldn't afford to get offended. Lives were at stake. ISIS were finally on our doorstep planning an atrocity that would bring London to its knees.

Five minutes later, a couple of counter-terrorism officers escorted me to Interview Room 2. With super-creepy eyes and grooves that dripped from the corners of her mouth, the lady reminded me of a ventriloquist's dummy. Way before she'd introduced herself as Detective Inspector Judith Clarins, I'd clocked her as the one in charge. Officer Redman I recognized from the awful night my dad reported me as a missing person. Only now he'd been sunburned. He kept scratching his ginger sideburns, sending flakes of skin falling on to his shoulders.

On the wall behind them was a large anti-terrorism poster. Major cringe. The word 'CONTEST' hovered over four smaller buzzwords: *Pursue*, *Prevent*, *Protect*, *Prepare*. There were other posters up too, covering everything from domestic abuse to human trafficking. My nervous eyes spied another terrorism one, this time advertising a confidential hotline number. My stomach dropped. Phoning this in would've been a *million times* easier.

'I'd like to speak to Officer Sealy, please,' I said, fidgeting with my hijab.

'As I explained to you before, Miss Saleem,' Redman said patiently. 'Officer Sealy is not part of the counter-terrorism unit.'

'You guys are making me nervous!' I shrieked, before getting a grip. 'Please. I need Officer Sealy to be here. She gets me.'

The officers whispered among themselves, then Redman got up and left. DI Clarins watched me wearily from under a creased brow, then silently placed a voice recorder on the table between us and took out a spiral-bound pad.

Officer Sealy arrived fifteen minutes later, greeting me like an old friend. With her friendly eyes, bouncy curls, and warm aroma of coconut oil, I started to feel *safe*. Like if things went pear-shaped, she'd have my back.

Sealy winked as she placed a cup of Costa's down in front of me. From the opposite end of the table, DI Clarins gave the recorder the 411: date, time, situation. All eyes settled on me. I swallowed, realizing it was now or never, then told them everything I knew about Jameel's terror cell.

'Well, Miss Saleem,' Clarins said, after I'd spilt my guts. 'Don't think we're not grateful for the intel you've provided, but we're bound by procedure. We'd need more to go on than that before we could consider organizing a raid.'

I threw down the memory stick like a smoking gun.

'Everything's on there. I found it in Jameel's cellar.'

'I thought you said he removed all the evidence from there?' said Redman, turning back a page in his pad, looking puzzled.

'That's what *he* thought,' I explained. 'But I found the USB on the floor, hidden in the dust. Must've dropped out or something.' My mouth kept flooding with saliva, and my eyes were wet. I hoped to God I didn't look like a psychotic attention-seeker.

DI Clarins muttered into her radio, summoning a digital forensics officer. While we waited for the expert to arrive, I described everything I'd seen on the drive.

'So let me get this straight,' Clarins said, consulting her notes. 'You believe Jameel Malik is the leader of a terrorist cell aiming to blow up the London Shard. You also believe he was behind the recent failed tube bombings, having seen evidence of this on eight laptops in his basement. Said laptops went missing shortly afterwards, but you recovered a memory stick. On it are three files: an Islamic State terror manual; a document written in code with only the date 2nd June readable; and a third file, which cannot be opened without a password. Correct?'

I nodded, ashamed that I'd wasted a whole hour telling her what could be summed up in about five sentences. *Some writer* . . .

She rubbed her chin like she was polishing a pebble. 'Unless we can find incontrovertible evidence linking Mr Malik to the tube bombing, or the intended bombing of the Shard, he'd be looking at a maximum of four years.'

'You're kidding,' I said. 'For goodness sake, we're talking about actual *terrorism* here!'

Jameel was a mind-thief and a mass-murderer. There could be no bigger crime. They needed to lock him up and throw away the key.

'You haven't told us what makes you think the Shard is their intended target,' Clarins noted, crossing her legs.

'Arif took me to the Shard yesterday.'

'Jameel's younger brother?' she asked, trying to keep up with the info dumps I was dropping randomly. I cursed myself again for not having thought this through. If I'd written it down first, constructed a proper timeline of events, it would have sounded way more convincing.

I nodded. 'Jameel gave him this wristband thingy.'

'Could you be more specific?' Redman asked, pencil hovering above his pad.

'Like a cross between a memory stick and a wristband? He told Arif to give it to a security guard called Aqil. I think . . .' I swallowed, realizing that what I was about to say next could never be taken back.

'Go on,' Sealy said gently.

'I think Arif's been radicalized by his brother.' I stared sadly into my lap as the words came out. 'Jameel might've sent him round with some last-minute instructions or something. Cos, well, nobody suspects teenagers, do they?'

My phone vibrated against my thigh.

'It's Arif!' Panic and shame heated my face. It was as if he'd been standing there all along, watching me land him in it.

'Stay calm,' Clarins said, galvanized for action. 'Put him on speakerphone. Watch for my signals. I might scribble you a note. Otherwise act naturally.'

I nodded, shaking like a leaf. Sealy squeezed my shoulder.

'Hey, Arif!' I said into the phone, inwardly cringing at how ridiculously happy my voice sounded. A dead giveaway.

'Did I wake you?' he asked.

'No, not at all. What's up?'

'It's about what you said yesterday. At the Shard . . .'

There was a long pause, then he cleared his throat.

'Can you get over here, fam?'

I looked up at the officers. DI Clarins nodded.

'Er, OK. Are you all right?' I said.

'Yeah, yeah. See you soon, babe.' He hung up.

DI Clarins congratulated me for keeping a cool head.

'Now listen carefully,' she said, as if I was one of her officers. 'It's going to take a while for Forensics to extract what we need from the memory stick, even with MI5 on board. How long? We don't know.' Her face hardened. 'Jameel Iqbal Malik has been on a surveillance list since 2015, so I *do* believe you're telling us the truth.'

I relaxed a little.

'But the police deal in facts not feelings,' she continued. 'From what you've said, we have under forty-eight hours left before the attack. If you can help us gather further evidence, perhaps even a confession, it would give us agency to make an immediate arrest.'

The cops told me it was my choice. That I didn't have to go through with any of it if I didn't want to. I understood what they meant. They were covering their backs. With or without them, I would have gone to see Arif anyway. Time was everything if we were going to prevent the attack.

From the moment I'd walked into the police station, I'd set the wheels in motion. Yet even now I had my doubts. Whichever way you looked at it, I'd betrayed my husband. I'd tried reaching out to him, reasoned and pleaded and begged. There'd even been that one moment at the Shard when I honestly believed he was going to make the right choice.

But extremism was a virus of the mind. If you didn't get help quickly, it took you over until you couldn't see where it began and you ended. I had to admit that Arif was beyond saving. Denying it could mean thousands of innocent people dying. I knew what Khadijah and Latifah would tell me: keeping quiet was haram.

It had begun to drizzle, and a cold wind rustled the leaves on the trees as I stood on the drive of Arif's house. The concealed microphone I wore burned a hole in my chest. I tried not to think about it as I rang the doorbell.

Jameel came to the door, greeting me with the ghost of a smile. 'Your husband is taking a shower. But feel free to wait up in his room.'

I took two steps towards the stairs, before he spoke again, making my skin crawl.

'Just before you go,' he said in a sibilant voice, 'may I ask you a few questions? We so seldom chat.'

And with that he steered me into the front room. I prayed he'd make a fatal slip and give the cops exactly what they needed to bang him up.

'Sure,' I said. 'Whatever makes you happy.'

'The only thing that makes me happy is earning the Pleasure of Allah, and safeguarding the welfare of true Muslims.'

He knows, I thought, before clamping down on my paranoia.

'And you, sister-in-law?' he said, sliding comfortably into the beige chair facing the window. 'What makes you happy?'

Jameel had changed my husband into a hardened jihadi. Taken his mind to a place where I could no longer reach him. Happiness was dead.

'Same,' I heard myself say. 'I want to be a good Muslima and do what's right.'

'Indeed?' he said, the hem of his thobe sliding up a stick-thin shin as he crossed his legs. 'And would you kill the enemy for the sake of Allah?'

I couldn't meet his penetrating gaze. Right then I hated him more than anyone in the entire history of the world. But killing him would never cross my mind. Life and Death weren't things for us to decide.

'You answer my question with your silence,' he said. 'It is disappointing. Have you forgotten the tale of Ibrahim and his beloved son Ismail? When Allah commanded Ibrahim to sacrifice his own flesh and blood, he obeyed. Truly in him was an example for us all.'

Classic Jameel. Take a story from the Qur'an and twist it to meet your own ends. Could he also quote me the passage where Allah told him to pose as hot teenage boys on social media and groom lonely school girls for jihad? Or where He commanded the death of hundreds and thousands of innocent visitors to the Shard?

'Do you know what the prescribed punishment is for a traitor?' he asked, eyebrows raised like guillotine blades.

Now I was *panicking*. He knew I had his memory stick and he wasn't happy. 'I don't . . . I'm not sure . . .' I mumbled.

'*Death*,' he said, squeezing the edges of the foam-padded armrests as if crushing sinners' skulls. 'It disrupts the harmony of the ummah and must be stamped out.'

I tried not to look guilty. No mean feat when the scumbag was being so damn spooky. Why wasn't DI Clarins breaking down the door and making an arrest? Hadn't he made enough threats? What if the mic had stopped working . . .

'Muz?' Arif called from the top of the stairs.

'Ah! Better not keep your husband waiting,' Jameel said, rising to his feet. 'I'm making chocolate cake. I'll bring you up a slice in about twenty minutes.'

I blinked. Jameel went from passively threatening to host-with-the-most, switching up so quick, I was left wondering if he wasn't an escaped mental patient. Could that be all terrorism was: an extreme mental illness?

'You bake?' I asked aloud.

'A Muslim must arm himself with a multitude of talents in order to survive.'

Excusing himself, he headed towards the kitchen.

I fled up the stairs. Arif drew me into a warm embrace, kissing me tenderly. He wore jersey shorts and a denim blue T-shirt. His skin was cool to the touch and smelt of sea minerals and bergamot.

Me and Arif sat side by side, leaning back against his bed. I removed my hijab, then stroked the soft blue pile of his noodle rug. Outside, storm clouds were gathering, blotting out the rising sun.

'I'm sorry,' he finally said, his throat making a dry clicking sound.

'Don't worry,' I said, patting his muscular thigh. 'My parents couldn't hate me any more than they already do.'

He craned his neck. Only now did I notice the purple shadows nesting beneath his large, mournful eyes. 'You deserve someone better than me.'

The sarcastic comment I dreamed up died in my throat. 'What have you done?' I whispered, suddenly afraid.

'Jameel said this is my final test. You and me get to be together forever as a reward. It's what we want, right?' His face was taut, jaw muscles like corrugated steel.

'You're scaring me,' I said, taking his hand.

He glanced down at our entwined fingers like the sight of it confused him. Then his eyes found mine.

'Run,' he said, nostrils flaring. 'Get out of here and pretend you never met me.'

'I-I don't understand . . .'

'Ten minutes from now, Jameel's gonna come through that door offering you a drink. It'll be spiked. Next thing you know, you'll be waking up in Syria. We both will. They'll train us in combat; teach us how to protect our new homeland. It'll be our new life together—' His voice broke, his hands shaking.

A million thoughts crashed through my mind like the mother of all storms.

A tear rolled down his cheek. 'Go!' he repeated, pushing me away from him.

'Come with me!' I said, holding my hand out to him.

He shook his head, turning his face away. 'I don't get a choice, me. But you *should*. You were right. All along you kept telling me about Jameel, and I wouldn't believe you. But the stuff you said back at the Shard got me thinking. I hacked into Jameel's cloud drive . . .' He sucked in his lips, like he was trying not to cry.

'Arif? What did you see?' I pressed.

'Messed-up shit.'

It was all I could get out of him.

'If you don't agree with what Jameel's doing, then you're not one of *them*. You deserve a second chance.'

'You don't know me!'

'Better than I know myself,' I promised.

He looked at me, pained. 'Not the real me, you don't. I'm weak, yeah? And a liar. I've done terrible things. I'm messed up in here,' he said, jabbing his temple.

I pulled his hand away from his beautiful face. 'I love you. Whatever that man made you do is on *him*.'

'You reckon? Time I did the right thing for once and told you the truth. I've had girlfriends before. Told you that, yeah? What I never said was . . . they became my wives.'

The rug was pulled from under my feet.

His cheeks pinked as he dropped his eyes. 'See, Jameel said Allah made me good looking so I could bring girls into His service. Said I was channelling their base desires into something pure.'

'Wait – what?' I yammered, my ears popping like the

room had been depressurized.

'Jameel'd lay down the groundwork for the girl, with his videos and lectures and that. Then we'd get married. Only I'd disappear. Jameel'd tell my wife I'd gone off to fight jihad in Syria. So she'd wanna go too, innit? But on arrival, she'd be told I'd been martyred. That'd leave her open to marry some other brother fighting for Islamic State. Keep the population growing . . .' His head sank between his knees. 'Meanwhile, Jameel'd shift me to another school. Rinse and repeat.'

I struggled to breathe. 'Is that why . . . ? Was I just . . . ?'

'No, never! Swear down, I married you for reals, Muz,' he said, clutching my rigid hands tightly. 'You're special.'

'Not what you thought at first though, is it?' A tear tugged at my lashes.

His silence was deafening.

Finally, he shook his head, confirming my worst fears.

'Jameel always told me to go for the quiet ones. Girls who got bullied or ignored. Said they had the most potential to become the best fighters. But something that wasn't supposed to happen happened. I fell in love with you. You're amazing, Muz! And it's like you don't even know it. You got passion like no one I've ever seen.' He wiped his hands over his face, gasping.

'All this time, yeah?' he said. 'I been fighting Jameel over sending you to Syria. He got proper mad. "What makes her different from the others?" he said. I told him I love you. So now he's decided my work here is done and that both of us can go together.'

'Are you hearing yourself?' I asked. 'Stop being a victim! Jameel isn't Allah, no matter how much he wants us to believe that. Help me bring him in to the police so this madness can stop. You *know* he's a criminal.'

He nodded. 'But if he's bad, yeah, then what am I? I gave Aqil the flash drive at the Shard.' He looked at me with the saddest eyes. 'Not gonna lie – I knew it were something bad. You knew too, didn't you?'

I nodded. 'It's why I tried to reach out to you. But I couldn't.' The tears that had been building up finally rolled down my cheeks.

'They're planning something *b-big*,' he stammered, turning haunted eyes on me. 'Took me an hour to decrypt one of Jameel's messages. There's going to be a massacre.'

I swallowed. 'But you know he's wrong?' I prodded, desperate for his response to be the right one. God, I hoped DI Clarins was still listening. 'Arif?'

'I don't know nothing!' he growled, shrugging me off. 'I'm messed up, OK? I friggin' hate myself!' He made a fist and punched himself in the face. Blood exploded from his nose, streaking his lips and beard. His eyes fluttered wide, as if he hadn't been expecting the pain. Then he grimaced, balling his fists for a second round.

'No!' I shouted, pouncing on his fists and hugging them to my chest.

'I'm dirty. I used my own body to trick girls.' He broke down into racking sobs that echoed in my gut. 'I deserve to die.'

I wanted to stroke his neck, tell him I forgave him, and that everything would be all right. But I couldn't. Arif had used me.

It was my fault. I should've known we could never be a thing. Not in the real world. He was the sun, lighting up the whole universe with his golden glow. But what was I? Nothing but space junk, knocking around uselessly. God, I'd been so basic, imagining we'd connected on some spiritual level. And literally everyone had been warning me that boys like Arif didn't fall in love with girls like me.

'Muz?' he said, cutting through my dark thoughts.

I gave him nothing.

'I love you,' he said. 'Do you still love me?'

My jaw was clamped so tightly shut, my teeth might've shattered. I was humiliated. Sarabi, Malachy and Mr Dunthorpe, even Salma, had all tried to show me the writing on the wall, but I'd shut them out.

'*I have spread my dreams under your feet*,' Arif recited, his voice quivering. '*Tread softly because you tread on my dreams*.'

He spoke the only words in the entire universe that could get through to me. I cut my eyes to him in shock. He *did* know me, better than anyone.

'Yeats.' He gave a hollow laugh. 'I laid my sins beneath your feet, Muz. *Wallahi*, you are the only girl I have ever loved.'

I glanced at the clock, then back at him. 'I don't know if I can forgive you. But if you don't come to the police with me right now, we'll never find out.'

His nostrils flared like wind tunnels. Then, slowly, he nodded. 'Let's go.'

Finally, finally I had got through to him. I praised Allah.

'So, you've told her,' said Jameel, standing in the doorway like the Angel of Death. In one hand, he held a plate with a slice of cake on it; in the other, a glass of coke.

Arif cowered away, covering his face with his hands. What the hell was wrong with him? He was twice the size of his evil brother.

'I know everything,' I confirmed. 'And so does Allah. Now get out of our way before He strikes you down.'

'Arif, it is as I feared. Break her neck, please,' Jameel spoke with a casualness that sent chills running down my spine.

'No,' Arif said. 'I *love* her!'

'No you don't,' Jameel stated. 'This she-devil is your final test. Believe me, Arif, fail in your task now, and Allah will visit upon you a punishment worse than any suffered by those before you. I would be powerless to help you.' The false sincerity in his face was sickening. 'Kill her, my brother, and spare yourself.'

There was a distant rumble in the heavens, then rain started to fall on the windows. They could've been tears.

Arif's face scrunched up. He clutched handfuls of his hair as he backed away, sobbing pitifully. I was gobsmacked by the power Jameel held over him. Gone was the brotherly banter, replaced by a real hypnotic fear. It awakened a powerful anger in my heart.

'Shut your dirty mouth!' I roared. 'Arif doesn't need you telling him what to do. He's twice the man you'll ever be.'

Jameel's eyes widened in surprise, as if nobody had dared challenge him before. 'So the mouse becomes a shrew. No matter. Allah's angels will rip out your sinful tongue with red hot pliers.'

Lightning flashed across the sky, bleaching the room white.

'You don't scare me, Jameel,' I said. 'You might think you have God on speed-dial, but newsflash: you don't.'

He was about to speak, but I beat him to it.

'You radicalize children in the name of Allah, and He will never accept it. You plan to kill hundreds and thousands of people. But it was God who gave them life.' I shook my head in disgust. 'And what sort of a sick, twisted man makes his own brother into a sex object to trap girls?'

'Who are you to speak to me in this way?' he demanded, spittle flying from contorted lips.

'I am Muzna Saleem,' I said, lifting my chin. 'I am the cloud that brings the rain.'

As if on cue, there was a clap of thunder, and naked terror flickered across Jameel's face. Then fixing his eyes on Arif he spat: 'You stand with this disbeliever, even though she will deliver you into the hands of the *kuffar* police?'

Arif swallowed. Then taking my hand, he nodded. 'Till death do us part.'

Jets of air blasted out of Jameel's nose. It was the first time I had ever seen him laugh. 'Do you realize what will happen to a pretty boy like you in prison? What our uncle did to you will pale in comparison.'

Arif's mouth fell open. The air became ionized as the room seemed to shrink. '*You knew?*'

Jameel licked his lips, realizing his terrible slip. I looked from one to the other. Arif had told me his uncle was 'violent'. Now the awful penny dropped, and I realized the violence had been sexual.

'You knew what Uncle was doing to me,' Arif repeated, advancing on him, 'and you still left me with him? *I was only eight fricking years old!*'

'It was your destiny,' Jameel countered, without a smidge of remorse. 'On no soul does Allah place a burden greater than it can bear.'

'Oh my God!' Arif said, looking like his mind was about to snap. 'You're demented!'

'It's over,' I told Jameel, pulling my phone out with numb fingers. 'Now you finally get what's yours.'

It happened too fast. Jameel flung both glass and plate at my head with enough force to break bones. I braced myself, too shocked to even raise my hands in protection.

Arif punched both out of the air. Fragments of china and glass scattered like pearls as his knuckles began to bleed. Only then did we see the ruse for what it was. A snick came from the door as a key was turned in the lock. Jameel had us trapped.

'Let us out!' I roared, twisting the handle and beating the door. 'You can't keep us in here forever!'

'That's the idea,' Arif said grimly. 'He's gonna torch the place.'

'He wouldn't!' I said, whipping round. 'Not his own *brother*.'

'I'm dead to him.' He bowed his head in shame. 'Only family he needs are people who think like him.'

There was a loud commotion from downstairs as if things were being thrown about. Arif flew into action, forcing the window. But no matter how hard he pushed, it wouldn't open more than a crack. I grabbed my phone and tried calling DI Clarins as Arif hunted under his bed. But there was no reception.

That's when the smoke first hit me. Although I'd known Jameel was a terrorist for a while now, faced with being burned alive for not bowing down to his crazy cult was next-level scary.

A moment later, I heard a roaring from outside the bedroom door. It grew in intensity, joined by the crackle and pop of wood being devoured by fire.

Arif emerged from beneath the bed brandishing a cricket bat. As he tested its weight, I saw the green-and-white decal of the Pakistan flag emblazoned on its side.

'Cover your eyes!' Resting the bat on his shoulder, he pelted towards the window. At the last moment, he swung the bat in a wide arc, unleashing fury on the pane. A spider web of cracks raced across the glass. The second blow turned the window into a hailstorm of shards.

Outside on the street, the hidden police cars glowed to life like Christmas lights as their sirens wailed. There was shouting followed by gunshots. Then a scorching wave of heat struck me from behind, nearly flattening me. I spun round to see little black pits sink into the carpet, which erupted into flame.

'We've got to jump!' Arif cried, getting a leg up on the windowsill.

'We'll never make it!' I protested, as the wind whipped my hair into my face.

'Yeah, we will.' He pointed at his mattress. 'Wrap it around us like padding.'

A man's voice boomed from outside the bedroom door. 'Step back!' it commanded. 'I'm going to break down the door.'

A thud came from the other side, rattling the door in its frame. The urgent sound of more sirens blared through the broken window. God, I hoped DI Clarins had called the fire brigade.

Just then, with the sound of a gigantic cork being pulled from a bottle, the door popped out of its frame and a sooty man came stumbling in. The contrast of his bright blue eyes against his blackened skin scared me. It was Officer Redman.

'Grab some blankets, cover your heads, and follow me!' he barked, taking in the flaming carpet.

Outside on the landing, everything glowed orange beneath a shimmering, oily haze.

'Nah, man,' Arif said, gripping my hand. 'Taking our chances through the window, thanks.'

'Do as you're bloody told!' snapped Redman. 'Jump and your spines shatter the moment you hit the ground. We've about two minutes before the stairs start to collapse.'

Arif's brows lowered as his shoulders rose like hackles. Redman glared right back. A macho pissing contest at a time like this? Were they *insane*?

'Let's try it his way, yeah?' I said, gently rubbing Arif's arm.

'Cover your heads!' repeated Redman, his voice cracking. 'Eyes'll get roasted before you even know it.'

Scared shitless, but buzzing with adrenaline, we followed him to the top of the stairs. Redman swore. Not a good sign, but at least he was keeping it real. He told us to stay put while he ran back to Arif's room.

Downstairs had transformed into a blackened pit from Hell. The stench of melting plastic and burning paint clawed at the back of my throat. How had Jameel managed to set fire to the house so quickly? Had he known all along that I was coming with the counter-terror police?

'Stay behind me!' Redman ordered. He held Arif's bedroom door like a gigantic shield. '*Do not get left behind.* We only get one shot at this.'

I reached behind and found Arif's bleeding hand. Redman glanced over his shoulder and gave the signal. Like a chain gang, we stumbled down the stairs as tongues of flame shot through the gaps in the banisters, snapping at us like angry dragons. A light bulb detonated above our heads, and I think I screamed, but we just kept going. Our lives depended on it.

We were almost out the door when a masked fireman blasted in, dousing the roaring flames with jets of frothy white water. The sight of us made him falter. He started to speak when the kitchen door exploded, hurling shrapnel and wood and thick plumes of smog into the already acrid air. I heard a male scream, then Redman was carrying me out the door.

Cool morning air surged over us as we fell to our knees, retching and choking from the burning in our lungs. Then paramedics descended on us, and I was lifted on to a stretcher. I glanced around wildly.

'Arif!' I cried out, splayed fingers reaching out for him as an oxygen mask was clamped over my mouth.

A jagged piece of wood was lodged in Arif's thigh; shorts soaked through with blood. I couldn't see his face for all the officers, firefighters and paramedics rushing about, until the mayhem cleared, and I saw Arif's closed eyes above the plastic cup of an oxygen mask. My insides shrivelled.

I thrashed about, trying to slip free of the forest of hands pinning me down. Voices everywhere telling me to calm down, not to move, fusing with the cacophony of sirens screaming like banshees. Blue lights flashed everywhere in the retreating dawn. How many police cars had arrived? I felt a sharp pain in my arm, then coolness spread swiftly through my body, numbing my nerves. I fought to keep my eyes open as I was lifted into the back of an ambulance. I was rushing towards a sky of deepest azure, passing through lily-white clouds as soft as dreams, looking for a rainbow.

CHAPTER 47

Crushing pain. Loud buzzing. Blinding lights.

I peeled open my eyes and blinked at the alien hospital room. A nurse hovered at my elbow, consulting an LCD display on a machine I was hooked up to. Her hazel eyes met mine and she smiled.

'Just let DI Clarins know you're awake,' she said, tearing open the Velcro fastenings on the blood-pressure cuff. My sore arm thanked her for it. 'Your parents are here too.'

I watched her leave, feeling dazed. I must have had the worst nightmare ever. My brain throbbed trying to figure it out, clutching at details, which escaped faster than smoke. Eventually I gave up, shifting my bruised body under the pale blue blanket.

'Welcome back!' Clarins piped as she entered.

Officer Sealy wasn't far behind. 'Hello, Muzna!' she said, waving.

I was glad to see her.

'How're you feeling?' she asked, squeezing my hand.

'I'm not sure,' I said in a raspy voice I didn't recognize as my own. 'Everything's all mixed up in my head.'

'You'll be fine,' Clarins said, while Sealy made sympathetic noises. 'The doctors have checked you over and given you a clean bill of health. Vocal cords are a bit sore, but that should soon settle. You're being kept in as a precaution. Your parents are eager to see you.'

'Oh crap,' I said. 'Am I in trouble?'

'Not in the least,' she said. 'I explained it all to them. I'm sure they're very proud of you, as are we all.'

Proud? That *had* to be an exaggeration.

A sudden vision of a wooden stake punching through Arif's thigh winded me. 'Arif!' I cried in alarm. 'Is he . . .' I trailed off, unable to finish that sentence.

'He's in surgery right now. Easy! The doctors have assured me he's going to be OK.'

'Why didn't you get us out before the fire started?' I asked, too weak to be angry.

'There was trouble with the mic,' Clarins explained. 'We believe Jameel disrupted the signal. Our best techies rerouted it as quickly as they could, but unfortunately it caused a delay. I am truly sorry.'

I remembered how my phone had lost reception too. I started to cry then.

'He wanted out,' I said, choking back tears. 'He didn't want to be part of Jameel's terror cell.'

'I know,' Clarins said in a softer tone. 'We heard that bit.'

'Don't judge him. Cancer took his mum; his own uncle raped him. Then he was stuck with Jameel preaching hate, day in, day out, every day of his life. What chance did he have? Why didn't you guys prevent *that*?'

Neither woman met my eyes.

'God, I hope Jameel suffered!'

It was a vicious thing to say, but Jameel had ruined so many lives and had intended to destroy thousands more.

'*What?*' I said, picking up on the awkwardness.

'Brace yourself,' advised Sealy, as she exchanged a look with Clarins.

'Jameel Malik is not dead,' DI Clarins said, face as stiff as a slice of burned toast.

'You what?' I said, sure I must have misheard her.

'We hadn't considered the presence of an armed guard.'

'Armed guard?' The tendons in my neck pinged painfully like elastic.

'Militants willing to die to help Jameel escape. We exchanged gunfire as he slipped through the chaos.' Clarins had the decency to look embarrassed. 'Somehow Malik knew we were coming. Maybe his suspicions arose when Arif hacked into his cloud drive.'

My brain hurt, trying to understand how a man could sacrifice his younger brother for an ideology. 'You are going to catch him though, yeah?' I asked with a hopefulness that bordered on the insane.

'That's the plan,' Clarins promised, jowls trembling with defiance. 'Scotland Yard and MI5 are cooperating with Interpol. We're trying to gain access to all the files on the memory stick you found.'

More promises.

'I need to be alone for a bit,' I whispered.

'Certainly,' Clarins said, getting up. 'But remember, there are people here you can talk to. Strictly off the record, of course. They're here if you need them.'

I stared out of the window, at the miserable British sky. Storm clouds were gathering in the west, bringing shades of grey and blustery winds that pushed against the windows.

My reunion with my parents was intense. Ami threw herself at me, blubbing and swearing oaths in Punjabi for Allah to take her life in exchange for mine.

'I'm OK, Ami,' I said, afraid of how I was going to be treated once they got over the fact I was still alive. After all, I'd been in a boy's bedroom when the fire broke out.

'Parveen, don't smother her,' my father chided. 'The

poor child has been through enough.'

DI Clarins had claimed my parents were proud of me. If that was true, they couldn't possibly know about Arif. So how much had she told them?

'Don't look at me like that, *beyta*,' Dad said, his eyes miserable and raw. 'Tonight I thought I'd lost you.' He looked like he was going to cry, then suddenly he was scowling. 'How could you lie to us? How could you put us through this?'

I met my dad's angry eyes and a tear rolled out of my eye. 'I didn't ask to be born in this country.'

Dad was silent then, his moustache twitching as if he was having some kind of internal debate. 'We tried our best to raise you right,' he said quietly.

'It's why I went to the police when I did.'

He blinked in surprise.

'You are British and you are Pakistani,' he said breaking his own contemplative silence. 'But before both of these, you are *Muzna Saleem*. And the world has never had one of those. Maybe you will make us proud, if we give you space?' His eyes searched mine. 'Can we trust you, *beyta*?'

It was the one question I had waited my whole life to hear.

'Everything OK, Muzna?' Officer Sealy asked from the door.

I nodded, as the tears flowed freely. Like me, Sealy had probably underestimated my parents. In spite of all the trouble I'd caused, they had never stopped loving me.

'I brought *gajar murabba*!' Ami said, opening a Tupperware container and filling a spoon.

I'm not sure why, but I started to laugh then. That set Dad off, and soon Ami was chuckling along too. Then we were all hugging and cry-laughing.

CHAPTER 48

Uncle Tanveer gave Dad the rest of the week off to look after me. Huge relief. Dad might've been cool with giving me space to figure things out, but Ami wouldn't stop asking me questions about who Arif and Jameel were and how I knew them.

'She'll tell us when she's ready,' Dad would say, drawing Ami away from me.

I had a sneaky feeling he knew more than he was letting on.

It took a tragedy for me to realize I'd got Dad all wrong. He moved to England because he wanted a better life for his family. And just like every immigrant, he'd suffered abuse along the way. Between the racists who wanted him to leave, and the gossipers in our community with their forked tongues, Dad had become a paranoid livewire. In Pakistan you lived or died by your reputation. So he'd tried to protect me with fear.

Arif Malik – the boy who'd seduced me for an international terrorist organization – had made a full recovery and was being interrogated by the counter-terrorism unit. In spite of everything, I still loved Arif as much as I ever had. But the obsession part was over. I'd been a headcase, willing to jump off a cliff to prove I was worthy of his love. Some days I'd hate him for getting me mixed up with extremism. Other days I'd hate myself for having gone along with Jameel's warped ideas for so long. What if I'd come to my senses sooner and got to Arif earlier? It was a question that never failed to bring on long episodes of crying.

I cried for what he must be going through with the anti-terror police. Not waterboarding or torture, obviously. But whatever it was, couldn't be fun. And Arif could be stubborn, which probably didn't help. Would I ever see him again?

DI Clarins gave me hope that his 'extenuating circumstances' would let him off from doing time in a Young Offenders Institute. After all, he'd never fully understood what Jameel was about. Groomed from childhood, he'd come to think everything Jameel said came from God Himself.

I developed a fear of sleep. Graphic nightmares would haunt me till I woke up screaming, flitting about on the floor, twisted up in sheets. Ami and Dad would be standing over me, worried half to death. If it didn't stop soon, I feared I might go insane. But then Jameel would have won.

On the third day, Dad came to fetch me from my room.

'Muchi, DI Clarins is here,' he said, poking his head round the door.

I stared at him blankly.

His lips formed a grim line, but his eyes were sympathetic. 'Make yourself a bit more presentable, *beyta*, then come and join us in the sitting room.'

In the past, a comment like that would've had me flying to the mirror, desperate to bury the ugly beneath a ton of cosmetics. But it didn't matter any more. Nothing did.

Throwing on a hoody, I joined DI Clarins and my parents on the horseshoe couch. Tea, biscuits and a bowl of Punjabi mix had been served, but no one was touching them.

DI Clarins made a few polite noises, then got down to business. 'It goes without saying that this is all strictly confidential.' She waited for some sign of consent before going on. 'There's good news and some bad news.'

'Makes a change,' I said. 'Usually it's just bad.'

Ami told me off for being so rude. I barely registered her.

'MI5 were able to decode and unlock the third file,' Clarins explained. 'You were right. Those men *were* planning to attack the Shard. The document contained personal details of the would-be suicide bombers and information about vast sums of money to be paid out to each of their families on completion of the job. Yesterday the Home Secretary authorized a take-down. In the biggest raid of its kind, twenty men were taken into custody, and two were shot for resisting.'

'Jameel,' I said, my nails cutting half-moons into my palms. 'You got him too, right?'

The DI played with a bit of fluff on her trousers. 'No.'

I fell back in my seat, shocked to the core. Craning my face up to the mini chandelier, I began to laugh. The DI considered my reaction, then sighed.

'I know it's difficult, but please have patience, Muzna. The hunt for Jameel has gone global. Everyone's involved: the Americans, the Pakistanis. It's only a matter of time before he's captured.'

I snorted. 'You said you knew about him since 2015. Why couldn't you have arrested him back then and spared us all?'

'You know it doesn't work like that. Jameel was a puppet master controlling several operations while hiding behind firewalls and fall guys. Which is why it's so important for people like you to join the fight. Without your help . . . well, I don't even want to think about what might have happened! The unprecedented loss of life and the damage to our city would have been *irreparable*.' For a moment she almost seemed human. 'Your vital contribution has not gone unnoticed. Which brings me to my final point. The prime minister has invited you to Number Ten this afternoon.'

I'd been so busy grinding my teeth, cursing each of Jameel's nine lives, that I now stared at her open-mouthed. It was Dad who put my question into words.

'Did you just say the prime minister wants to see *my* daughter?' he asked, poking himself in the chest.

Clarins served confirmation with a smile. 'The PM would like to congratulate your daughter in person. No one underestimates the bravery Muzna showed in coming forward. Or the tremendous sacrifices she made.'

All I could do was stare. Dad patted me on the back and – after he'd explained it to her in Punjabi – Ami hugged and kissed me.

'Congratulations, Muzna,' DI Clarins said, appraising me like a cadet who'd come good. 'You're a *national hero.*'

While DI Clarins sketched out the details of the meeting for my parents, I began to realize bailing out would be *impossible*. Don't get me wrong, if it'd just been about me, I'd be on the next bus out of town. But whether I liked it or not, I'd become The Face of an entire community. How did you get your head round something like that? If my experiences had taught me anything, it was that being Muslim meant different things to different people. One person couldn't speak for all of us.

CHAPTER 49

I sloshed through puddles, hunched under Ami's embarrassing brown granny umbrella. The sound of rainwater in the gutter was like a troll gargling. Good things never lasted. The summer had been blink-and-miss short. In under a week it would be September and I'd be back at school, studying for November resits.

Mr Dunthorpe kept uploading study resources to the school portal, as well as getting all my other subject teachers to do the same. The guy still believed I had it in me to ace my exams. Low-key annoying, but I was totally nominating him for Teacher of the Year.

Back in June, I'd received a giant card from Falstrum.

Congratulations! We all knew you were 'Great British bravery at its finest' long before the PM!

was emblazoned on the front. Under it was a mosaic girl in a hijab with a fantastic smile on her face. I guessed she was supposed to be me.

Everybody had signed it, including Mr Dillinger, who had retired to a villa in Monte Carlo. Malachy, Amie and Latifah had all written especially sweet messages, urging me to keep in touch. Even Sade had decided I was 'all right'. Sarabi might've been absent on the day of the card signing, but more likely hadn't forgiven me. I got it: I'd been through the same drama with Salma and my own parents.

I stopped outside the newsagent's, shaking off Ami's umbrella.

The bell jingled above my head as I entered. Like every other teenager in the country, I was shot with a suspicious look before the man behind the counter went back to frowning at his scratch card. I headed straight over to the fridge and grabbed the two-pinter Ami needed to make *kheer*. I placed it on the counter along with a packet of gum.

My phone pinged. Another upbeat text from Khadijah, keeping me positive.

I smiled sadly, thinking about the number of versions of Islam I'd tried on for size before finally coming back to Khadijah's Allah. It didn't mean I couldn't respect Muslims who practised faith differently, like Latifah or even my parents. Neither was it about 'othering' non-Muslims. I knew from experience exactly how hurtful that could be. For me, faith was my way of being a better person. It had helped me find a way to fight Jameel's warped version of Islam.

As the cashier rang up my total, my eyes were drawn to a surly woman's face splashed across every newspaper. She'd been charged with running a brothel using refugee kids. Apparently two MPs and a retired children's TV presenter had also been hit by the sting operation. Stuff like that made you physically sick. But honestly? I was relieved that for once the papers weren't harping on about Muslims and terrorism.

'I'll take this too,' I said, handing the guy a newspaper.

'Excuse me,' said a woman queuing behind me. 'Are you the girl from the telly, the one what stopped the Shard bombing?'

I bit my lip. I could've lied. She would never have known.

But then I wouldn't be Muzna. 'Guilty,' I said.

'Cor! Can I get a selfie?'

Five minutes later, the rain had stopped, and the sun was playing peek-a-boo with the clouds. The smell of old pennies grew stronger as I strode towards the park.

It was empty apart from a couple of mothers pushing kids on swings, and an old man taking an Irish setter for a walk. Using my sleeve as a squeegee, I scraped the water off the bench and sat down. The wind rifled through the edge of my newspaper, giving me previews of celebrities who were too fat, or too thin, had too much sex, or hadn't worn enough make-up.

As I adjusted my hijab, a rainbow leaped across the sky. It should have made me smile. But lately my Should Do list had got longer than a loo roll. I stared at the bloated rain clouds teetering at the edge of the sky, wondering why my parents had named me after them.

The afternoon sun shifted, plating everything in 24-carat gold. My heart started to beat faster, every sense was suddenly tingling. His silhouette appeared in the ethereal golden light, and I *knew* it was him. As Arif's terrified face appeared and he opened his arms wide, I leaped up before shyness and fear rooted me to the spot.

I am thunder, the cloud that brings the rain.

I lifted my chin and walked slowly towards him.

ACKNOWLEDGEMENTS

Thank you, Pan Macmillan, for welcoming me into your family and caring so passionately about inclusive representation. You guys are WOKE!

To my incredible editor, Lucy Pearse, who championed Muzna's story from first draft to published article. You brought the thunder and the lightning. I can't thank you enough.

Massive props to Kat McKenna and Beatrice Cross who got my book out into the world and shouted about it. I love you guys!

Thanks to Venetia Gosling, Alyx Price, Rachel Vale, Sarah Blackie, Catherine Alport, Kris Doyle, Rory O'Brien, and everyone else at Pan Macmillan.

Special thanks to Penny Holroyde, who rescued me from the Slush Monster, stuck me in a rocket and launched me at the stars. I am honoured to have you as my agent and friend.

Thanks to Yasmin Rahman for her sensitivity reading and very helpful suggestions. And to Fiona Noble and Darren Chetty for being so passionate about BAME stories and authors.

To Bryony Pearce for your help and advice.

To Chris Mould for thrilling my students with your amazing skulls.

To Sabah Mehmood, Carrie Goodgame, José Alvarez, Sophia Daire and Andrew Hall – teachers of the highest order, all.

To Jonathan Gibbs and the gang at St Mary's Uni: thanks for everything!

To the hundreds of teenagers I've had the pleasure of teaching and knowing. This book is totally your fault!

To the sassy South London slang-checkers. I see you.

To the librarians, reviewers and bloggers who embraced this tale.

And lastly to YOU dear reader. Your imagination transformed a stack of pages into a full-blown quest for identity and more. From the bottom of my heart: thank you. Hope you'll join me for the next one – coming 2019!

ABOUT THE AUTHOR

Muhammad Khan is an engineer, a secondary-school maths teacher, and now a YA author! He takes his inspiration from the children he teaches, as well as his own upbringing as a British-born Pakistani. He lives in South London and is studying for an MA in Creative Writing at St Mary's University. He is working on *Kick the Moon*, his second novel for Macmillan Children's Books.